RISK

IMOGEN WELLS

Risk

Cover Design by LJ Designs

FOREWORD

Note from the Author

This book contains scenes and themes that some readers may find upsetting and/or offensive. Scenes of explicit sex and violence and profanity can be found in the pages that follow.

The author is British, and British English spellings and phrases are used throughout.

RISK

When Camryn Moore set out to start a new life, she always knew that her past would catch up to her.
She thought she had more time before he found her. Before she'd have to face her nightmares, her guilt and her shame.
When she receives a message reminding her of why she left, she makes a decision that will change her life forever.

What Camryn wasn't expecting was Ryder 'Blue' Hawkins. Blue barrels into her life exuding danger and a darkness that should have her running the other way.
Camryn never expected that his kind of darkness would call to her and have her wishing for things she'd given up hope of ever having.

Can Camryn take the risk she vowed never to take again?

ONE

Kasey

For me right now, life sucks big time! At 25 years old you'd think that the world would be my oyster. Cliché, I know. It couldn't be further from the truth, though. I'm currently hiding out in a rundown B&B in some shit town I don't even want to be in. This room is about as appealing as a case of gastroenteritis and most likely what I'll end up with after staying here. I don't even have the small luxury of my own bathroom, oh no, instead I have to share one pokey little bathroom with the rest of the unsavoury occupants. It's like a walking advertisement for an STD!

The room contains a single bed that looks ready to collapse as soon as you touch it, with a throw that's completely threadbare and faded. The wallpaper is a throw-back from the 60s, with a vulgar green floral pattern that's peeling from damp in the corners of the room. There's also a questionable stain splattered above the rickety metal head-board. Ewwww!

Dumping my bag on the floor, I head to the one window in the room. Dark brown velvet curtains block any light from outside, and as I attempt to draw one back, the distinct pinging sound of a hook breaking echoes around the room. Outside, the rain continues pelting the window as a cold draft seeps through, sending a shiver through me. Yeah, inside's just as dreary as outside. Like I said, life sucks, but at least I'm alive.

Snatching my bag up, I pull out the map I've been using and tentatively lower myself to the bed. I hold my breath, the old frame creaks and groans as I finally rest all my weight on it, but it holds. Spreading the map on the bed, I begin to plot my next move. This would be so much easier with my phone, but it's one of the many things I had to leave behind.

To be honest, I'm safer without it right now, *he* probably put some sort of tracking device or app on it anyway. With limited cash, a phone is the least of my worries.

I shake my head to clear the images racing through my mind. My bruises throb in recognition of memories I refuse to get sucked into. I need to focus on finding somewhere I can start afresh and forget the last four years of my life. I also need to see about getting a new identity.

Luckily, before I left, I was able to get an address from Tyler for someone who might be able to help me. For the right price, of course.

The question is, what's it going to cost me, and will I be willing to pay no matter what?

I spend an hour trying to decide where to go next, then finally narrow it down to a couple of places. Unable to make a definite decision, I decide on a quick shower. I need to wash away the grime and sweat from travelling for the last 24 hours. Grabbing a clean set of clothes and the limited toiletries I was able to pack, I head to the bathroom. Thank the lord there's a lock.

I hurry through my shower and get dressed just as my stomach growls in protest at not being fed. Seeing the time is just approaching 7pm, I decide to venture out for some food.

The B&B sits in a small side road just a ten-minute walk from Peterborough train station, and I head back that way remembering that there was a small café across the road. It's almost dark outside, and the street is quiet. Pulling my hood up over my head I walk quickly. The rain has stopped, thankfully, and a damp, earthy smell lingers in the air.

Once I get out on to the main road, I turn right towards the café that sits just up ahead on the corner. I cross over and make my way through the throng of people that just got off the train. Most are men in business suits, carrying brief-cases. A few are younger, dressed ready for a night on the town. Young and carefree. That used to be me, before *him*! Or more accurately when I met him.

Twenty-one, dressed to the nines, happy and confident. Me and the girls, Laura and Sam, had gone out to celebrate Laura's new job.

After graduating with a degree in marketing and adver-tisement, Laura had landed a job at a huge London based marketing firm, and in celebration we'd gone to one of the many clubs in London. We'd had a blast, drinks a plenty and laughed so hard my sides had hurt.

Towards the end of the night I'd been on the dance floor, completely lost in the music. Body swaying, arms in the air, next thing I knew there were hands on my hips and heat at my back. Before I got the chance to spin and face my 'handsy' dance partner, warm minty breath brushed my neck, followed by a deep, husky voice whispering in my ear.

'Hey, beautiful'. Utterly mesmerised by his beautifully rich voice, and with a buzz from all the cocktails I'd drunk, we danced till the end of the song. When I finally turned around, I was met by the deepest, darkest brown eyes I'd ever seen. The rest, as they say, is history.

Now, had I not been young and naïve, or in hindsight, stupid, and completely enamoured with the hot, well mannered, flatterer, I may have seen beneath the beautiful veneer to the manipulative, arrogant arsehole of a man he was. Like I said, hindsight!

A bell above the door rings as I enter the café, and the smell of fried food and oil assaults my nose. Inside there is a short, bald Turkish man behind the counter frying chips. The only other customer is an elderly gentleman, reading a newspaper and nursing a cup of tea. Nodding in greeting to the man behind the counter, I head to a table and take a seat. Picking up the laminated double-sided menu, I scan it for something to fill the hollowness in my stomach. If only it was that simple.

This hollowness is a deep, dark pit of despair and fear, nothing to do with food.

When the waitress comes to take my order, I pick the first thing on the menu. It's not going to matter what it is because I won't taste any of it. I order a tea to wash it down.

While I wait for my food, I watch the world outside. Purposely picking a table near the back and facing the door gives me the advantage of watching who comes and goes.

My dad was a Marine, and I always remember that no matter where we were, he would take up the best vantage point. I can hear him now, *"You gotta cover all entrances and exits Kasey. It means the difference between breathing another day"*. God! I loved my dad.

The day he died was the day my life turned to shit. I was the epitome of a 'Daddy's girl'. In my eyes that man was God, and I believed that he could've walked on water. It's funny how one event can cause such devastation; a domino effect that would change the course of my life. Ultimately leading to me sitting in a shitty little café on the fucking run, from *him*!

If my dad were still alive, would I be here now? Who the fuck knows! I guess that depends on whether you believe in fate, destiny, kismet, all that shit. Would things be as bad? I'd like to think not. I'd like to think that my dad would kick his scrawny little arse! Okay, so it's hardly scrawny, but my dad would still kick his arse.

Christ knows why I'm sitting here thinking about all this anyway, it's not like just thinking about it will magically make it happen. Dad isn't here, so suck it up Kasey!

Lost in the memories of my dad, the swooshing of the double doors leading from the kitchen have me almost jumping out of my seat. The young girl who took my order earlier approaches with my food and tea, placing them on the table, she gives me a forced smile before walking back the way she came.

I look down at my plate, stomach roiling at the idea of food, but I know I have to eat. Apparently, I ordered omelette and chips. The omelette looks a little grey, and the chips, obviously frozen, could have done with five minutes more in the fat fryer. Mind you, with the amount of oil covering them, I'm surprised they're not still cooking on the plate. Reluctantly, I load my fork and eat.

Pushing my plate away, I throw my napkin on top and pick up my tea. It looks like piss in a cup, but it's wet and will have to do.

The old man is still sitting in the corner when I get up to leave, and he looks up as I near his table.

"It hurts to see such a pretty little thing looking so sad. How about a smile, you know, make an old man happy?" he rasps out, a wide, almost toothless grin on his face. I bite back the snarky reply itching to break free. I simply smile and keep walking. Just as I pass him, he murmurs, "Running is never the answer." I stumble at his words but keep walking. I wish that were true, but I don't have a choice.

If I want to survive then I need to run and never stop.

My walk back to the B&B is much quieter as most of the commuters from earlier are home in their cosy little houses with their lovely families.

Then there's me. I used to have that but not since I was a kid, before dad died. How many times over the years have I wished to turn back the clock? Quite honestly, I've lost count.

Clearly from the old man's comment my face must be really telling. Guess I better up my game and perfect my poker face.

The following morning, I set out to meet Rick, Tyler's contact, who's hopefully going to help me with a new identity.

Short on cash, I have no other option but to walk the three miles to where Tyler told me I would find this Rick guy.

After an hour walk, I finally arrive at the address Tyler scribbled on a scrap of paper and palmed to me.

The house sits on a quiet, well maintained and, surprisingly, wealthy well-off road. Hardly the type of road you'd expect a person involved in criminal activity to live, but what the hell would I know, right?

As I approach the door, I can hear a voice inside, a child's excited voice. I pause to listen and am surprised when the front door springs open. I don't have time to breathe let alone move before a small boy barrels into me, almost knocking me off my feet. The only reason I don't hit the deck in a crumpled heap is thanks to the hand that grips my forearm like a vice and propels me forward into a rock-hard chest.

"Whoa there, darling. I got you." His voice rumbles through his chest. I should know, seeing as my face is smashed up against it. I push back, and he releases me.

My eyes widen as a tremor of fear runs through me, and my heart beats manically inside my chest. I take a couple of deep breaths to stave off the panic slowly rising in me. I tune out the worried voice of the boy who ploughed into me, who is currently clutching onto this guy's leg. Instead, I focus my attention on inspecting the—Wow! Big guy. I mean, I'm no dwarf, and with heels I wouldn't be far off his height, but this guy has muscles in all the right places.

He's wearing a pair of black ripped jeans and a black tee that does nothing to hide the muscles underneath. One arm is alive with swirling black tattoos that continue way beyond the cuff of his tee.

My eyes rake over him, and when they reach his face, I'm met with a chiselled jaw covered in scruff that my body would love to feel brushed against my cheek. Woah. Where the hell did that thought come from. I've not felt an ounce of arousal in a long time, but I can't help looking at his mouth and the perfect cupid's bow and full biteable lower lip. Unable to take my eyes off his lips, I watch as one side kicks up in a devilish smirk. When his lips start moving, I'm so mesmerised I don't even hear what he's saying. The sudden click of fingers brings me out of my reverie.

"Uhm. Sorry, what did you say?" I ask, shaking my head and looking up at him. I'm met with a pair of aviator sunglasses.

"I said, see something you like, sweetheart? But I guess from that little display, verbal confirmation is not required," he states with a chuckle, as he removes the glasses. He drops his head slightly making his browny-blond hair flop forwards. I feel a blush rise in my cheeks, and the blood in my veins begins to heat at the utter gall of the man.

Yeah, I mean I was totally checking him out, but talk about ego the size of Everest. Before I can cut him to size, the boy, still clinging to his leg pipes up.

"Can we go now, please? I'm real sorry, I didn't mean to knock into the lady."

"Sure we can, and I know you didn't. It's all good, little man. I just need to talk to...." he pauses, waiting for me to give him my name. Ah, shit. I don't want to give him my real name. Come on, think Kasey, think, but I don't get a chance to reply as he answers for me.

"Bambi here, then we'll shoot, okay?" The boy nods. "Why don't you go back inside, and I'll come get you when I'm done, alright, bud?" Turning to me, the boy drops his chin and apologises before running off back into the house.

"Bambi?" I look at him questioningly, his eyes light with humour. Sensing he's not going to answer, I get back to why I came here. "I'm looking for Rick, is he here?" At that he grabs his chest in mock pain.

"And there was me thinking it was my lucky day." Noting the serious look on my face, he laughs. Dropping his hands, he turns back towards the house calling out for someone inside.

This guy exudes danger, and alarms bells should be blaring in my head, but they're not. I look him over, this time pausing on his arse in the tight black jeans that hug his figure. Not wanting to get busted checking him out again, I quickly look away down the road. I don't think I was as subtle as I thought when I feel eyes burning the side of my face, and I nervously bite the inside of my cheek.

Relief floods me when I hear footsteps coming down the hall, and a few seconds later a guy, a few inches shorter than 'pretty boy' here, appears.

"Blue. What's up? I thought you and Max were heading to the park to..." the guy cuts off when he spots me. "Oh, man! I thought we talked about you bringing your latest fuck buddy round when Max is about." His brows pull together in a fierce frown.

I snort with disgust. Seriously. What in the hell kind of place has Tyler sent me to? I'm starting to think I don't want or need this guy's help. Turning around, I head back down the path and away from them. I can hear their muffled voices as I reach the gate.

I guess I shouldn't be surprised that the hottest guy I've ever seen, is a total man whore, and the other one, well, he helps people disappear. From the looks of him, literally and metaphorically. This might be a nice neighbourhood but these two, look like a kind of trouble I don't need.

Feet pound the pavement behind me, but I don't stop. I don't falter, just keep walking. I need to get out of here and find another way to disappear, screw the new ID.

I do, however, almost fall flat on my face when the guy behind me calls out my name.

"Kasey! Kasey, wait up." A hand latches onto my arm, spinning me around. I flinch, throwing my hands up to protect myself. I hate that it's my body's natural reaction now. Because of *him*. The guy immediately releases me, holding his hands palm up to show he's not a threat.

"I'm sorry. Please come back to the house, and we can start again." His voice is softer than before, trying to put me at ease. "I'm Rick. Tyler told me to expect you, I guess you're not quite what I was expecting." This throws me for a loop. If Tyler called him does that mean he knows too?

He must see the panic spread across my face. "It's okay, Se...."

"Please, don't say his name. I can't.... I just. Don't." My heart is racing, and my breathing quickens as panic grips me again. I can't bear to hear or say the name of the man that haunts my every waking hour, and my nightmares too.

"He doesn't know where you are, I promise, Kasey." He lowers his hands, then gestures towards the house.

I start to relax as Rick guides me back to the house. When we arrive, the house is empty. 'Pretty boy' and Max must have left, and I'm glad too. Nothing more humiliating than having a panic attack in front of an audience. Bad enough that Rick got a small glimpse of how fucked up I am.

Rick leads me through the house to his kitchen as my eyes take in my surroundings. The walls of the hallway are lined with a dozen candid, black and white framed photos of a beautiful brunette and the little boy, Max, from earlier. I assume she's Max's mum and I wonder where she is, but it's not my business. I'm not here to make friends, just to get a new ID and get as far away from *him* as possible and pray like fuck he never finds me. Because if he does...it doesn't even bear thinking about.

The kitchen is clean, almost clinical, but still manages to be warm and homey. Decked out with top of the range appliances and every possible gadget you could ever wish for. There's an island in the middle and one end acts as a breakfast bar with sleek black, high-backed stools. Rick gestures to them, and as I move that way, I take in the rest of the room.

At the far end, the whole wall is made up of bi-folding doors that lead out to a long, well-manicured garden.

There's a dark oak dining table that looks to seat 12, and to the left is a matching Welsh dresser.

I take a seat on the nearest stool, closest to the door in case I need to run. God! I'm such a fuck up. A throat clearing has me almost toppling off the stool, and I turn to see Rick looking at me from the other side of the island as he leans back against the work top behind him. Ha, totally proved my point on my fucked-upness.

"Sorry, I didn't mean to startle you. Do you want a tea or coffee, or maybe something stronger?" he asks, giving me a wink. I appreciate his attempt to put me at ease and offer him a small smile.

"Thanks, but I'd rather just get this done if you don't mind." He nods his head in acceptance, before turning slightly and reaching into the drawer behind him. My heart beats a little faster at the thought of what he's getting, and several scenarios run through my mind all at once. I watch every movement he makes like a lion watches its prey. When he turns back to face me, he's holding nothing more sinister than a large manila envelope in his hand. Well, sinister is completely subjective as blackmailers usually use manila envelopes, and I guess this could be classed as sinister due to the fact I'm here for a new identity. Not exactly legal and above board, or so I assume. I shut my ridiculous thoughts down and focus back on Rick.

"So, I managed to get you everything except a new passport." One side of his face kicks up as he says it, almost in apology, but there's something else in his eyes I can't quite put my finger on. I shrug in reply.

Whilst it's a lovely idea to leave and set myself up on the other side of the world, I just can't. There are things keeping me here.

I leave Rick's with my new ID, and a business card for a

security firm that he and 'pretty boy' run together. He refused to take any sort of payment, instead making me promise to call him if I ever need anything, but I have no intention of calling him.

I head back to the B&B, not exactly relishing the idea of spending another night there, but I have no other option. The reason I picked it certainly wasn't for its luxury that's for sure but for its location so close to the train station.

Back in the room, I remove the documents that Rick gave me, checking everything.

I am no longer Kasey Smith, now I'm Camryn Juliette Moore.

Considering I had no say in my new name, I'm actually very happy with it. I repeat it several times in my head and out loud, getting used to the sound of it. I thought I'd be upset about the loss of my name, especially as my dad named me, but I'm not.

Honestly, I've not felt like me in a very long time.

After checking everything over, I take another look at the map Tyler gave me. Deciding that I'm probably safer nearer a larger town or city, you know hiding in plain sight and all that shit you see in the movies.

I look at Norfolk and wistfully remember we visited once when I was younger, taking a trip on the Broads, it was the one of the best holidays. I don't think I ever saw my parents look so happy. It was always their love that had me wishing for the same. Now, I'm not so naïve because my hopes for the same have been tainted. I know how lucky they were, but that won't ever be me, not now.

I decide against Norfolk, it's somewhere *he* knows I've been, and I talked about fondly. Before I spiral into dark thoughts and things I wish I could forget but never will, I decide to take a walk to the station.

It's early afternoon and there are plenty of people milling about, but I'm not sure if that's better or worse. As I enter the station, a guy comes rushing out and nearly barrels me over. He doesn't stop, not even a 'sorry' called over his shoulder. Bastard!

My heart is pounding inside my chest, and my breathing has spiked. Please, god, don't let me have a panic attack right here, right now. I step to the side and lean against the wall, taking in some slow, deep breaths right from the gut. I rest my head back on the wall and close my eyes, conscious that it's not the best idea, but if I want this to pass and the heavy weight settling in on my chest to go away, it's what I need to do.

I don't know how long I stand there, but slowly the tightness lessens, my heart rate slows and breathing becomes easier. As I open my eyes, I become aware of someone standing off to the left of me. From my periphery, I see it's a woman holding a little girl's hand.

"Excuse me, Miss, are you alright?" she asks. As I turn to look at her, I can see a small, but concerned smile on her face. I pass a quick glance at the little girl by her side before looking back to the woman in front of me.

"Yes, I'm fine. Thank you." I can see the question on the tip of her tongue, so I quickly add, "I was running for my train, but I missed it. No bother, there'll be another along any minute." Whilst it's clear she doesn't believe me, she nods, accepting my lie before going on her way. I watch them as they leave and can just make out the little girl, who appears to be around four years old, ask her mother "Why was the lady so sad mummy?" and my heart breaks a little bit more. If that's even possible. Pulling myself together and drawing in a deep breath, I head for the counter.

Sleep evaded me last night, not surprising in the slightest. My panic attack, although minor, combined with the little girl and her mother, left my mind in turmoil. And now, I need to lock that shit up tight. I can't afford for my mind to take me back there, last night was it, the last time.

The sun is just coming up and as my train doesn't leave until 8.30am, I decide to take a shower and go for breakfast.

After I paid for my train ticket last night, I realised I had enough money to get breakfast, and with hardly any food yesterday and no idea when the next time I eat will be, I take this opportunity.

At the café near the station, I order the biggest breakfast I can afford, and then board my train to Manchester and my new life.

TWO

Camryn

Six months later

"Camryn, get your nasty arse outta that pit you call a bed, or you're gonna be late." Jamie calls from the hall. I groan as I roll over, stretching my sore body out and cracking my eyelids open.

You would never guess that Jamie's parents are loaded based on the way she speaks, but that's one of the things I love about her. She hasn't let the fact she has money change the fabric of her being.

"Why are you shouting? It's too early, and my head hurts, like really fucking hurts." I knew I shouldn't have had that last cocktail, jeez. What the hell was I thinking! Before I can think any more about it, the bedroom door flies open, and there stands Jamie with her hands on her hips and a smirk on her lips. Bitch! How can she look that good at this time in the morning after last night? Like I said, bitch! But I love her, sometimes.

Right now, I want to slap that silly look off her face, and

then bury myself in the warm, comfortable quilt and sleep for eternity. A girl can dream, right?

"Come on, up. I didn't set this up so you could crash and burn before you even get there," she says, raising a brow at me.

Jamie's dad owns a newspaper, and she managed to get me an interview working in the human resources department. It's not the glamorous journalism job I dreamed of when I did my degree, but it sure as fuck beats serving overpriced cocktails to jumped-up suits and barely legal girls looking for a sugar daddy. Besides, it's not like I can follow my dream now anyway. There is no way I can risk putting my name out there, even if I'm not Kasey Smith anymore.

"Okay, okay, I'm getting up," I say, as I roll, yes, literally roll out of bed. My body is most definitely still asleep. "What sort of friend are you, anyway? Who lets their friend get wasted the night before an interview?" I stumble as I get to my feet and look at Jamie. "More to the point who conducts interviews on a Saturday. I mean really, come on," I whine, while pointing my finger at her. Jamie just shakes her head at me and laughs before walking out the door.

As she moves down the hall, she calls out that I have exactly 40 minutes to shower and be ready to leave. Ugh! Fuck my life!

Despite my snarky mood this morning, courtesy of a hangover to end all hangovers, I don't know where I'd be without Jamie. Actually, that's a lie. I'd still be begging on the street and sleeping anywhere that was dry.

When I stepped off the train in Manchester six months ago with nothing more than the clothes on my back and the one small bag I managed to escape with, I had no choice but to sleep rough. Those first few weeks were hard, but I'd been through worse. I refused to have made it that far, only to give up. So, I sucked it up and got on with it, all the while hoping that my luck would change, and it did. Jamie literally saved my life that day, and every day since.

I'D BEEN SLEEPING in the same doorway for the last three weeks, claimed it as my own, the way of the street, apparently. I'd had a good day begging and had enough money to eat and buy a bottle of whiskey. Having drowned my sorrows, I'd crashed in my doorway around 2am, with not much chance of sleep before that on a weekend. The drink helped me on the way, but not as much as in those first few days.

I woke to a crushing weight on my chest, at first, I thought I was dreaming about one of my panic attacks, but then I heard someone grunting. When I opened my eyes, I found a guy kneeling on my chest. I immediately started shouting at him to get the fuck off, but he didn't listen. Then I lashed out with my fists, hoping to land one on the arsehole's nose. I almost did too, until he pulled out a blade and held it to my throat.

He leaned in real close, I could smell his rancid breath, and as he spoke spittle landed on my cheek, "Shut the fuck up, bitch, or I'll cut you from ear to fucking ear, then I'm gonna take whatever I want anyway. Maybe have a little taste of you before you take your last breath too."

At the time, my stomach almost turned inside out with disgust, I gripped the edge of my sleeping bag, knuckles turned white. Surprisingly, I wasn't afraid, I guess it not being the first time having a knife held to my throat or the threat of rape, meant the effect wasn't quite as potent.

Still kneeling partially on my chest and restricting my

movements regardless of the knife, he started searching for the zip on my sleeping bag.

As his attention was elsewhere, I scanned the area, as much as I could, looking for anyone that might help, but the sun hadn't even risen in the sky yet. I remember my mind was racing with how I was going to get out this without my head hanging off my shoulders and my life flowing into the filthy gutters.

Death hadn't really scared me in a long time, but when I made the decision to run, to escape, I chose to live. To fight back and not allow the deaths of those I loved the most to be in vain. Surviving their loss hadn't killed me, although it came close, and that meant that I could survive anything this shitty life threw my way. I refused to let him hurt me, tear me apart anymore, to win.

His hand brought me back to reality as it brushed past my breast before coming back to cop a feel completely, squeezing tightly. Immediately my whole body tensed up, muscles locked tight and a grimace crossed my face at the pain, but I refused to make a sound and give him even an ounce of satisfaction. A soft groan filled the air as he eased his grip only to squeeze again.

"These tits would look fucking delicious with my cum all over them," he groaned, and I could almost picture him licking his lips. My stomach roiled and acid burned in the back of my throat at his words, but I swallowed it back down.

A car turned the corner allowing the headlights to shine on his face, and I saw the delightful smile spread across his face, just as he moved to the other breast.

"Let's see about getting these titties out so I can admire them before I pierce through this smooth skin..." he moved his face closer again, his mouth right next to my ear then whispered the next words, "and slice those pretty pink nipples off, while I fuck that juicy little cunt of yours." His eyes lit up and his lip turned up in a smirk. I could see as the images he described flashed through his mind.

He moved his hand away from my breast, grabbing his crotch, and then he started to pull at my clothes. He realised he'd need both hands as I started to struggle against him. He pushed the knife further into my neck, and a small droplet of blood trickled down my neck.

"Stay the fuck still, bitch, and I promise I won't hurt you, too much." He threw his head back and released a psychotic laugh that sent a shiver through my entire body. It was cut off just as soon as it had started, and his eyes glazed over before he fell forwards on top of me.

When I finally got the sick fuck off me and took a second to breathe, there stood a petite redhead in gym clothes, and a bag hanging from one hand.

"Did you...Oh my god, thank you so much. How?" I asked, shocked and a little in awe. She wasn't more than 5'5" and though it was clear from her outfit she worked out, she wasn't exactly packing it. She lifted the bag as though that answered all my questions. "What the hell have you got in there, Bricks?" I asked on a chuckle.

"Nah, although, there might be a dumbbell or two in here," she replied, shrugging and winking at me. "I'm Jamie, by the way."

THAT IS how I met Jamie, the feisty little redhead, with a heart of gold. This girl has been my absolute rock. She took me in, helped me get a job, fed me, bought me clothes, like I said, she saved my life.

Emotionally I feel much stronger too, I haven't had an attack for almost 3 months now. Although we've grown close, I haven't shared much with her, and I feel bad about that. But I don't want to put her in any more danger than she already is just by knowing me and having me here is even more of a danger to her, so the quicker I can move out the better.

I'm ready to leave with 5 minutes to spare, and I head down the stairs meeting Jamie in the kitchen.

"How do I look? Scrub up pretty well, don't you think?" I ask, giving her a little twirl. I have on a black pencil skirt, that fits snug to my flared hips and accentuates my hourglass figure. I've paired it with a simple white bell-sleeved blouse and a pair of black kitten heels. No time or inclination for straighteners, I've put my unruly, long dark curls into a neat chignon at the nape of my neck.

"You know, you don't look half bad, Cam," she says, with a smirk on her face, "If I was a college guy trying to study in the library, I'd absolutely do you," she snickers, before clutching her sides, unable to hold it in anymore. I walk over to her, slapping her good-naturedly before picking up the coffee she obviously prepared for me.

We pull up to a stunning glass building, and as I step from the car, I strain my neck to take in the whole building. A 'holy shit' whispers from my lips as the doorman greets me, opening the door and permitting me entry.

The lobby is vast but light and welcoming despite the plain decor. Directly in front of me is a half-moon reception desk behind which a stunning blonde sits with one of those fancy headsets on. I scan the rest of the floor as I approach the desk. To the left is a bank of lifts and on the right are several doors, all closed, with little plaques denoting the purpose of each room. As I near the desk, the blonde lifts her head and smiles wide, almost blinding me with her perfectly straight and bleached to within an inch of their life teeth. Her hair is in a high ponytail that falls down to the middle of her back, and she's wearing a pant suit that probably cost more than my current wardrobe.

"Good morning, how may I help you today," she asks, still smiling wide. Her jaw must be locked in place having to smile like that all damn day.

"Hi. I have an appointment with Miss Hudson at 11am." She looks me up and down, assessing me, before bringing her eyes back to me. She thinks I didn't catch the slight sneer on her face, but I did. I return the gesture, scanning her attire, scrutinising her. I glance at her name badge and store that information for later.

"Of course. Please take a seat and I'll let Miss Hudson know that..." she trails off, clearly waiting for me to fill in my name. I give it to her. "Yes, thank you, Miss Moore, she'll be with you shortly. Have a good day." I don't miss the fact she almost chokes on those words. Jeez, what's her fucking problem? I really hope the rest of the women in this place aren't super bitches like Chantelle here.

I take a seat at the small waiting area just behind and to the right of the reception desk. I watch people come and go for a couple of minutes then look to the small coffee table and the magazines there, picking one up and flicking through the pages.

Suddenly feeling eyes on me, I look up and glance around, seeing nothing obvious for the strange feeling. Just to the left of me something catches my attention, looking over I see the back of a man talking to a woman. As I begin to drop my gaze, the man turns more this way. He's broad, easily topping 6', and wearing a pair of snug black jeans and a black t-shirt, with a pair of light tan, almost grey, Chelsea boots. I can't see his face clearly, but he has short, dark hair, shorn sides and slicked back on top. I can just make out part of a tattoo on the left side of his neck, but he's too far away for me to see exactly what it is. Possibly wings of some sort.

A voice to my right makes me jump, dropping the magazine I was holding. Looking over I see an older woman smiling warmly at me.

"I'm sorry, Miss Moore," I wave her apology away, and try not to look like I was staring at some guy in the foyer. "Would you like to follow me, and we can get started." I nod, placing the magazine back on the table as I stand. I risk a glance back to the man and woman, only they are no longer there.

The interview takes over an hour, and I breathe a huge sigh of relief when I finally exit the building. I spot Jamie over the road leaning against the car, parked in a 'no parking' bay, not a huge surprise. I roll my eyes at her as I get to the other side of the road.

"You honestly don't give a shit, do you?" I mock, shaking my head. She's almost bursting at the seams to ask how it went, and whilst I'd love nothing more than to leave her hanging, I put her out of her misery as I round the car. "Yes, I got the job, and I start Monday. Salary was better than I expected too. Are we going to grab lunch, 'cause I'm starving, and this hangover is still kicking my arse." I look up when she doesn't answer, she's looking at something up the road, "Jamie!" She's still looking down the street. I follow her line of sight and see a guy in his late 50s, just as he greets a woman, pulling her into him and kissing her cheek. Looking back to Jamie, I see a deep frown on her face, "Jamie, who is that? Do you know them?"

"Yeah, I know him. It's my dad, but that is most definitely not my mother!"

THREE

Camryn

After Jamie dropped that bombshell she didn't fancy going for lunch, and to be fair, I don't blame her. We headed back to the house, ordered pizza and decided this shit required alcohol in the form of gin, lots of gin.

From what Jamie has told me, her parents are happily married, now I don't know much about that, but I sure as shit know that kissing another woman in the street doesn't equate to happily married. We watch classic 80's movies all day, eat junk and drink gin until we pass out.

I wake Sunday morning to an incessant pounding on the front door. It's at this point I realise that I'm on the sofa, with one leg on the floor, and the other thrown over the back. Not exactly ladylike but hot if you're getting your freak on, and I store that little nugget away for another time. Then it hits, that's the first time I've thought about sex since...The banging starts again.

"For fuck's sake!" I grumble, "I'm coming, keep your fucking pants on!" I shout, as I stumble off the sofa and stub my toe en-route to the door. I pull the door open, holding my sore toe in one hand and trying to keep my balance, pretty sure I look like a hot mess.

Outside the door, the guy's eyes widen and his mouth drops open "Ah, sorry...err, but are you...erm," he quickly looks to the parcel in his hands, then back to me, "Miss Moore?"

"Wow! I look that bad, huh?" I snort a laugh.

"Oh, no. I...uhm, no you look just fine." His cheeks blaze, and he drops his eyes to the floor.

"Sorry that was kinda mean. I'm just messing with you. To answer your question, yes, I'm Miss Moore. I take it that's for me?" I say, pointing at the parcel. I take him in and notice that he doesn't look like our usual deliver guy, he's much younger, hence the blushing. Poor guy. He's not wearing any sort of uniform either, which is a little strange, but before I get a chance to question it any further, he thrusts the parcel at me. I manage to hold onto it and watch completely dumbstruck as he spins so fast, I'm surprised he doesn't give himself whiplash, stumbles down the drive and books it up the road. "Well, that was fucking weird," I mumble to myself, looking down at the parcel in my hands. Then it hits me that it's Sunday. There are no deliveries on Sundays!

I shut the door and carry the parcel into the living room, placing it on the coffee table. Jamie is still passed out on the floor. How the hell she slept through that racket; I don't know. I sit and look at the package. It's about the size of a book, but it has the hair on my arms standing on end and fear flooding through me. *Please don't let it be from him.* If it is, how the fuck did he find me?

Before the fear takes complete control, I grab it and rip the paper off, immediately dropping it to the floor when I see what it is. *It can't be. It can't be, no, no, no!*

It's a copy of one of my favourite books, *Rebel at Raleigh High*, I have—had the whole series back home. He hated me reading, but it was my escape. I needed it to keep me sane. This is the one and only book he took any interest in, and not for anything other than he liked one of the characters. And it wasn't the hero.

I begin to feel my chest tighten, and my breathing becomes choppy. I'm aware it's happening, and I put my forefinger to my thumb and start to rub, applying pressure as I do.

After Jamie rescued me from the pervy tramp that day, she convinced me to see a counsellor about my anxiety and panic attacks. Whilst I was sceptical at first, I can't be too mad now, she taught me some techniques to stave them off before they take complete control. I continue with my finger hold and take some slow, deep breathes until I start to relax.

"Urgh, my mouth tastes like a whore's arsehole," Jamie mutters, as she sits up, "That image just had my stomach turning over. Ooh, your book came, yay!" She picks it up off the table, turning to read the back. I just sit there in utter shock, not knowing how I feel about that. I can hear Jamie talking, but it sounds fuzzy, like I'm under water. I really thought he'd found me, and I'd have to run again. I don't want to run. I like it here, and I'm finally living like a normal 26-year-old should. Not in fear, not worried about when the next punch is going to come, or when I'll have to give my body to someone who doesn't cherish it but takes what they want, abuses it, sees it as a piece of meat. The fear from earlier has gone and been replaced by anger. An anger that I've not felt in a long time.

"Cam, did you hear me?" I look at Jamie, the smile on her face drops away and worry creeps in. "What's the matter, don't you like it? You said it was one of your favourites, and I wanted to get you something to congratulate you on your new job." She seems unsure, and I hate myself for making her feel that way. So, I suck it up, put my big girl pants on and plaster a smile on my face, hoping she doesn't see right through my fake arse happiness.

"I love it, thank you. I can't believe you did that." I smile wide, even though I actually can't believe she did that, but I know it's not her fault, she doesn't understand. How could she possibly understand when I've kept everything from her. It's been nice to pretend that none of it happened, but that's not realistic. This incident has made me realise that if I ever want to have a shot at a normal life then I need to trust a little more and expel some of this baggage that's weighing me down. I dive out of my seat and hug Jamie. Hugging her tight and hoping she gets it. When I pull back with tears in my eyes, I take a deep breath.

"I think it's time I tell you my story."

"WELL SHIT! That's one hell of a story, Cam." She's sitting at the other end of the sofa from me, and I can see the many questions running through her mind.

"Yeah, it is," I say, and although I haven't told her everything, I've told her enough without, at least I hope, putting her life in any danger. Looking to change the subject, I ask her if she fancies coming into town as there's a few bits I need for work, plus I need the fresh air after that conversation.

When we get back from town, Jamie goes off to cook dinner. She decided that we needed some meat and veg. Take that however you like, I know I'm not getting any, and I don't think she is either.

I head to my room to put away the new clothes I

purchased, well, Jamie purchased if I'm honest. Once I get paid, I intend on paying her back, for everything.

I start hanging the clothes when I spot my duffel bag in the bottom of the wardrobe. I pull it out, opening it, not sure what I'm hoping to find as I haven't looked at this bag since I first moved in with Jamie. I'm not surprised to find it empty as there was never much of value in there anyway. I go to drop it back in the wardrobe when I feel something heavy in a side pocket. I put my hand in and wrap it round...oh my god! I pull out the phone Tyler gave me before I left. I'd forgotten it was even in there.

Plopping to the floor with it in my hands, I just sit and stare at it. Several minutes pass and although I doubt it will work, I push the 'on' button, so I'm surprised when the start-up screen lights up. As it loads, several message alerts ping across the screen that have my heart rate rising and dread falling in the pit of my stomach.

There was only one number saved in the phone and just one person who had this number, but a couple of these messages appear to be from a different number. With shaky hands and fear wrapping round me like a snake round its prey, I click on the first message.

UNKNOWN: Kasey, please come home. I need you. I'm not mad, just come home and we can work it out.

I flick through a few more, all similar to the first one, but as I get to the most recent ones the tone changes. This is the man I know, and dare I say, once loved.

UNKNOWN: You little fucking bitch! I will find you and, baby, when I do, I'm going to make you hurt so bad.

UNKNOWN: You have blood on your hands

too now. He screamed like the little pussy he was. I'm coming for you next, baby, and it's gonna be so fucking pretty watching your blood run. It's making me hard just thinking about it.

There's a link with this message, and when it opens, I watch in horror as Tyler comes in to view. *Oh my god. What did I do?*

Tyler is strung up, arms above his head, but his head is dropped to his chest, so I can't see his face. But I can see the blood that runs down his body in rivulets and pools on the floor below him. I can't see *him* from this angle, but I can see as he swipes out with a switchblade, slashing into Tyler's skin. I drop the phone, running to the bathroom and drop-ping to the floor then heaving into the toilet. Sweat forms on my neck and forehead as I slump back and lean on the bath panel. I grab some tissue, wiping my mouth and closing my eyes as I try to rid my mind of the image of Tyler, but I can't. It will be forever etched into my brain, alongside the pictures of the two people who were most precious to me that he felt necessary to show me; to torture me with as though he hadn't done that enough. The man knows no bounds.

I feel sick to my stomach, and acid still burns in my throat at the thought of Tyler suffering. He didn't deserve to die and certainly not for helping me, but I refuse to let his death be in vain. And I refuse to allow *him* to play the guilt trip on me. I can feel tears well in my eyes, but I won't let them fall. He doesn't deserve any more of my pain or sorrow.

I crawl back to the wardrobe and pick the phone up. I see another message from a different number, and while I'm conscious that it's possible my phone is being tracked, I get the feeling this message is important.

UNKNOWN: Camryn, it's Rick. I know when you left that you had no intention of contacting me, and I totally understand that. However, things have become a little complicated. I know you're probably wondering how I got this number; Tyler gave it to me. He knew things were going pear shaped and gave this to me to ensure your safety. I need you to contact me asap, but don't use this phone. Once you've read this message you need to get rid of the phone. Here's my number, 0784 619 7721, it's secure.

I scramble to my feet, going to my desk and grabbing a pen then quickly writing the number down on a scrap of paper. I double check it before shutting the phone off, putting it on the floor and go to stamp on it, but at the last second, I stop. I know Rick said to get rid of it, but it has evidence on it.

I don't know what the fuck is going on or who Rick is, but I have to believe that if Tyler trusted him then maybe I should too.

From what I know, if a phone is off then it can't be traced, and though there may be ways to get round that, it's been in my bag for over 6 months and so far, I'm safe. He obviously has the number but not where I am. Yet. I take that thought and lock it up tight and pray it stays that way. I put the phone in my desk drawer, and then sit and think about my next move.

FOUR

Blue

Three months ago

"Have you heard from her?" I take a seat at the dining table, grabbing the coffee pot. I turn my nose up as I bring the cup to my mouth. Rick and his fancy arse coffee. I'd much rather have a cup of tea than this sludge.

"No, nothing. Do we still have eyes on her?" Rick asks, and I see the worry in his eyes. He feels bad for letting her walk away, for not trying harder to get her talking. I understand how he feels.

I had no idea who she was outside Rick's that day, although to be honest, I was more interested in getting to know her for another reason. Shit! This is what happens when I let my dick have control.

"No, and we haven't since she left the streets. It's like she just disappeared." I pray to god that's not the truth. "I have a contact in the Manchester area that's doing some digging." I tell him, rubbing my thumb and forefinger across my brow and trailing my hand down my face, across the stubble that's growing. Rick nods just as his phone rings, pulling it out and answering as he leaves the room.

I sip my coffee while running different scenarios through my mind and none of them are good. I can't believe we just fucking let her walk away.

At the time, we had a man on the inside, and now he's fucking dead. Tyler was a fucking good man, and it makes my blood boil that the bastard took him out. I've been in touch with his wife and made sure that she and the family are well looked after, but it's no fucking consolation.

Now, without Tyler, we have no idea of Sean's movements or even if he has any leads on where Kasey is, which is pushing my stress levels through the fucking roof. I can't wrap my head around how such a beautiful woman could get mixed up with a twisted motherfucker like Sean Donovan. I just have to hope that my contact comes through for us.

Rick comes back in with a deep frown on his face. "Something up?" I ask, not sure I really want to know the answer.

"I'm not sure," he says, as he grabs the folder sitting on the table, chucks back the last of his coffee then turns to me. "We have a possible sighting of her. And before you get too excited, it's not concrete." I jump up from my chair, but before I can get a word out, Rick cuts me off, "I thought maybe you would like to go check it out?" I see the fucking smile in his eyes, and I can almost feel the ribbing he's dying to give me but won't if he knows what's good for him.

"Too fucking right I do! What do we know?" I ask, as we head out the front door.

Within the hour I'm on the road to Manchester, and although we don't have much of a lead, it's something. I'm to meet a guy called Lee, who apparently works at an upscale bar in Spinningfields. It's the financial district and best known for its entertainment and cocktail bars. Lee thinks that he worked with Kasey for a while, but he can't be one hundred percent until he's seen a picture of her. It would have been easy to send a picture to his phone, but neither of us wanted to risk it. Sean has eyes everywhere.

FIVE

Camryn

It's been almost a week since I found the messages on my old phone, and I'm still not sure what to do. I know I can't, or shouldn't, leave it too much longer. But what the hell do I do? I'm so scared that if I get in touch with Rick it will lead *him* to me. But if I don't, then not only does he get away with murder, but there are no guarantees he won't find me anyway.

I don't know exactly what Rick does, but I remember the card he gave me the day I met him. Unfortunately, I don't have it anymore, only remembering that he works for a security company. Whatever the fuck that means. I could speak to Jamie about it, but I don't really want to drag her into this anymore than I already have. Although, I could use her laptop and see if there is anything online about him. Shit! I don't even know his last name. That's the end of that fucking idea.

Just then I hear the door downstairs and head to the kitchen to find Jamie putting bags of shopping on the counter.

"Hey." She turns to look at me as I near the breakfast bar, I nod to the bags, "You planning on cooking up a storm? Shit, did you buy the whole supermarket?" I laugh.

"Nah, I invited a couple of the girls round, thought that we could have a girl's night. A few movies, several drinks and some nibbles. You know, a sort of celebration of your first week at work," she says, while she unpacks the mountain of snacks she bought. I walk over to help her, picking up the last bag which just so happens to be the drinks.

"Ooh, are we making cocktails?" I ask, pulling out ingredients for Mojitos, "Now that, I'm definitely down for." I clap, then rub my hands together excited to see the girls. We spend several minutes chatting about our day, and then I head to my room to shower and change.

After my shower, I pull out some comfy joggers and a slouch, off-shoulder tee before heading to my dresser for underwear. As I shut the drawer, my eyes land on the scrap of paper with Rick's number on it. My eyes quickly flick to the phone on my bedside table, and before I have time to change my mind, I grab the number, walking to the phone and dialling it without a thought to what it will mean. As it rings, part of me hopes no one will answer and absolve me feeling any guilt when I don't bother to try again. But I know that's no good. I made the choice to run, I made the choice to live, and now is my chance to make sure that all the precious lives lost because of me weren't for nothing. I don't want to live my life in fear, forever looking over my shoulder, so I need to man the fuck up. As that thought goes through my head the line connects, and I'm met with a voice that as the fear inside me settling.

"Hello, Rick Sullivan speaking." I try to speak but nothing comes out. "Hello," another pause and then, "Camryn, is that you?" I gasp, shit! How does he know it's me?

"Yes, it's me." I hear him sigh down the phone, and then rustling noises as he moves around. "How did you know it was me?" I ask, a little unsure now. My fear spikes again, but I push it down refusing to let it control me or stop me from doing what's right.

"I didn't, not for sure. I guess I just hoped it was you. Are you okay? Are you safe?" I can hear the hesitation in his voice, and almost see him holding his breath while he waits for me to put his mind at ease.

"I'm safe, well, at least I think I am. What's going on Rick, do you know what happened to Tyler?" I hear a mumbled 'shit' and then him whispering to someone before he comes back to me.

"Look, I'm sending someone to you." I shake my head before realising he can't see me through the phone, but just as I go to speak he cuts me off, "Don't be scared, you've met before, and I trust him with my life. He'll be there soon, and then he'll fill you in, as much as possible anyway." The last bit is mumbled, but I still heard him. "Did you hear me, Camryn, is that okay?"

"Yes, okay" And before I can say anything else the line goes dead. Fuck! What does this mean, who's he sending here, and how the fuck does he know where I am?

I lay back on my bed, grab a pillow and scream into it. Afterwards, I get dressed, and then go and make cocktails because, boy, do I need one right now. By the time Jamie comes down, I've made two jugs of Mojito and am already on my second glass. Jamie grabs a glass from the counter and pours herself one, taking a large gulp and nearly chokes.

"Fuck...How much did you put in here?" She manages to splutter. Oops, I think I may have been a little overzealous with the rum. We spend the next thirty minutes setting out the snacks in the lounge and drinking more of my strong as fuck Mojitos.

I don't think any more about my call with Rick and just plan to enjoy the evening. And that is exactly what I do.

It's just past midnight when we call it a night, the girls, Jess and Marie are at the door. They are attempting to put their coats on, very badly at that. After all the usual hugging and air kissing bullshit, Marie opens the front door and steps out, but then spins around, almost falling and breaking her neck.

"Who's the hottie, do you know him?" she whisper-shouts, throwing her head over her shoulder and drawing our attention down the drive to the road.

Once I'm sure she's not going to topple over, I lift my head looking in the direction she gestured to, and lo and behold...Oh, you've got to be fucking shitting me! Leaning against a sleek, black car, one leg crossed over the other and arms folded across his massive chest, is none other than 'pretty boy' from Rick's house.

Obviously hearing us, he lifts his head, and his eyes immediately find mine. Woah! That is fucking hot as hell. His head is tilted slightly allowing his hair to fall forward as his stare penetrates right through me. To the very bones of me. A shiver runs through my body that has goosebumps spreading across my skin like waves on the shore. I break our gaze when I hear Jamie behind me asking if I know him.

"Yeah. Yeah, I know him." Without another word, I walk down the drive towards him, and it's like my feet have a mind of their fucking own. When I reach him, he rises to his full height, towering over me, and now I'm face to face with his broad chest. I have to crane my neck to be even close to looking him in the eye, but it does make me realise just how close to him I am. More than that, I'm not even afraid, and that thought has my mind in a complete spin.

Taking a step back, so as not to end up with a crook neck, I finally meet his eyes. And boy, are they pretty fucking eyes. I remember seeing them at Rick's, but I certainly don't remember how stunningly blue they are. They are an azure blue, the exact colour of the sky on a clear day and it feels like I could take a swim in them.

"Hey," is all I manage to get out of my mouth before it dries up like the Sahara dessert. The corner of his lip quirks up, and a dimple appears that has my heart literally skipping a beat at the sight. I'm so screwed.

"Hey, Bambi, good to see you again. You going to introduce me to your friends?" he says, flicking his eyes over my shoulder to where I'm absolutely certain the girls are standing with their jaws on the floor.

After quick introductions, to Jess and Marie, whose taxi couldn't have arrived at a better time, we say our goodbyes and head inside. I can feel eyes on me the whole way into the house, in fact, I can feel two sets of eyes on me, and it's making me nervous.

We move to the lounge, and as Blue takes a seat, Jamie acts the perfect host offering him a drink. I already know what's coming.

"Err...Cam, can you join me in the kitchen for a second, please?" Jamie asks, before heading that way. To be honest I'm grateful for the reprieve because I feel like I'm caught in a riptide and the sea is about to swallow me whole. I have no idea how I'm supposed to explain this to her. *'Jamie, this is Blue. We met when I went to his friend to get a new identity.'* You know, 'cause that's an everyday occurrence. When I shared my story with Jamie, I left huge parts out, and now I feel like it's all going to be exposed.

I'm not ready for that, not ready at all! My chest begins to tighten, anxiety kicking in as I move towards the kitchen.

The instant we enter the kitchen, Jamie whirls around on me and I brace myself for the questions.

"Start talking. I want to know everything." I can see the sparkle of excitement in her eyes, and I'm a little surprised. "I'm assuming, you know, as you're not screaming the walls down, he's not the ex?" She moves around the kitchen as she waits me out. Come on Camryn, think for fuck sakes, think!

"Err...No, not the ex. He's just a guy I met before I came to Manchester, no one important," I say, with a shrug.

"You wound me, Bambi." The sound of Blue's rich, velvety smooth voice right behind me has my hand flying to my chest in fright, but I don't turn around, I can't. My feet are stuck to the floor.

I hear the slight rustle of clothes then the warmth of his hands on the tops of my arms and that's it. That right there is my breaking point. I spin away so fast it makes me dizzy.

"Don't touch me!" The venomous edge to my tone has Jamie arching a brow in surprise. I hold my hands out warning them to stay back as Jamie takes a step forward.

I try to take a few deep breaths, but my chest feels like it's in a vice slowly crushing me in its jaws and every breath tightens the screws. My eyes dart around the room looking for an escape, and then they land on Blue's. His brow is drawn together, but his eyes remain soft. I see the confusion in them and the apology, but it's not enough to calm me. I'm lost to the vision of another's hands on me.

WE'D BEEN out for our usual date night when Sean had taken a call halfway through the evening, and ever since, his mood had soured. I had assumed it was because of the call, and maybe it was partly, but once we arrived home it become all too clear that wasn't the only reason.

As soon as we entered the house, he lost his shit, shouting and screaming in my face about how I had flirted with the waiter, giving him the eye all night. I knew what was coming, and that my night would end with me bruised and broken, again. I just had no idea how very bad it would be. He slapped me across the face, and as I tried to run, Lewis grabbed my arms from behind, his grip on my biceps was bruising.

"Fucking hold her still. This little whore needs to learn a lesson, and I'm going to enjoy it so very fucking much," he shouted, sneering at me. He grabbed his crotch, and I could clearly see the outline of his hard dick.

Sean started slapping me again, my lip split, and blood trickled to the floor. Lewis was still holding me, and I could hear the smile in his grunt when I tried to pull my arms free.

"You want to act like a whore, then I'll fucking treat you like one." Sean pulled his favourite knife from his pocket, and the colour drained from my face. I already knew the pain of that blade. Stepping forward, he grabbed my chin in a vice like grip, yanking my head back to him when I tried to turn away from him. "I'm going to show you how I fuck whores, and then maybe I'll let Lewis here have a go too."

Then I begged. "No, Sean. Please, I'll be good, I'm sorry, it won't happen again. I'll keep my eyes to the floor, I prom- ise." I remember searching the room looking for someone that might help me, but it was pointless. Nobody gave a shit.

He slapped be again, and before I could recover, he ripped my dress open, running the flat edge of the knife down my cheek to my collarbone. When he reached the centre of my breasts, he flipped it, pressing the pointed tip into my flesh and piercing the skin. I felt the flow of warm blood as it seeped from my skin. The metallic smell had made my stomach clench and bile rise in my throat. Pulling the knife away, he slid it under my bra and yanked forward, slicing my bra in two. A whimper left me, and I felt the first tear fall down my cheek.

I started begging again, but it made no difference. Sean cut the rest of my underwear away, leaving me standing there in the shredded remains of my dress. Lewis' hold on me remained, and when Sean reached out to touch my naked breast, I flinched backwards. Lewis practically purred as my arse made contact with his crotch. He held me, watched and enjoyed every second of Sean's assault on my body, and when Sean removed his belt, undoing his trousers, I knew right then that this would be the worst night of my life.

COMING OUT OF THE MEMORY, I watch as Blue steps back, holding his hands up and mirroring my own.

"It's okay, I won't come any closer, I promise." I can feel his sincerity, but my fucked-up brain won't allow me to believe it. "How about…" he pauses, looking to Jamie, and from the corner of my eye I see the silent conversation pass between them. This time when Blue speaks, he's more confident, assured about whatever it is he's going to say. "How about I go back to the lounge and leave you two alone for a minute? Jamie can make that drink she promised me, and then we can talk, huh. That sound good?" He's talking to me like a frightened child, it's patronising as hell, but I get it.

I feel like a cornered animal. My body is ready to fight back without a thought for the repercussions, and adrenaline has flooded my system as my fight or flight response kicks in. I just nod my head; it's all my body is capable of right now. Immediately, Blue edges backwards, lowering his hands as he goes. He doesn't turn or look away until he reaches the door to the lounge, and then he disappears from sight altogether.

My breath leaves me, one I didn't even know I was holding, and I sink to the floor, drawing my knees into my chest with my head back on the kitchen cupboard. I'm conscious of movement, but I don't open my eyes or look to the sound because I know it's just Jamie. She's giving me time and space, and she has no idea how thankful I am for it. I sit there as a whispered conversation floats to me from the lounge, one I only catch snippets from.

And I sit.

I don't know how long I stay there for, but it feels like the longest time. Eventually, I become aware of someone sitting next to me.

"Cam? Blue left." I roll my head along the cupboard until I'm looking at her. I guess she must see surprise or shock in my eyes and adds, "He didn't want to, trust me. I practically had to force him out the door," she says, rolling her eyes, "But you've been sat here for almost an hour..."

"An hour? I've been sat here for an hour?" I ask incredulously, she just nods in reply. "I'm sorry, Jamie."

"What on earth are you apologising for?"

"For everything. Freaking out on you, bringing shit to your door." *Fucking your life up, putting you in possible danger.* But I don't voice those because I'm a fucking coward. Jamie just tuts like it's no big deal but it is. She thinks it's no big deal because that's what I've let her think. What's she going to say when all my secrets poor out of the bulging closet? The doors are already straining at the seams, lie upon lie, secret upon secret, and they will all come crashing out. Like a tsunami they will consume and destroy everything in its path.

I help Jamie lock up, and without another word between us we go our separate ways. I'm not sure how I feel about that; part of me thinks it's probably for the best, but then the other part is sad for the loss of a friendship. One that has kept me tethered and sane.

SIX

Blue

Fuck! Fuck, fuck, fuck! I slam my hand on the steering wheel. And again, when that doesn't even touch the aggression flowing through my body right now. I don't know what I'm angrier at; the fact that I scared the shit out of her, or the fact that I even care that much. Yeah, that makes me sound like a complete arsehole, but why change the habit of a lifetime, right? Don't get me wrong, I'm not completely devoid of emotion or feeling, but I don't get these feelings. What is it about this fucking woman that has me twisted up like the cords of a rope?

From the moment I met her, and at that point she was a target for the next notch on my man-whore bedpost, there was something different, something appealing about her, and she hasn't left my mind since.

When Rick finally filled me in on exactly who she was it just fuelled the fire already burning within me. A fire I've not felt since...Well, let's just say in a long time. I don't have time for relationships or romantic shit, and there sure ain't no white picket fence and 2.4 children in my future. That hasn't stopped me searching all over Manchester looking for her and following every fucking lead possible, and though I might not want to admit it right now, it sure as shit wasn't just because of the job.

My phone starts ringing in my pocket, and I pull it out to see it's Rick, then drop it to my lap. It rings off, then immediately starts back up again, which tells me he won't give up till I answer. Before it can ring off a second time I answer.

"Yes." I wince at my tone, "Sorry, man. What's up?"

"Oh, wow!" he chuckles, "Is Cam proving to be impervious to your charms, you must be losing your touch."

"Shut it, Sully, this is fucking serious." I blow a breath down the phone, "How much do you know about her, Sully? 'Cause from what I just witnessed; we don't know the half of it. Are you sure Tyler gave you everything because I feel we are missing something? And I ain't talking no little something either." I'm met by a few choice words before Sully asks me to meet him at a hotel. Obviously, he's in town and that has me concerned.

On my way to the hotel, I go over my conversation with Camryn's friend Jamie. From what she said, it would appear we are not the only ones in the dark. Which tells me that Camryn doesn't trust anyone, and that's going to make our job twice as hard. I need to remember, that despite what my dick thinks or wants, this is just another job.

Jamie wasn't able to tell me anything about Sean, in fact, she seemed surprised when I mentioned his name. I'm not stupid enough to have given her his surname because being in Manchester means nothing to men like him. Him and others like him have eyes and ears everywhere, that's a big worry, and the main reason why I'm just glad we found her before he did. At least I hope that's the case.

I won't know for certain what Camryn knows until I speak with her in the morning. What I do know, is that if Sean Donovan finds her, it will be game over. Whatever she did or took from him, has him gunning for her like he's at war.

When I arrive at the hotel, Sully is leaning against his car, looking casual as hell and not at all like it's almost 2am. Jerk!

We find a corner in the bar, near the back and away from nosey bastards. I catch him up on what went down tonight, and when I'm finished, he doesn't look surprised in the slightest. When I ask him what he knows, he gives me a pained sigh and rubs both hands down his face, leaving them cupped around his mouth. Then he tells me the one thing no man, no real man, wishes to hear. I knew it was bad, but this...It explains her reaction tonight. Now I feel doubly shit for touching her.

Tyler had told us that Sean liked to be heavy handed with her, but he never mentioned anything about rape or sexual assault.

Men like Sean Donovan don't have an ounce of respect for their women. They are nothing more than property, and there to be used and abused as they see fit. For a man who has ties to several gangs and has been mentioned in relation to sex trafficking, it's not a big leap to imagine how he treats his own woman.

His ties to the sex trafficking world are the reason for our interest in the first place. Amongst other things.

We talk for a little longer, now we have no man inside things are a damn sight harder. Without Tyler we have no idea of Sean's movements and despite the fact we have Seb and a few of the other guys keeping tabs, it's not enough.

Sully plans to head back to London tomorrow and meet

with Seb, and I'm going to stay here with Camryn. I've been here three months chasing every lead we had, and now we've found her there's no way I'm leaving. This is just another job, and it will get done one way or another. That's what I keep telling myself anyway.

SEVEN

Camryn

What little sleep I had was like a show reel of every bad memory. What happened in the kitchen last night, when Blue touched me, has me feeling all kinds of screwed up. I know he won't hurt me; I mean the guy is a giant and gives off a 'don't fuck with me' vibe, but I've never felt safer than when he's near. Which is utterly ridiculous because I hardly know him? Besides, my arsehole radar must be broken, or I wouldn't be in this fucking position in the first place.

I smack my hand on my forehead a couple of times hoping to knock some sense into myself. I don't have room in my mind to sort out my feelings towards Blue, and I certainly have no idea how to make sense of my reactions to him. Before my mind threw me into that terrible memory, Blue's touch was warm, I could feel his rough callouses brush over my skin and even pictured his hands travelling my body. I shake my head, clearing the image, as if he'd ever be interested in damaged goods. The man is hot, like feel the burn from another county hot, and no doubt has women lining the streets to get a piece of him.

Urgh! I get up and shower hoping it will wash all the shit away, but it doesn't. I'll never be clean again, I'm tainted. My body has scars that nobody can see, has endured pain and suffering that is buried deep below the surface, and now I have blood on my hands. The blood of the most precious person, the one person that gave me purpose and a reason to live, to fight.

"MUMMY, MUMMY, LOOK WHAT I DID." Faye runs to me where I'm sat on the patio. As she reached me, I scooped her up and set her on my lap. She's waving a piece of paper and talking incessantly. I grab the paper and lay it on her knees to get a better look at it.

"Wow! You did this? It's beautiful, just like you," I told her, bopping her on her tiny little nose. She grins up at me and then tells me.

"It's for you, that big star is me though." I chuckle, of course it is. A small frown formed on her cute little face, and when I asked her why, she said, "You said that I'm the bright that lights up the dark, is that not true?"

My heart aches at that statement, and then I tell her, "Oh, baby girl, it is all true, you are the brightest star in the sky, and when you get older you will shine for everyone."

AS THE MEMORY fades tears slide down my face. Who would have known how significant that conversation has become.

When I was sleeping on the streets, I would often look at the night sky and search for the brightest star. My daughter. The one good thing that bastard gave me, only for her to be snatched away. I was so stupid to think that we could live in his fucked-up world and remain safe and untouched.

I hear the front door downstairs and hushed voices, but I'm so lost in my mind it doesn't really register. It becomes clear exactly how lost to my thoughts I am when I don't hear Jamie come into the room, and it's only as she crouches in front of me, I realise she's there.

"Hey. You okay?" She searches my face, I know she can see the tears, but she doesn't mention them. I don't try to stop them from falling, I can't hold them in anymore and I won't. Faye deserves more than to be hidden away like a dirty secret. That is one thing she'll never be. She was my greatest achievement, the reason I'm here now, and why I'll fight to the end. I look at Jamie, who is now kneeling before me, and she takes my hands and nods, telling me it's okay.

Taking a deep breath and gathering the courage I need to get through this conversation I say, "I had a daughter." She lets out a little gasp but doesn't interrupt. "Her name was Faye, and she died a couple of months before her 4th birthday along with my mum." I close my eyes against the pain mentioning her name brings. "My mum and I had been shopping while Faye was at nursery, but I got a call saying she wasn't well and could I pick her up. Mum had persuaded me to get my hair cut while we were there, and I was halfway through." I shake my head, wishing I had just left then instead of staying. "My mum said she would get her and come back for me, but I told her to take her straight home if she wasn't feeling well. It wasn't a big deal I would get a cab, but on the way home they were hit by a truck and forced into a ditch. Apparently, they both..." the words get stuck in my throat, but I swallow the pain back down determined to get them out, "they both...d-died on impact, they were there for over an hour, Jamie. Nobody knew. Nobody knew and they just lay there dead." A sob breaks free, dropping my head in my hands. After several seconds, I sniff, swiping the tears away. "It wasn't until I got home and realised they weren't there, that I knew something had happened." The tears fall down my face and pain stabs at my heart, ripping and shredding the walls I built to block it all out. Tearing me wide open.

Jamie moves to sit next to me on the bed, taking me in her arms, and I drop my head to her shoulder and sob. I thought I'd cried all my tears. I thought I locked my grief away, and I did, but grief can't be contained, it will eat away at you until there is nothing left.

"It's all my fault, Jamie. I killed my daughter, she died because of me." Jamie pushes me back, holding me in place by my shoulders.

"No, Cam. That is not true, it wasn't your fault. You can't really believe that?" she says, tilting her head to the side, her brow raised in disbelief. "Why would you even think that? You weren't driving, and you can't control other people's actions." I start shaking my head at her, it doesn't matter what she says, it's my fault because I stupidly fell for a man who is the personification of the devil himself, and I foolishly believed he loved me.

"You don't understand," I pause, aware that now is the perfect time to tell her about *him*. But it seems I don't have to.

"You're talking about Sean, aren't you?" she asks, and as soon as the name falls from her mouth, I'm up on my feet.

"What the fuck! How do you know that name? I never told you his name. Shit, shit, shit! Does he know I'm here? I should have died on the street that night. Should never have come here with you." I'm pacing the bedroom, head down and chewing my thumb nail. I need to leave; I can't stay here anymore. I know how this goes, I watch the TV, I've read those books, but there ain't no happy ever after for me.

I walk to my wardrobe and start pulling out clothes, I grab the duffel and instantly feel sick at the thought of going on the run again, but what choice do I have. If I stay here, he will find me, and he will rain down hell on everyone I know. I don't want more blood on my hands. I start thinking about where I can go while I load the clothes into my bag.

"Woah, hold on, what do you think you're doing, Cam?" But I don't stop, then she's in front of me, and the bag is snatched from my hand, "Stop, you can't leave."

"I have to, Jamie. If he knows I'm here, he'll come for me, and he won't hesitate to ki..." I'm cut off as Blue charges into the room, heading straight for me. My breath catches in my throat at the anger on his face. I take a step back as he advances, my back hits the wall, and then he's there.

"He won't even get close," he growls, caging me in with an arm either side of my head, "he won't lay one finger on you..." His velvety voice washes over me as he leans in closer, breath whispering across the shell of my ear, "Because if he does—I'll kill him. I'll make him beg for his life and wish he'd never laid a finger on you. Do you understand?" I open my mouth to speak, but nothing comes out. I've never been so scared and turned on at the same time. I just nod, it's so subtle if he blinked, he'd have missed it. "Good. Now, I'm starving," he pauses, I turn my head, our lips are almost touching, and I get the feeling he's not exactly talking about food, "get dressed, we're going for breakfast." With that, he turns and leaves the room as quick as he came. I slump against the wall and blow out a deep breath.

"Holy fucking shit, that was hot!" I look over to Jamie,

raising my brows. "What? Come on, you can't tell me that didn't make your fanny flutter." I screw my nose up at that. "Bitch, please," she says waving me off, "I need clean underwear and a couple good orgasms. Enjoy your *breakfast*."

I'm so confused. Firstly, I didn't even know he was in the damn house. Secondly, that damn man brings out the strangest feelings in me. I mean, how can you be scared and so turned on you think you're going to come without so much as a kiss. Jamie was right, it was hot, but I shouldn't feel like that about a man that oozes danger. I can see it in his eyes and feel it in him, he's a man that has blood on his hands too. But somehow, deep in the very pit of my gut, I know he's nothing like Sean.

I find that Sean's name doesn't produce as much fear as it once did. Maybe I gave him too much power over me by not saying his name, scared he'd appear behind me like the fucking Candy Man.

As I finish dressing, I think about what Blue said, the whole 'wish he'd never laid a finger on me', and what that means. He can't possibly know about all the beatings and— the other things Sean did to me, can he? Nah, there's no way, I'm being stupid, but I plan to ask him about it later.

Downstairs there is no sign of Jamie, guess she wasn't lying about the underwear and orgasms. The less I think about that the better.

I do, however, find Blue in the lounge scanning the bookcase. I watch him from the door, but I'm not daft enough to think he isn't aware I'm here; he'd hear a pin drop in a crowded room. Several minutes pass before he turns.

"You ready to go?" he asks, striding towards me.

"Yes. Where are we going?" He doesn't answer just walks straight past me. I shake my head as I follow after him, "You knew I was there the whole time, didn't you?" I ask.

"Sure did, I'll always know where you are." He chuckles.

See, I fucking knew it! Dangerous and veering into stalker territory, but I'm surprised to find it doesn't worry me. Not sure what that says about my own sanity.

EIGHT

Camryn

We drive into town in Blue's fancy arse car, the same one he was in last night. Apparently, it's some high spec armoured car, an Audi RS7, that him, Sully and Seb all have. When I ask him who Sully and Seb are, I'm surprised to learn that Sully is Rick, who they call Sully because of his surname, Sullivan, and Seb is their other partner in the business.

"So, if Rick is called Sully, I'm guessing Blue isn't your real name?" I ask, as I shift in my seat so I'm facing him more. Watching his reactions, but all I get is a little smirk.

"What makes you think that, something wrong with the name Blue?" His face is all serious, but there's a teasing tone to his words. Okay, if that's the game he wants to play.

"Well, no, but…" I pause just long enough to see him flick his eyes to me, trying to read if I'm serious or not, "it's not exactly, you know—"

"No, I don't know. Not exactly what?" All trace of teasing is gone now, this is his serious voice. I stifle a laugh, but the bastard hears me, as I thought, eyes and ears like a fucking hawk. "Oh, you think you're funny, huh. If I wasn't driving right now, I'd span—" he cuts off abruptly, and I turn to see a frown cross his brows.

I don't need to be a genius to work out what he was about to say. Before Sean I wasn't afraid of a little spanking, but it's been a long time since the thought of a rough hand slapping my arse turned me on. Blue, however, seems to have jump started my libido as it snaps awake and has me squeezing my thighs together at the thought of how good his hand on my body would feel. I have no idea what possesses me to do it, but I turn to face him.

"Is that right, pretty boy," I say, my voice sultry as I lean over, I lower it to just above a whisper, "you'd like that wouldn't you?" I watch his throat as he swallows, realising I know what he was going to say. He shifts slightly in his seat. "Guess what...it ain't ever going to fucking happen." Immediately moving back to my seat and looking out my window to avoid looking at him. I can feel his eyes on me, but I can't look at his beautiful blues right now.

I give a mental fist bump to the return of my former sassy self. It feels good, more like the me before Sean came into my life and destroyed my very soul. Crushing and tearing down everything that made me, me. He's taken too much from me, and I refuse to let him have anymore of me.

We travel the rest of the way in silence, the previous tension has ebbed away and it's nice. I don't look back to Blue until we pull up outside what looks like apartments, but the lower floor is made up of a bar and a restaurant.

This is not the usual tower block, in some run-down part of town, no, this is something else. There's a freaking concierge, and someone coming down to park the car. Blue hands over the keys as he steps out before coming to my side and opening my door. Where I'm still sat in some sort of shock. I'm not stupid, I've stayed places like this with Sean, and yes, I'm being unfairly judgemental, but it's just not what I expected when I look at Blue. Yes, he has an armoured car, but I just assumed it was a company car.

"What is this place?" I ask, taking his offered hand and stepping out of the car.

The building sits on the corner of two roads, with the front entrance at the apex of where the two corners of the building meet. On one side of the entrance is a bar, currently closed but looks to be the kind where if your name's not down, you ain't coming in. And the other side is a restaurant, and here was me thinking we'd go to some greasy spoon. He doesn't let go of my hand as we walk up the steps to the entrance, where the concierge opens the door.

"Welcome back, Mr Hawkins," he greets, tipping his head to Blue and offering me a smile. I smile in return, uttering a barely audible 'good morning'.

The inside reminds me of a hotel with what looks like a reception desk but is actually a security desk, where a security guard sits. He is surrounded by a bank of CCTV screens. Off to the right are several lifts, with a small seating area, but we walk to the left, past the security guard to a single lift there. Blue's long strides have me practically jogging to keep up as he's still holding my hand, and I'm still none the wiser about where we're going.

As we enter the lift, Blue pulls a key card from his back pocket, swiping it through the access panel. The doors close, and we begin to climb. There are no numbers displayed to indicate what floor we are heading to, and we don't stop until we reach what seems to be the top floor.

When the doors open, I'm faced with an open plan living space that must cover nearly the whole top floor of the building. Wow! To the left of me, there a couple of steps that lead down to a curved, sunken lounge area, with cream leather seating set in semi-circles, and a large grey coffee table shaped like a pebble in the centre. The far wall has bi-folding doors from end to end leading to a balcony, with a small bar area, and seating around a fire pit. As I walk further in, I see a kitchen area with a breakfast bar to the right, and directly in front of me there is a large dining table and chairs. Just past the kitchen is a hall that must lead to the bedrooms and bathroom.

Blue lets go of my hand, "So, what do you fancy for breakfast then?" he asks, as he walks towards the kitchen. Looking over his shoulder when he realises I'm not following him. "You can close your mouth now. Come on, I'll give you the big tour after we've eaten."

He's not wrong, my jaw was dragging on the floor. I'm kind of speechless, this is not what I was expecting at all.

I take a seat at the breakfast bar as Blue moves around the kitchen, gathering everything he needs from various cupboards. I watch shamelessly, especially when he gives me a great view of his arse in those jeans. They fit so snug to his toned backside, that I can almost see his glutes flexing with every move he makes.

He's broad with powerful, well defined muscles that taper to a trim and toned waist, covered by another black t-shirt. I bet he has a six-pack and a happy trail leading to the most spectacular... Okay, knock it off.

Completely lost in my ogling, I hadn't noticed Blue now stands on the other side of the breakfast bar in front of me, with two glasses of orange juice, the smell of bacon cooking, but here he stands with the cockiest smile on his face. He absolutely knows I was checking him out, but you know what, I don't give a shit.

"Don't get too excited, pretty boy," I say, plastering a devilish smile on my face, while he quirks a brow at my nickname for him. "I'm not adverse to a little window shopping, doesn't mean I want to buy it or even try it on for size. One of them for me?" I ask, pointing at the drinks in his hands and winking at him. Damn. What is it about this guy that makes my lips so loose and me lose all self-preservation of life because I'm pretty sure he could crush me with one hand.

The cocky grin on his face doesn't even falter, taking a step forward and placing the drink in front of me forces him to lean closer. My back straightens, and I lift my chin, giving him the impression I'm not afraid. But I'm very afraid. Not of him but of what he does to me, and how he makes my body react to him. My thighs automatically come together, and I feel my nipples harden at the hooded look in his eyes.

"Oh, Bambi." He drops his eyes to my chest, a knowing look on his face. "Don't kid yourself, you and I both know one taste would never be enough. Mmmm, the things I could do to your body would have you screaming for more and begging me to never stop. I'd own you."

Those words reverberate around my brain, penetrating through the fog of lust that Blue created. It's not the first time I've heard those words, but they never meant anything more than just possession in its rawest form. I thought I'd be disgusted hearing them again, from another man no less, but I couldn't have been more wrong. The way Blue said them has me tied up in knots, not from fear or anger but with want, and that confuses the hell out of me.

The soft caress of fingers on my cheek brings me back, "Hey, where did you go? I lost you for a second there." I look at him and take a swim in the deep blue depths of his eyes. It's like they've hypnotised me, drawing me in closer and closer, lips just a breath apart. A blaring siren has me jumping back, and the smell of smoke and burnt bacon assaults my nose.

"Shit!" Blue spins away, grabbing a tea towel as he turns off the hob, moving the pan to the sink, then waving the towel at the fire alarm. I attempt to curb a giggle, not very successfully. Blue eyes me over his shoulder, he looks pissed, but I'm not sure if it's aimed at me, or the burnt bacon.

Deciding it's probably best to remove myself from the firing line, I tell him I'm going to go sit in the lounge, grabbing my drink as I leave. If you can't stand the heat, get out of the kitchen, and that kitchen was definitely packing some heat.

On my way to the lounge I check out the view, it's stunning. I also notice that the balcony wraps around the whole of the outside, and I spot a hot tub too.

Stepping down into the lounge area, I place my drink on the pebble coffee table and take a look around. The artwork on the walls is a little dark and unusual, but I find I quite like it. I don't see any photos except one on the far wall, as I draw closer and the picture becomes clearer, I realise it's of a group of army soldiers. I recognise two of the three front and centre. Blue stands in the middle with his arm around the two either side of him, Rick being the one on the left. I don't know the other guy on the right, but I'm not at all surprised they're ex-army. They look close, and I wonder if the third guy is Seb, Blue and Rick's other colleague.

I hear movement behind me, but before I'm able to turn around, a warm body brushes against my back. He doesn't touch me, and I'm so grateful, clearly remembering what happened the last time.

"That's you and Rick, right, and I'm guessing the other guy is Seb?" I ask, turning my head so I can see him when he doesn't answer. He nods, then reaching past me he points to another of the guys in the picture, but I don't even hear what he says. His close proximity mixed with the earlier sexual tension has my brain short circuiting, which becomes even more obvious when I try to turn around and escape. I literally bump into his chest and bounce back off. I wait for the inevitable pain from landing on my arse, but it never comes. Instead, I'm hauled up against Blue, with his arm wrapped tightly around me. And I mean tightly. I can feel every inch of his hot as fuck body, and my breath lodges in my throat. My hands rest on his pecs, palms sweating and my breath choppy.

"Steady, Bambi." His voice is husky, and thinly veiled lust pours off him. "Breakfast is ready," he says, his eyes glisten with the blatant innuendo, and then he slowly releases me.

Jamie was right, my fanny is fluttering, and I seriously need some new knickers.

NINE

Camryn

We sit at the breakfast bar to eat, and Blue tells me a little about his time in the army. I can tell he's holding back, not giving too much away, but I don't blame him because I know that being in the army holds some memories you wish to never speak of again. He's particularly reserved when it comes to Rick's past, but again, that's not his story to tell, and I totally understand his loyalty.

Blue talks about their security firm, Triple R Security, that him and Rick set up after leaving the army four years ago, and Seb joined them a year later.

He finally tells me that his real name is Ryder. When I test it out in my head, my dirty little mind is very vocal about how she'd let him 'ryde' her any time, but I shut her down.

The conversation flows until the topic of me comes up, my first reaction is to clam up, but I realise if I want to move forward then I need to open up a little. I give him the basics, single child, parents both dead, it hurts like hell to say it out loud, but I do it. I tell him how I went to university and studied journalism, completely avoiding Sean altogether, but I know it won't stop him from asking. I'm not stupid enough to think that Rick hasn't told him what I was there for that day, otherwise, why else would he be here. I'm also curious about why Rick was so keen to get hold of me. When Blue asks me about Sean, and he does, I'm as ready as I can be.

"So, how did you and Sean meet?" It almost sounds casual, but I catch the underlying tone in his voice that tells me it's anything but. I feel the anxiety creep in, but I tamp it down and try to disassociate myself, to tell it like it's someone else's story.

"The usual, night out with the girls." I'm surprised by how steady my voice sounds, not a tremble in sight, but inside my whole body is vibrating. Adding a shrug of my shoulders to drive home the indifference that I don't really feel but attempt anyway. I don't think Blue's convinced, not even one bit. "It didn't work out, no biggie, it happens, end of story."

"Come on, Cam, a four-year relationship and what, summed up just like that?" he scoffs, rising from his stool and clearing the plates away.

A spark of anger rises in me at his tone, and the implication that my explanation isn't enough. Yeah, I'm not being completely transparent, but he has no bloody right to question my relationship. Who the hell does he think he is?

"How dare you..." then I pick up on something he said, "Hold on, how do you know how long I was with Sean?" I demand, as my brain goes into panic mode, and I jump up from my seat, stepping further away from him. He has his back to me at the sink, but I don't miss the way his shoulders tense at my question. Don't panic. There could be a reasonable explanation, just hear him out first.

Spinning to face me, I finally get a look at his face and him mine. Obviously sensing the panic battling inside of me, he hesitantly steps forward, but I raise my hands, warning him to stay there. Confusion briefly crosses his face. "I'm not going to hurt you, Bambi, let…"

"Stop fucking calling me that!" I shout, letting the fear get the better of me.

"Okay. Camryn, I can explain, if you'll just hear me out." He watches me closely, unsure whether I'm going to run or not. Well, that makes two of us pal. I fight my natural instinct to run and allow his words to register through my adrenaline addled brain. I give him the smallest of nods, and he moves to take up his seat again. I don't move a muscle.

"It was Sully that told me how long you'd been with Sean." He spits Sean's name like he wouldn't piss on him if he was on fire. To be honest, neither would I. I'd pour petrol on him and dance round the flames as they engulf him. "You don't work in my line of business without knowing or hearing about some of the less… pleasant, shall we say, members of society." I grunt at that, and it's not missed by Blue. "We've heard of him, know the circles he runs in and even knew a member of his close team, Tyler, as you know, he's the one that gave you Sully's details." At the mention of Tyler's name, I remember the video Sean sent me, nausea washes through me, and I feel the blood drain from my face as the images flash through my mind. My knees buckle, but Blue catches me, picking me up bride style and setting me down on the sofa in the lounge.

"Oh my god, he's dead. Tyler's dead. I can't believe I forgot. How fucking stupid am I, and how did I forget that?" Blue crouches in front of me, his hands resting on my legs and gently rubbing slow circles on the inside of my thighs with his thumbs.

Aware that I'm not making much sense, I take a couple of deep breaths and try again. "He's the reason I called Rick, Sean sent messages to my phone, like Rick did, but Sean also sent a video. A video that showed him torturing Tyler because of me, it's my fault. Someone else died because of me, their blood is on my hands again." I drop my head into my hands in shame. The tears fall freely as my heart fills with guilt at causing someone else's death.

"Hey." Blue pulls my hands away from my face, replacing them with his own. "You listen to me right now, this is not your fault, none of it is. Do you hear me, Camryn?" I go to argue, but I'm stopped in my tracks when his lips land on mine in a punishing kiss.

It takes a split second for the shock to fade, and then I'm opening to him, letting his tongue war with mine when it demands entry. I grab his wrists where his hands still hold my face, not sure if I'm trying to pull him closer or push him off, but when he groans into my mouth, I give up the fight and melt into him.

Blue's intoxicating, masculine scent invades my senses and has my body arching towards him, as he moves one hand into my hair at the nape of my neck. I release his wrists and run my hands up his chest, over his shoulders and wrap my arms around his neck, pulling him further into me.

My legs drop open, inviting him into the space between my thighs, and my core throbs as his hips meet mine. I've lost all sense and just allow my body control, which clearly wants to climb him like a damn tree. Blue breaks the kiss, and I gasp for breath as he kisses across my jaw and down my neck. Before I know it, I'm laid out beneath him as he towers over me, running his hands all over my body. I don't feel an ounce of the fear that usually comes from being beneath a man, trapped and unable to escape or fight back.

I feel Blue slide a hand under my top, his warm, rough fingers glide up my stomach to my breast and squeeze enough to cause a spike of pain, but it's a good pain. I throw my head back on a groan as he rips the cup of my bra down, pinching and tweaking my taut nipple. At the same time, I feel his hard length push against my core, and the roughness of our clothes causes friction in all the right places but it's not enough. I want more. No, I *need* more. I reach for the button of his jeans, but Blue's hand stops me. Confusion and shame wash over me at the thought that he's come to his senses and realised what I already know. I'm damaged goods.

Just as that thought passes through my mind he jumps up, pulling me with him, and then I hear it. The ping of the lift arriving, and the doors whooshing open. He grips my hair, pulling my head back and whispers in my ear, "We'll finish this later." Kissing me quick then releasing me just as Rick walks in.

Rick looks surprised when he sees me, but that could be the fact the heat in my cheeks, my swollen lips and my messed-up hair are a dead give-away for what he just interrupted.

After a quick greeting, I excuse myself to the bathroom in the direction Blue pointed.

Once inside the bathroom, I slump against the door and wait for my heart to slow its crazy pace. Going to the sink I finally get a look at myself in the mirror, as I thought, a hot mess. I touch my fingers to my lips, still tasting Blue and feel how his mouth moved against mine, just imagining it has my thighs clenching together. Urgh! My mind spirals with the thought of what would have happened had Rick not turned up.

I must be more fucked up than I thought, one minute we are talking about Tyler being dead, and the next I'm under a man who is dangerous to my very soul, dry humping him like a hormonal teen.

Embarrassment has me taking my time, in no rush to face either of the men in the other room.

TEN

Blue

What the fuck was I thinking kissing her like that, forcing myself on her. I know her history I'm not a complete arsehole, although some may disagree. The guilt over the death of Tyler so clear on her face. She actually blames herself, and what a fucking load of shit that is. I needed her to feel something good, and my dick was in total agreement with that stupid fucking plan. Still is, painfully so, I might add. Spouting that bullshit about having blood on her hands made me so fucking angry, and as I'm a twisted son of a bitch, it made my dick stand to attention too.

I watched as the shame washed over her when I stopped her, and I saw the thoughts running through her mind clear as day. She thinks she's damaged, that I stopped her because I wouldn't want someone like her. Well, fuck that shit! I don't want no pampered fucking princess, and I see the darkness in her eyes, it calls to me. Like I said, twisted son of a bitch.

"You want to explain to me what the fuck I just walked in on?" Rick demands, stepping down into the lounge.

"Not really, no." I take a seat, running my hand over my face. "Look we were talking about Tyler, she got upset and almost passed out. I was trying to be a fucking gentleman."

"What by fucking her?"

"Fuck you, man. It wasn't like that, and besides, I don't have to fucking explain myself to you," I say, then lean back, putting my hands behind my head. Looking over to Sully, I say, "She thinks it's her fault Tyler's dead, and she..."

"Hold on a second, how does she know Tyler's dead? I never told her that," Rick says. Then I remember what she said before I kissed her, about Sean sending messages to her phone with a video or something. When I tell Sully, his face pales and mines not far behind when I think of the implications of Sean knowing her number.

"Do you think he knows where she is? Maybe Tyler gave her up before Sean finished him off. Fuck!" I slam my fist into the seat beside me.

"So, let's assume that Sean told her about Tyler, to make her feel guilty, which obviously worked, but just because he has her number doesn't mean he knows her location. I don't believe Tyler would give her up, not for a second. The phones a burner and difficult to trace, as we well know, and I told her to destroy it after reading the messages." Sully doesn't say *let's hope she did*, but we're both thinking it.

While we wait for Camryn to return, Sully tells me he brought a couple of the guys I asked for with him to help watch her while she's at work or if I can't be there. I can't say I'm happy about it, but Russ and Scott are good guys and I trust them. Despite the fact I want to fuck her, make her body sing and hear her screaming my name, I have a job to do and that has to come first. This job has been in the works for the last three years, we can't afford for anything to screw it up, especially as Tyler paid with his life getting the intel we need to take Sean Donovan down.

I didn't lie to Camryn about my job, the three of us do run a security company, I just didn't disclose the other side of our business, and the shady shit we do for the even shadier clients that employ our services.

As well as the usual security guard detail for businesses, events and the rich and famous, which mostly consists of babysitting spoilt little daddy's girls, we also work for the police and government. We have several private investigators and undercover operatives, like Tyler, who we use to infiltrate corrupt businesses and criminal organisations, and being ex-army means the wonderfully corrupt government get to take advantage of all our skills with no comeback if it goes tits up. Like with Tyler. He won't get the funeral he deserves without blowing our op and that's fucked up.

I hear the bathroom door and minutes later Camryn walks back into the room. As she walks towards us, I watch her carefully, but she's put the mask back in place. Just as she reaches us I catch her eye, I see it, the shame and embarrassment, but I also see the want in her eyes right before she drops them to the floor and taking a seat across from me. That move has me clenching my fists at my side, and no matter how much I try to catch her eye again she refuses to meet mine.

"Blue tells me that you may have had some other messages, and that Sean sent them to you," Rick asks, getting straight to the point. It pisses me off, but I keep quiet.

Camryn sits with her hands in her lap, and I can see her rubbing her thumb and fore finger together, a clear sign of her anxiety. Bypassing me all together she raises her head, lifting her chin and looks straight at Sully.

"Yes, there were messages," she swallows, taking a breath before she continues, "and a video that—" she licks her lips, then places her hands under her legs, "that showed Sean torturing Tyler." Her voice breaks a little on that last bit and has me itching to go to her, but I stay where I am. She's not as weak or fragile as she thinks. I've seen the darkness that glints in her eyes, and I've felt her need for vengeance. It's beautiful. Whatever Sean did to this beautiful woman hasn't broken her, like he thought. No, this is a woman who is ready to fight back.

"Where is the phone, Camryn? Did you destroy it like I told you to?" Rick's gaze flicks to me before going back to Cam.

"No, it's at the house. I know you told me to get rid of it, but I thought that maybe you could use the video as evidence," she says, a little unsure now. She watches Sully, but she doesn't give away the fear that I know is just below the surface. "I've had that phone for the last six months, and yes, he may have got the number, but I know they aren't easy to trace and it's switched off. I'm not a complete idiot." A little indignation coming into her voice.

"Okay. Blue can collect it from you when he takes you home. Just as a precaution I have a couple of guys that will be tailing you." I see the moment she goes to argue but Sully cuts her off, "They will be discreet, you won't even know they are there. And, like I said it's a precautionary measure."

"One you'll take" I add, and that has Camryn finally looking my way. The glare she's throwing me would cut a lesser man down. Me, not so much. I just want to spank her arse before I take her hard against the nearest surface. I shift to ease the discomfort of my raging hard cock, as an image of Cam laid out on the coffee table flashes through my mind.

"You think one kiss gives you the right to order me around? I don't fucking think so!" Now she's looking at me. There's a fire in her eyes that sets me alight. I lean forward, elbows resting on my knees and offer her a dimpled smile. Then I mask my emotions and show her I mean business.

"No, *sweetheart*, I don't, but my job does. So, in that vein, you'll do as you're told." Then I drop back in my seat. The shock on her face tells me I hit a sore spot, and the devil on my shoulder preens at that. I can see Sully in the corner of my eye cover a smirk with his hand.

She doesn't engage me further, instead turns back to Sully, where they continue to discuss her security detail. I'll let her think that Sully's in charge, for now. But she's mistaken if she thinks she or Sully have any say in her safety. I protect what's mine. Mine, now there's a word I've never used in a sentence when talking about a woman before, but I put it to the back of my mind. Where it's going to fucking stay.

A half hour later, Sully is ready to leave and asks me to show him out. After saying goodbye to Cam, I follow him to the lift.

"What's up?" I ask, once we are out of ear shot.

"I've had a message that Sean might have a man in Manchester." I scowl at him. "It only just came through, so it's a new development, and I don't know how accurate it is. It also doesn't mean that they are here for her, although it's highly suspicious. You just need to be on your guard, that's all. I'll keep you posted, oh and, Blue, try and keep it in your pants, yeah? We can't afford for your dick to fuck us all over."

"What the fuck ever, man. I already told you, it's not like that, and just because I might want her riding my cock doesn't mean I'm going to let her. I can handle some blue balls until we finish the job."

Sully scoffs at that. "You and I both know that when you want something you always get it. And you sure as shit didn't get your name because of your ability to deal with blue balls." He offers a sarcastic pat to the shoulder before getting in the lift. I offer him the middle finger just as the doors close.

ELEVEN

Camryn

Unbelievable! I sit here quietly seething over Blue's last comment while he sees Rick out, no doubt having a laugh at my expense. I think I should be done with it and become a damn nun. I can feel my libido pitching a fit in the box she's currently locked up tight in at the thought of never having sex again. Well, good. It's her fault in the first fucking place and would serve her right.

I always thought any man that tried to control me I'd send packing, and I would have too. Being with Sean changed that, somewhere along the way I let him take charge, and by the time I realised, it was too late, he'd changed. Gone was the loving boyfriend I'd fallen in love with, and in his place stood a man I no longer recognised. A man so full of anger and rage, possessiveness became the definition of our relationship. I remember the first time he hit me, I was so shocked, and he was so remorseful afterwards, that I just put it down to a one-off.

.   .   .

I THOUGHT I would surprise Sean at the office with lunch and maybe a little dessert too. So, I had dressed myself in my sexiest lingerie and a simple black dress with some killer heels. On the way there I'd contemplated calling ahead to make sure he was free, but decided against it, not wanting to ruin the surprise.

As I exited the lift on his floor, I noticed that Tina wasn't at her desk, thinking she'd probably gone to lunch I continued to his office. The door was closed, and I could hear voices, that should have been my first clue. As I got closer, I realised it wasn't voices I could hear but moans and grunts, at one point I even heard the sound of furniture being scraped across the floor. Feeling sick at what I had heard, I raced to the bathroom, emptying my stomach as I reached the toilet bowl.

Once my stomach was empty and the retching stopped, I'd gathered myself together, touched up my make-up, smoothed down my dress and checked my hair in the mirror and attempted to remove all hints of tears from my face, then headed back towards his office. Just as I rounded the corner, Tina was coming out of his office, and I'd watched as he smacked her on the arse before sending her on her way. I'd paused, making sure neither of them saw me. Not wanting to see either of them for fear of what I might do, I had turn-tailed and ran down the fire escape stairs.

When Sean came home that afternoon, I was waiting for him in the kitchen, with my bags packed ready at the front door.

He came in just like any other day, but I knew the instant he'd seen my bags, as I watched his reaction from the doorway.

"Kasey? Kasey, where are you?" he called, repeating it when I still hadn't answered him. As he made his way to the

stairs, he spotted me and instantly changed direction, coming straight for me. "Hey gorgeous, what's with the bags," he asked, as he leaned in to kiss me on the cheek. At the last second, I moved out of his reach. He frowned, and confusion covered his face.

"How was your day at the office?" I asked, trying to keep the contempt from my voice, but not doing a very good job. "How's Tina?" And this time I'd let my derision show. Taking a step back I watched the frown turn to a sinister smirk that had made my blood run cold.

"No need to pretend, Kase, I know you came to the office today. It's a shame you didn't stick around, you could have joined us. There's nothing better than having two whores servicing you at the same time," he sneered.

"Fuck you, Sean! I'm out. I won't sit around and let you make a fool out of me." I moved past him, then span back round, "I'm nobody's whore, you make me sick." And I stormed towards the front door. I didn't make it five steps before I was twirled back round, so disorientated that I didn't have a chance to dodge the palm headed for my face. It landed with a crack, throwing my head to the side. Immediately, I had raised my hand to my face and could feel the burn there. I had been so shocked I just ran upstairs instead of away. Maybe that had been the first nail in my coffin.

THAT WAS the first time I let a man lay his hands me, and the first time I knew Sean cheated. But they were by no means the last. My thought process at that time was so messed up. I allowed him to sweet talk me, fell for his charms all over again. God, what a fucking fool I am.

It was good for a while after that, until it happened again and again and again. He became angrier, more possessive, and when I found out I was pregnant, I stupidly thought things would change. If anything, they got even worse, hitting me was no longer enough. A shiver runs down my back at the thought. Shaking it off, I focus back in the now.

Blue asserting his authority certainly got my back up, but it's not the same. I think what irritated and confused me more was I liked it. Maybe Sean took more than my heart, ripping it out, crushing my resolve, breaking my backbone and leaving me a shadow of my former self. He doomed me with some innate attraction to possessive, domineering arse-holes for the rest of my life. Destined to become a statistic, just another battered wife, but that's wrong. With Blue it doesn't feel like that, and that scares the absolute shit out of me.

Getting up, I walk to the balcony doors taking in the view. The sun sits high in the sky, meaning it must be around midday. My mind is a tumult of emotions that will only get worse over the next few weeks as the anniversary of my mum and daughter's death approaches.

My beautiful, bright, baby girl, who didn't deserve to have her life snatched away before it had even begun. The worst part is I can't even visit her grave or mourn her properly. I can't do any of that, and I guess in some way, that's just another way to punish me. That's what I deserve for bringing her into this world, causing her pain and suffering, even before she was born. I can never absolve myself of the guilt I feel, and I'm okay with that, it can have me. Festering away, writhing inside like maggots in a dead carcass, and reminding me every day of what I have done.

I feel the tears pricking at my eyes, but I don't let them fall, not again. I've already cried enough today.

I know Blue is behind me and has been for the last

couple of minutes. I can feel him, sense his every move, hear his breath that has all the tiny hairs on my arms standing to attention. He steps up close, this is becoming a habit, brushing his front against my back, and for a split second I close my eyes and revel in the feel of him there. Then I lock it away, shut down the safe, comforting feeling that he induces in me and spin on my heels to face him.

I lock eyes with him, although I have to crane my neck to do it, "Don't ever think you have the right to tell me what I will and won't do again. Do you understand me?" My voice is strong despite my recent thoughts, and I watch a small muscle in his jaw tick before I continue. "I just escaped one domineering arsehole, and I damn well didn't go through it all to fall into the arms of another." My last words are punctuated by my finger poking his chest. His all muscle, sexy as fuck chest. *Don't think about it*. Move your finger away, don't do it. I don't listen. Instead, I push my open palm to the centre of his chest, splaying my fingers over it. I can feel his heartbeat, just as erratic as my own. Our eyes are still locked onto each other, and I see the desire in his eyes. Hell, it's reflected back in mine.

He takes a step forward, keeps coming until my back hits the window, and then he lifts his hand toward my face, and I flinch. It's minute but I know he saw it, dropping his hand back to his side.

"Are you done?" he asks, and I nod. "Let's get one thing straight, don't ever compare me to that cunt of an ex-boyfriend. I am not nor will I ever be anything like him. I would never lay a finger on a woman. Especially not one that I love." He pauses, searching my face, for what I don't know, but he must find it there because he nods and carries on. "When I fuck you, and I will, make no mistake it's gonna happen, there won't be a drop of fear in your face, in your eyes or your heart. The only look on your face will be one of pure pleasure as I drive my cock into your tight little pussy, and you'll love every second. You'll be begging me to never stop." And with that he turns away, walking to the lift. "Come on, Bambi, let's get you home so you can change that sexy little thong I know you're wearing."

Holy fuck, shit and damn! I'm fucked. Or I will be, thoroughly so, according to Mr I'm-the-dogs-fucking-bollocks-at-screwing. "Hey, how did you know I was wearing a thong?" I call out as I jog to catch up to him. Out of everything he just said, that's what I ask?

"Lucky guess," he calls over his shoulder.

"Perv."

"And proud I am too. Took me forever to get that title." He chuckles, as we enter the lift.

"Is that how you get your women? Stalker alert."

"Nah, don't need to, they usually follow me like lovesick puppies."

"Cocky much," I say, rolling my eyes at him.

"Nope. Not cocky if it's true. Statement of fact, simple as that, Bambi." And now he fucking laughs, a fully on belly laugh. I've barely seen a smile cross his face, but that has him laughing. Figures.

"Jerk!" I mutter, as we step out of the lift and cross the lobby. "And why the hell do you keep calling me Bambi, for fucks sake?" And as the words leave my mouth, my ankle rolls, and I almost hit the deck, again. Blue grips my arm and holds me up.

"And there, Bambi, is your answer," he snickers, as he releases me.

"So fucking funny." I humph, but when I look over at Blue, I can't help the laugh that escapes. It feels good, freeing and I can't remember the last time I did it.

As we exit the building Blue grabs my hand again. I don't know why, and I don't question it. I'm happy in this moment. His car is already there waiting, and he leads me round to the passenger side, opening the door for me to slide in. Once I'm settled, he leans over, and for a second, I think he's going to kiss me, but he reaches past me, plugging in my belt. I watch him as he passes the front of the car to the driver's side, and the smirk on his face brings a smile to my own.

TWELVE

Unknown

I watch as Ryder and Kasey walk down the steps to the waiting car. Grabbing my phone, I push dial and bring it to my ear as it starts to ring.

"Well?"

"It's her, she's with him, just like you said she would be. They've been at his apartment for hours, probably fucking," I say, knowing it will piss him off. Shame he can't see the smile that brings to my face.

"Fucking cunt!" he shouts down the phone. I pull the phone from my ear so he can't hear the laugh bubbling up from me. "Where are they now?"

"They are just leaving his apartment; do you want me to follow?" I ask.

"No, I fucking don't. What are you some kind of fucking idiot? Just do what we discussed and nothing more. If you fuck this up for me, you can forget that little promise I made you, instead you'll be digging another grave. For yourself." Then the line goes dead. Fucking prick! If he thinks I'm gonna screw this up and miss out on a free ride of that nice bit of arse right there, he's deluded. There's got to be some perks to this shit show of a job.

After checking my watch, I have enough time to get rid of the vehicle I borrowed, head back to the hotel and change ready for later. Switching the engine on, I spin onto the other side of the road and head off.

THIRTEEN

Camryn

When we arrive back to Jamie's place, her car isn't in the drive, and I assume she must have gone shopping. Despite all the bags she came in with on Friday night, there was nothing that would constitute a meal. I head straight for the stairs when we enter, keen to get the phone so Blue can go.

"Two secs, I'll grab the phone so you can get going," I call out, as I take the stairs two at a time. Reaching my room, I grab the phone from the drawer I stashed it in and head back down. When I get there, Blue isn't in the hall, no, the cheeky fucker has taken up residence on the sofa in the lounge, and even switched the TV on. Feeling slightly irked by his assumption that he's welcome to stay, I march towards him and thrust the phone at him.

"Here you go, is there anything else I can get you? A drink, maybe?" He takes the phone without even taking his eyes off the TV and proceeds to tell me a cup of tea would be great. Completely missing, or more likely, ignoring my sarcasm. The absolute gall of this man! I bite my tongue, but just as I decide I'm going to give him a piece of my mind the front door opens, and in walks Jamie, shouting out for a hand with the shopping. Before I even have a chance to reply, Blue is up and out the door carrying bags through to the kitchen like he damn well lives here.

After helping Jamie with the shopping, she makes a start on dinner and Blue returns to the lounge, but not before reminding me about that cup of tea. So, I make him his damn tea, taking my frustrations out on the cupboards. I can feel Jamie's eyes on me the whole time as I crash and stomp around the kitchen. I even contemplating swapping out his sugar. Petty, I know, but I'm feeling— I don't even know what I'm feeling.

Coming back into the kitchen after taking Blue's tea to him and damn near throwing it over him, Jamie asks how my day went. That's it, that one question opens the flood gates to me spouting off my anger at Blue, at Sean, although I don't actually mention him, the fact that I haven't had sex in forever, and that infuriating man in there has me wound tighter than a damn spring. All the while Jamie just stands there watching me before declaring.

"You need to get laid." Waving her knife at me and telling me sexual frustration is as bad for your health as stress. "You should totally jump his bones," she casually announces. Seeing my face, she shrugs. "Well, at the very least you should go and rub one out."

"Jamie," I cry, then lower my voice, not wanting Blue to hear, "Do you have to be so— vulgar?"

"What? Come on, Cam, It's only natural. Nothing wrong with getting yourself—"

"What's only natural?" Blue asks from behind me. God, I wish that voice didn't do delicious things to my body. I'm sitting at the breakfast bar, and of course, he comes and takes the seat right next to me, his thigh brushing against mine as he settles onto the stool. I know what's coming. I look to Jamie, narrowing my eyes at her and imploring her not to do it.

"You know, flicking the bean, paddling the pink canoe, buttering your muffin, auditioning the finger puppets." She actually fucking waves her two fingers in the air like puppets. "Basically, getting yourself off," she states, shrugging, and then carries on with chopping whatever the fuck she's chopping. Absolutely no shame. I hang my head in my hands, as Blue lets out a laugh beside me.

"Now that's fucking funny. Paddling the pink canoe, I've not heard that one before," Blue says, humour lacing his words.

"I'm out," I say, jumping down from my stool and heading for the stairs. I can hear them laughing and talking as I reach my room, it's kind of nice, but it makes me nervous too.

After I got with Sean most of my girl friends slowly disappeared, but Laura and Sam stuck with me—for a while. They would complain that I didn't spend enough time with them, that Sean controlled my life, but I was in love and wanted to spend all my time with him.

Then when Laura accused Sean of coming on to her, claiming he groped her at a club one night, I put it down to jealousy. God. I was so fucking blind. I should have listened to my friends. Friends that I'd grown up with, especially Laura. We'd known each other since primary school, but after that we drifted apart. And now I see it for what it was; Sean isolating me.

Listening to Blue and Jamie laughing and joking seems so natural, like that's how it should be, and that makes me uncomfortable. How can a man I've only known for five minutes fit into my new life so perfectly? I feel so confused when Blue's around because I know that he's a dangerous man, strong and powerful, yet there is something more than that. He has my body wanting and feeling things I never thought it would again. Blue doesn't scare me physically. Emotionally? Without a doubt.

I throw my hair up into a messy bun and take a quick shower. Stepping back into my room, I find Blue sitting on the end of my bed, elbows resting on his knees, head down. Given that he hasn't looked up, I guess he didn't hear me come in. Suddenly, I'm all too conscious that I'm only wearing a towel and horny as hell, and this guy sets my blood racing faster than a McLaren F1 car.

"What the fuck, Blue!"

He raises his head just enough to look up at me, "Sorry," he says, his lip curls up as his eyes rake over me, taking in my lack of clothing. "Nice shower?" he asks with a wink, trying to get a rise out of me, but I just glare at him. Rising to his feet he says, "I got a call, I need to head out, and I didn't want to leave without saying bye."

"What a gentleman," I scoff, "I'm not your keeper, so, please don't feel you need to inform me of your every move." There's a bite to my words, and that vexes me even more.

Blue slowly comes towards me. He doesn't say anything, but he doesn't need to because the look on his face says it all and then some. Coming to a stop, our toes almost touching, he reaches out and tucks a stray lock of hair behind my ear. His fingers graze the edge of my ear as he does, sending tiny little shock waves all over my body. He's invading my space, surrounding me, towering over me, his scent, something masculine with a hint of leather, has my synapses firing off everywhere. I feel my skin begin to heat and my breathing changes, becoming slower but heavier.

"I'm a perfect gentleman when it counts. Now, in the bedroom, that's another story, let's just say all bets are off. There's only one gentlemanly thing I do in the bedroom, and do you know what that is, Camryn?" he asks, rolling the 'r' so it sounds like a purr. Unable to speak, as is usual around this infuriatingly, cocky but sexy arsehole, I just shake my head. "I make sure the lady always comes first, at least once." I literally have to clamp my mouth shut to stop the moan that is hellbent on escaping, and the bastard knows it too.

Determined to turn me into a puddle on the floor, he traces his finger along the inside of the top of my towel. Then yanks me forward, slamming me up against him. I grab his hips to steady myself, oh dear God, have mercy. He lifts my chin with his finger, running his thumb over my bottom lip before leaning forward so his lips just brush mine. It's the most erotic 'almost' kiss I've ever had. "I really do have to go, but I'll see you soon." he whispers. I can feel his erection through his jeans, and it takes everything in me to not rub up against him like a dog in heat. Then he kisses me, taking my mouth like it's his very breath. His lips leave mine just as quick as they came, and then he's gone. Fuck. I really need to go and paddle the pink canoe now.

When I get back downstairs, Jamie is dishing up dinner. We sit at the table and talk about crap, avoiding the topic I just know Jamie really wants to talk about.

In the six months since I met Jamie, we have become really close, and it's amazing how much we have in common. Especially given our differing financial status. Don't get me wrong, we weren't poor by any means, we lived comfortably, but nowhere near the luxury that Jamie is used to. You would never know it to look at her, though. More often than not her red hair is wildly untamed, she wears very little makeup and shops in high street stores the rest of us common folk use. She could throw on a bin bag and take a walk down the catwalk, turning every head in the place.

Several times whilst clearing the plates away I catch Jamie watching me from the corner of her eye, and I can practically see the questions bursting to get free. Feeling generous and knowing there is no escape from them, I decide to put her out of her misery.

"Just ask, Jamie," I tell her. She looks over at me, a look of mock surprise on her face, "Oh, please. Don't pretend you don't know what I'm talking about."

I wait it out, and it takes all of two seconds for her to grab my hand and drag me to the lounge, pulling me down onto the sofa with her. She sits facing me, one foot on the floor and the other bent at the knee in a half-crossed leg position. I mirror her, our knees touching, with a small smile on my face at her excitement.

"Okay, spill the beans. I want to know everything."

"I don't know what you mean," I mock.

"Now who's bullshitting who. Come on, give me something. Have you kissed? What was it like?" The excitement on her face matches that of a kid in a sweet shop. I feel like a teenager that just had her first kiss and am telling my best friend all about it.

"Jeez, Jamie, we're not twelve," I say, rolling my eyes with a small laugh. Realising she's not going to drop it, I tell her about Blue's apartment, and when I tell her how he caged me in against the window and what he said to me, she literally squeals. Falling back on the sofa, with her hand over her heart she sighs.

Sitting back up just as quickly she's says, "Please tell me you let him fuck you, there and then up against the window? 'Cause that shit is hot."

"Of course I didn't!" I exclaim, like it's the most ridiculous thing I've ever heard.

"You're telling me you didn't want to jump that man's bones and have his babies? 'Cause I would have been all over that shit, and he's not even my type. But I'd take one for the team, if he talked dirty to me like that. You know, like can you imagine how gorgeous his baby would be—" she tails off, looking at me. I feel the tears well in my eyes, and I know she sees them too. "Ah, fuck. I'm sorry, Cam. I didn't...I wasn't thinking. I just..."

"It's fine, Jamie." I sigh, feeling bad that my grief has marred what should be a funny moment between us. My sorrow turns to anger when I think about what I've lost because of my own weakness, naivety, better yet, stupidity.

Giving birth to Faye was the happiest day of my life, erasing all the pain and suffering I had endured. Having her gave me the strength to survive. I'd take every punch, kick, all of it again, if only I could hold her in my arms one more time.

The day she died my whole world fell apart. I look at Jamie, the pain I know she's feeling for bringing up my daughter couldn't be clearer. Feeling it would be good for both us, I decide to push my grief aside and share a little about Faye with her. Remembering the one photo of her that I was able to bring with me, I tell Jamie to hold on and rush to get it.

When I return, I hand her the photograph. It's of Faye laying on a picnic blanket under a cloudy sky with the sun trying to shine behind the weight of the clouds. It's kind of how I feel now, trying to move through the darkness and forward with my life. To forget all the bad and shine again, only my light isn't as bright or strong as the sun's, but I'd like to think it will be one day.

We talk for hours, and Jamie just listens. I'm so lucky to have found her, and it's amazing how light I feel afterwards. When I finally crawl into bed later that night, lying there thinking over our conversation, I think back to my reason for leaving in the first place.

Sean's hold on me broke when my mum and daughter died, he no longer had leverage to keep me under his control, but I was drowning in a world of sorrow and pain. I was like a fucking zombie for those first few weeks, and even after that I just went into autopilot.

Tyler was the one to finally help me, that's why Sean's video hurt so much. Tyler joined Sean's team two years after we got together, and I always liked him from the moment we first met. He was always careful around Sean, but when we were alone, he was sweet and caring.

For a while I thought I had a crush on him, but I soon realised it wasn't reciprocated. He was married, and I just wanted someone to rescue me, I guess. In the end that's exactly what he did, and now I'll never be able to thank him properly.

After Faye's death Sean went crazy, the worst he'd ever been, worse than when he found out I was having a girl. His anger knew no bounds and anytime I was close by, it was me that took the brunt of it. Part of me didn't care, I wanted the pain, to feel something, anything. The guilt was already slowly killing me, and Sean was grieving too, so it didn't matter.

Tyler would always clean me up after and make sure I was okay when he was there. I got the impression he didn't much like Sean, but I was never sure. Why was he working for him if he hated him?

Then around two months after Faye's death I overheard Sean talking with some businessmen in his office. They were discussing a new shipment, I had no idea what that meant, but I took a chance and asked Tyler about it the next time we were alone. I remember him seeming angry, and then he peppered me with a shit load of questions that I didn't know the answers to. He told me not to worry, but when I didn't see him for several days, that's just what I did do.

During Tyler's absence I overheard several more conversations, mostly phone calls. I even braved searching Sean's office while he was away, finding a folder containing shipping consignment documents, and took pictures. At the time I didn't know why they were so important, but when Tyler returned, I told him everything I knew. He asked me to send the pictures to him, and then delete everything from my phone.

Over the next couple of weeks, I watched every move Sean made, it gave me a new focus, taking my mind off the loss of Faye and my mum. A couple of weeks before I ran, Tyler came to me and asked if I could access Sean's computer. At first, I told Tyler it was impossible, and that if Sean caught me, he'd kill me. Tyler said he understood and left it at that.

A few days later Sean called me to his office, I was nervous, I thought he'd found out what I'd been doing, but I was wrong. No, the bastard had decided that enough time had passed, and we should go ahead with our marriage, and he wanted to try for another baby as soon as possible. I remember how the bile rose in my throat, and my stomach turned over then sank at the thought of having another child. Never, it was never going to happen again. I would never allow myself the joy a child could bring for it to be ripped from me. I would never survive a second time.

That cemented my decision to follow through with Tyler's plan, but I was adding a stipulation of my own. If I was going to do this, then Tyler had to get me out.

When I put my proposal to him, he agreed instantly and told me he had already begun work on how to get me away safely. The next chance I got, I accessed Sean's computer and plugged in the little USB Tyler had given me. He said I didn't need to do anything except plug it in, and it would do the rest.

Then two days later I was gone. I never asked Tyler what he wanted on Sean's computer and he never told me. I didn't care, I just wanted to get out and as far away from that monster as I could.

Now Tyler's dead, and Sean is looking for me. I always knew there was a chance he'd come looking, but the smallest part of me hoped he'd just let me go. I should be so fucking lucky. I just hope that he never finds me, and that no one else has to suffer at his hands because of me.

FOURTEEN

Camryn

I wake feeling refreshed, having slept really well considering the heavy conversation last night and my thoughts before finally falling asleep. Talking to Jamie about Faye must have been better for me than I thought.

After showering, I go in search of tea and food. Following the delicious smell of bacon and eggs, I find Jamie in the kitchen cooking breakfast. This girl. If I was a lesbian, I'd marry her tomorrow.

"Morning, how did you sleep?" she asks, as I enter the kitchen.

"Surprisingly well actually. It's been a while since I slept without nightmares plaguing me all night." I go to the kettle and start making tea for us both. Jamie is just finishing plating up as I bring the tea over. "I meant to ask, did you talk to your dad about that woman we saw him with?" I say, looking up as I shovel the first forkful in my mouth.

Jamie fidgets in her chair, and then says, "Not exactly, no." She looks at her plate, pushing the food around it, but not actually eating any of it.

"What does 'not exactly' mean, Jamie?" I probe with a smidgen of suspicion in my tone. I may not have known her long but she's like a damn cat, curiosity always getting the better of her. She's also just as crafty. "Jamie, what did you do?"

"Well, I may have—erm, I might have followed him," she states cautiously.

"Jeez, you are insane. Why didn't you just ask him about it?"

"I was going to, but then I went to see my mum and she seemed upset. Said something that had my spidey sense going haywire, so I thought I'd do a bit of digging." She finally starts to eat, but I can see the worry on her face.

"And...? Come on, Jamie, spit it out," I say, throwing her words from last night back at her. She gives me a scowl at my choice of words, and I just laugh, trying to lighten the moment.

"Nothing happened. Well, nothing out of the ordinary." I can see there is something else bothering her, but I decide not to press. Jamie is not good when pushed. Trust me I know. I remember her telling me what happened when her dad tried to force her into getting a law degree. She went ballistic and went all out the other way, enrolling on an art degree instead. When he realised that she was serious, he relented. Now Jamie does what she always wanted and is a nurse working in the emergency department.

"I'm sure it's nothing. Maybe they just had an argument and that's why your mum was upset. And, despite how it looked, I'm sure his meeting with that woman the other week was completely innocent." I paint on a smile that I hope she doesn't see right through. Changing the subject, I ask what her plans are for the day, and she tells me she's working later this afternoon.

Just as we finish up clearing away from breakfast there's a knock at the door. Jamie goes to answer it while I finish loading the dishwasher. She comes back carrying a box, and I immediately get a sense of deja vu of the last time I got a delivery on a Sunday. I take it from her when she holds it out to me, trying to keep my nerves from getting the better of me. Ripping it open, I tip the contents onto the counter, a brand-new iPhone and a note fall out. I pick up the note first.

CAM,

I noticed that you don't have a phone, and well, now you do. I have pre-programed mine and Sully's numbers in already, in case you need them. I have also loaded a program that prevents anyone from tracking your device, so you don't need to worry about Sean using the phone to find you.

See you soon, stay out of trouble, or I'll have to spank that tight little arse of yours. ;)

Ryder

I'M a little shocked that he signed it Ryder, I thought for sure he'd use the opportunity to take the piss in some way. I'm even more surprised to find that I really love his name. And the spanking my arse, yeah, that elicits little butterflies low in my belly. Ones I never dreamed would return, especially not when threatened with a spanking.

While I've been reading the note, Jamie has the iPhone out of the box and switched on. She passes the phone to me, and I open it up just as a new message comes through from someone labelled 'Pretty Boy', I don't need to be a genius to work that one out. Shaking my head, I open the message.

Pretty Boy: Make sure you setup the facial ID!

Bossy arsehole!

Begrudgingly, I set up the facial recognition and program Jamie's number in too, then call her so she has mine. I spend the rest of the day doing washing and housework, I even do a little in the garden.

Jamie goes off to work just before four, leaving me on my own. Not too bothered about cooking for just me, I throw in a microwave meal and take out the rubbish while I wait for it. I chuck the bag in the wheelie bin and then drag it down the drive ready for the bin men tomorrow.

Hearing a noise from across the road, I lift my head, but see nothing obvious. I notice that the house across from us is still empty, it's been up for sale for the last month. Just as I go to turn back to go indoors, I spot a shadow in the upstairs front window, but then it's gone and seeing the car out front, I assume it's probably the agent waiting for a viewing, although, it seems a little late. I guess people that work all day don't have a lot of options.

The microwave pings as I get back inside, and I forget all about the house over the road. I eat my half decent dinner, and then go and run a bath.

I may have overdone the bubbles, but who cares. Getting in, I quickly wash my hair, then lie back and allow the water to do its job. I must have dozed off when I'm suddenly woken by a loud bang. I sit up so fast, water sloshes over the edge of the bath and onto the floor. It's then I realise the water is tepid, confirming my thoughts about falling asleep. Not hearing anything else, I hastily shave and wash my body, jumping out just as goosebumps appear on my skin, and not the good kind.

Drying off and wrapping a towel around me, I use the other to roughly dry my hair before pulling on some pyjamas. I return the towel to the bathroom, brushing my hair and teeth while I'm there. I grab my new phone off the bed and head downstairs.

As I enter the kitchen, a cold draft creeps over my bare arms and up the bottom of my pyjamas. Looking around for the source of the cold air, I notice the door to the utility room is open. The hairs on my arms stand to attention as I walk towards it, and a little fear crawls into my throat. The only lighting is from the downlights below the cupboards, and it casts eerie shadows around the room. I slowly push the utility room door open fully, and as the room comes in to view, I see that the back door is open.

The room is only small, one side houses the washing machine and tumble dryer and the other has a sink unit and a few wall cupboards. The back door is at the other end of the small room, and from my position I can see straight out to the pitch-black garden.

Seeing nothing out of the ordinary in the room, I hurry to close the back door, making sure to lock it and removing the key just to be on the safe side. I'm almost certain that I closed it earlier when I came in from the garden, obviously, I didn't. I double check the door is secure before making my way back to the kitchen.

Feeling on edge, I switch the main kitchen light on, going to the lounge and doing the same. Back in the kitchen I make myself a hot chocolate with marshmallows and whipped cream. Hoping that the overindulgent drink will ease my fear somewhat.

I settle on the sofa, pulling the throw from the back and

snuggle up under it. I flick through the channels, finding nothing, and just as I'm about to give up, Julia Roberts and Richard Gere fill the screen. Ah, one of my all-time favourites.

I WAKE BLEARY EYED, a complete contrast to the day before. After dragging myself out of bed, I quickly dress for work in a pair of black cigarette trousers and a black shirt. Throwing on a pair of nude heels and grabbing a matching purse before heading downstairs.

There is no sign of Jamie, but I'm not surprised after her late shift last night. Not having a car means I have to rely on Jamie or public transport, which I'm lucky enough to have right on my doorstep.

Making sure I have everything, I open the front door and crash into...looking up, a hard chest belonging to— "Blue! What are you doing here?" Then I spot the two men standing next to a car parked on the street. "What's going on, is something wrong?" When I look back at him, he's openly staring at me, eyes hooded and blatant desire shines in his eyes. It suddenly feels extremely hot out here, despite the early spring chill in the air. Waving my hand in front of his face, his gaze locks back on to mine. "Are you done eyeing me up like I'm your next meal?" I jest.

Snapping out of it, he grabs my hand, leading me down the path, "Hey! Hold on I need to shut the door," I say, as I pull against his hold on me. For a split second, his grip tightens before letting me go completely. I rush back, pulling the door shut and double checking it's closed fully before moving back to Blue, who immediately takes up my hand again. Feeling nervous now, I ask him again what's wrong.

"Nothing, everything is fine. I came to introduce you to your security detail," he replies, as we approach the two men.

Both are standing with their hands in front of their bodies, hands crossed over like soldiers and dressed in black suits. The one on the left is wearing sunglasses making it difficult for me to get a good read on him and it makes me weary. He's tall, around 6' with almost black hair that's cut close on the sides, a little longer on top, but not as long as Blue's. He has a strong jaw and a few days growth that makes his baby face more manly. He appears to be about the same age as me, probably in his mid to late twenties. He offers a simple head nod as Blue introduces him as Scott.

Turning to the guy on the right, who Blue tells me is Russ, I'm greeted by warm brown eyes and a smile that no doubt has the ladies tripping over themselves to get in his bed. Russ is a little older, early thirties maybe, there are flecks of grey peppering his dark brown hair. He's lean and slightly taller than me, and I notice a tattoo hidden below the cuff of his suit jacket, but I can't make out what.

Blue tells me that they will drive me to and from work every day and anywhere else I need to go. To say I'm pissed about this arrangement would be the understatement of the fucking year. And it's so far from what I agreed with Rick, it's out the ballpark as the Americans would say. I wear my distaste like a badge, but all that does is have Blue chuckling like a five-year-old. The man is insufferable.

I quietly fume all the way to work, while Russ attempts to talk to me, but I reply with short and to the point answers. Scott drives, and apart from the occasional grunt doesn't say a word. The man has some serious 'don't poke the bear' vibes going on.

The rest of my day goes by quickly, as does the whole week. I don't see or hear from Blue at all.

RETURNING FROM LUNCH ON FRIDAY, Gloria the receptionist on my floor, tells me that I had a delivery while I was out, and she put it on my desk. Adding what a lucky lady I am. Confused by her comment, I head to my desk, but as I round the corner, I don't even need to go any further. Sitting on my desk is a huge bouquet of black lilies. Before I can catch my breath or take another step, my eyes glaze over, black spots appearing in front of me, and my legs give out from underneath me.

I come to laid out on a couch in one of the offices. I try to sit up but am stopped by a large hand on my shoulder, and when I look up, I'm met by those sky-blue eyes I'm coming to love an awful lot.

"Take it easy, don't try to get up too quickly, you might have banged your head when you fainted." I bristle at his words, which is a little unfair given he has no clue how many times I've likely had a concussion over the years. Refusing to be fussed over, I sit up, and this time I brush his hand away when he tries to stop me.

"I'm fine, stop fussing." I swing my legs round so I'm facing him from his position kneeling on the floor. "What are you doing here anyway?" My head feels a little woozy, and my mouth is dry. Licking my lips to moisten then a bit, Blue notices and passes me a bottle of water from the floor beside him. I take it, gratefully. Before he can answer, the door opens and Sandra, my head of department, pops her head in.

"Ahh, Cam, it's good see you're okay." Then she turns her attention to Blue. "Your car is out front and ready when you are Mr. Hawkins." Blue thanks her, and then she tells me she'll see me Monday.

"What does she mean she'll see me Monday? I still have half a day of work to do," I exclaim.

"No, you don't. You're going home—with me," he states definitively.

"Excuse me? The hell I fucking am!" I shout, then remember where we are. "If I can't work, then I'll be going back to Jamie's, she'll be expecting me," I tell him, getting to my feet. My legs feel like jelly and my head is pounding, but I stay on my feet.

"I've already spoken to her, and as she is working again tonight, she thinks it's a good idea," Blue tells me, his manner matter of fact and leaving no room for argument.

I place my hands on my hips and glare at him. I swear if my eyes were lasers, he'd be in teeny tiny pieces right now. He doesn't even look at me, just moves to the door, holding it open for me, and follows behind me till we reach his car.

I don't bother arguing with him on the drive, instead I sit and think up creative ways to castrate him. Cocky, arrogant, bossy, bull-headed arsehole! *Sexy you forgot sexy*, whispers my sex starved libido. Oh, shut up! My head is throbbing, and I'm still a little woozy. All I really want to do is go home and curl up in my bed. But no—instead, I've got to endure Captain-fucking-Hawkins all night.

I had hoped that by the time we arrived, my anger would have subsided, but I couldn't have been more wrong.

As soon as we enter his apartment, the dam bursts, and I let him have it, both barrels.

FIFTEEN

Camryn

"What gives you the right to come to my work, laying down the law and telling me what the fuck I'm going to do? I didn't call you." Now I come to think of it, "Actually, who even did call you, how did you know I fainted?" I fire questions, all the while advancing on him with fury in my blood. I don't give him the chance to answer even one, they just keep coming. "You're not in the army now, I'm not one of your little soldiers you can order around. My god, where do you get off," I say, throwing my hands up in the air. "I don't need a damn babysitter, Blue! You can't just stroll into my life and take control. I don't need another fucking controlling, psycho wanker in my life, I've had more than my fair share. I've also had more than a few concussions in my short life. Here's a list of other injuries for your notes; broken ribs, broken wrist, knife wounds that Freddie fucking Kruger would be proud of and more bruises than Muhammad Ali had in his whole damn career." I pause, leaning over to rest my hands on my knees and pull in a couple of breaths.

When I raise my head to look at Blue, he's got his fists

clenched at his sides, and his nostrils are flaring like a dragon about to breathe fire. Who knows, maybe he will.

As I slowly stand back up, he takes a step towards me. A trickle of fear scatters up my spine, but I straighten my back, lifting my chin and standing my ground. I don't fear what he'll do to me. I fear the look in his eyes, and the lick of arousal that's mixed with the fear inside me. My body is like a tightly wound coil, ready to snap at any moment.

"Are you fucking finished with your tantrum? Good, now it's my turn. Your work called me because I had my details added to your emergency contacts." Oh, my fucking god! I'm speechless. "And you're right, I might not be in the army anymore but giving orders is par for the course in this job. Lastly, where I get off is, this is my job and—"

Yep, there it is. Ping! "Yeah, and I'm just another job, right, Blue?" I wave him off like it's nothing. Well, apparently it is fucking nothing. "Do you flirt and kiss all your female *clients*, Blue? Why I'm so surprised, I don't fucking know," I sneer at him, spinning on my heels and storming off—where exactly, I have no fucking clue. I just know I need to get away from him before I lose my mind.

I don't make it more than two steps before he grabs my arm, spinning me round and catching my face in his hands. He slams his lips to mine, and my body instantly reacts to him. My hands grip his shirt as he pushes me back until I hit the wall, crushing his hips against mine as our tongues battle against each other. Feeling his arousal through the thin material of his trousers. I break the kiss on a soft moan, and as though a fire has been lit inside of me, I start tearing at his clothes. Running my hands up his chest, pulling at the buttons of his shirt as he slides a hand down the side of my body, brushing my breast as he goes before gripping my hip. His other hand slips to the back of my neck, grabbing my hair and yanking my head back to trail kisses and tiny nips down my throat, across my collarbone, and when his tongue licks at my pulse as it beats likes a trapped butterfly, I groan low in my throat.

The sound elicits a growl that rumbles up Blue's chest as his hand dips inside my trousers, I'm so completely lost in the moment I hadn't even realised he'd undone them. I gasp as his fingers slide beneath my underwear, slowly slipping through my wet folds. Fuck! He slides his finger back and forth, spreading my juices to my clit before focusing his attention there, rubbing in slow, torturous circles that has another moan falling from my lips.

I grab his hair pulling his face back to mine, kissing him, and in the exact same moment as I bite down hard on his bottom lip, drawing blood, he thrusts two fingers into my throbbing pussy. I convulse around the delicious intrusion, gripping his shirt so hard I hear it tear, but I don't care. I don't care about anything else at this moment. All I want is to chase the pleasure he's creating in me, I want more, all of it.

With an unrivalled need, I yank at the last few buttons of his shirt and shove it down his shoulders, unable to get it all the way off, I push him back a step. His fingers slip from me, and I moan at the loss. Blue throws his shirt off before gripping mine, he rips it open, buttons flying off and pinging as they hit the floor. As soon as I have his trousers undone, I reach in, wrapping my hand around him, he's rock-hard, as smooth as silk and big. So fucking big. That has me hesitating for a beat, then Blue pulls away, ripping my trousers and underwear down, and lifting me up in one fluid action. My back slams against the wall as I wrap my legs around him, his hard cock rubs on my clit as he gently rocks his hips making my eyes roll, and my head fall back, hitting the wall.

As the pressure low in my belly builds into a delicious peak, I grab his shoulders, moving my own hips in time with his, making him growl so deep that it sets my body alight, and just before I explode, he pulls back and thrusts forward, impaling me on his cock, both of us moaning at the contact. He holds himself there inside me, as if he's on the edge, and the thought that he's just as wild and turned on as me, at being inside me, stretching me perfectly, has my pulse racing. His scent envelops us as he moves his hips back slowly before ramming back into me. It drives me over the edge, and I let go. That one thrust has me falling apart in his arms, and I shout out my release as he continues to pump his hips.

"Ahhh, fuck, Ryder!" I shout, as I rake my nails down his back. I grip his shoulders tighter as he speeds up, fucking me harder, and when he hits that sweet spot inside, I fall over the edge again, convulsing around him as he roars out his own release.

We stay locked together, breathing heavily, his head resting in the crook of my neck as we come down from the high. My body feels boneless, but as my mind slowly returns, my thoughts turn to what we just did. Shit, shit, shit!

"Are you okay?" is whispered against my heated flesh stopping my mind from spiralling.

"Yeah, I'm good," I rasp. My throat is clogged with mixed emotions, and I barely get the words past my lips. Ryder, almost unwillingly, lowers my legs to the ground, but maintains his hold on me, ensuring I'm steady on my feet before releasing me fully. He drops a tender kiss to the side of my neck, sending a spark of pleasure rushing over my skin before pulling his head away to look at me. His eyes search mine, and when he finds what he's obviously looking for, he drops another kiss to my forehead before picking up our clothes and passing me mine.

"You know where the bathroom is if you want to clean up. I'll just be a second," he says, before walking away.

As he leaves, I see the tattoo that covers the whole of his back. It's a fallen angel. The wingspan reaches from one shoulder blade to the other, in greys and black ink. Below is some writing in gothic script, but I'm too far away to be able to read it. It's beautiful, just like the man it adorns.

Once he disappears into, what I assume is his room, I grab my handbag, which I dropped when I arrived, and hurry to the bathroom. The evidence of what we just did drips down the inside of my thighs, and I'm suddenly aware we didn't use any protection. Thank the lord I can't get pregnant.

I slam the door closed, leaning my head on it while I try to make sense of whatever the fuck that was. My phone pings with a message, and I fumble around inside my bag, pulling it out when I finally find it.

Jamie: Hey, girl, I hope you're okay. Blue told me you're staying at his, time to get yourself laid. I'm off to work but call if you need anything. Xx

I immediately go to hit call, then stop. What the hell do I even say, *'Oh, hey, by the way I just let Ryder fuck me against a wall. You know, the guy I've only known for a week, but it's cool, I got laid, right.'* I'm so fucking stupid. I hardly know the guy, and apparently, he's just doing his job. I guess that entails screwing his clients when he can. Despite feeling like a complete fool, I decide I need to talk to Jamie. I hit call, and she picks up on the second ring.

"Hey, what's up, you okay?"

"Jamie." Her name is all I manage before my throat closes up and tears form in my eyes.

"Shit, Cam, what's the matter," she rushes out, the panic clear in her voice.

"I'm fine, but I screwed up." I scoff at the irony of that explanation. "We had sex," I blurt out.

"Okaaaay, that bad, huh," she laughs, I shake my head, aware that she can't actually see me, but my answer is still true. It wasn't bad at all, and that right there, is the fucking problem. "Cam?" Jamie calls down the phone.

"Sorry. No, it wasn't bad."

"So, what's the problem? Did he hurt you? I'll fucking gut him if he did!" And I don't doubt the truth of that threat.

"God, no. Nothing like that." I pause, unsure of what saying it out loud will mean. "It...It was—argh! It was fucking hot, the best sex I've ever had. There I said it. Now what the fuck do I do? I don't know what to do or say. I'm not the 'friends with benefits' type of girl, Jamie, I catch feels too easy, and I can't—I don't have room for that right now."

"Cam, just calm down. I may have only met Blue a few times, but I know guys, and I don't think you're just another notch on his bedpost. I've seen the way he watches you. Do you like him?" she asks.

I think about that question for second, and whilst I'm not convinced that I'm more than another notch, she's right, I've caught him watching me too, and I do like him. Probably more than I should, and that scares the crap out of me.

I've just escaped from a man that spent the last four years abusing me, so how can I fall back into a possible relationship with a man that clearly has demons. I should be running a mile in the other direction, but I find myself wanting to stay, to take a risk. The big question is not whether I like him, or him me, but more about if I'll survive being broken by another man if I let him in. Will he even want me when he finds out the truth? I don't know, and I'm unsure whether I can risk it to find out.

"Yeah, but it's more complicated than that, Jamie. There are things I've not told you, not told anyone, and they mean I need to protect myself."

"I'm not stupid, Cam. I know they're things you haven't told me and that's fine, but you need to know that I'm always here when you're ready to talk. On the issue of Blue, I think you should take the time you have with him now to figure out exactly how you feel about him. If you trust him enough to open up to him, share your fears, maybe some secrets. You may not be the type to sleep with someone without feeling or trust but the fact you had sex with Blue tells me you trust him on some level already." As though she can read my mind she says, "You're not broken, Cam, you're here, still standing, still fighting. Don't let your past stop you from taking a risk."

I let the tears that her words have brought slip down my face freely. This girl who saved me, took me into her home, looked after me, brought back the girl I used to be and who I would give my life for, has slain me with her words. She's never asked anything of me in return for all that she's done, and I can't thank her enough.

"You're amazing, and I'm so glad to have you as a friend," I blub down the phone.

"Ahh, don't be so soppy, or you'll have me crying too. Now, I assume you're hiding out in the bathroom, hmmm?" I can picture her raised brow as she says it. "Get yourself tidied up, get out there and enjoy yourself, girl. No paddling the pink canoe for you this weekend." She chuckles, then the line goes dead.

I hurriedly splash cold water on my face, hopefully removing any signs of my tears, then after relieving myself, I dress back in my work clothes. As I pull my shirt on, I realise the buttons are missing from around halfway. Fucking perfect. Ryder's magic fingers must have gotten some undone before ripping my shirt from my body. With no other option, I use the two sides of the shirt, tying a knot that rests at my midriff. Making sure that everything is covered, I leave the bathroom in search of Ryder.

As I near the end of the corridor, the sound of voices reaches me. Ryder's voice is instantly recognisable, and I'm certain the other voice is Russ. I'm conscious that Blue, has now become Ryder to me, and that is another confusing factor of what happened.

I enter the room to find Ryder and Russ standing at the dining table, a bag sits on the table between them. Ryder's head lifts, locking eyes with me, while Russ continues talking. At Russ' mention of the flowers, my spine stiffens, but thankfully Russ cuts off when he sees that Ryder's attention is focused elsewhere. He follows Ryder's line of sight, looking over his shoulder and spotting me there. A brief look of annoyance crosses his face, I assume at the intrusion, before he smiles.

"Hello, Camryn. I'm glad to see you back on your feet. I was just dropping off an overnight bag for you."

I look at Ryder in question, but he keeps the mask firmly on his face. "Thank you, that's very kind," I say, feeling a little pissed at the idea of a stranger going through my belongings. Clearly, I don't do a good job of hiding my irritation because Russ informs me that Jamie put the bag together for me.

"Right, is that all, boss?" Russ asks, directing his question to Ryder, who simply nods, "Good, then I'll see you later." He turns to me, "I'll see you soon, Camryn, enjoy your weekend."

Well, this isn't awkward in the slightest.

SIXTEEN

Camryn

After Russ left, we moved to the lounge to wait for the takeaway that Ryder ordered. The tension is palpable, almost unbearable. Deciding I've had enough, and I need to clear the air, I tell Ryder I'm sorry for going off at him.

"It's fine, Cam, you don't need to apologise. But you damn well best understand that I'm not like your ex. I have never laid a hand on a woman in anger, and I don't appreciate the comparison, especially as it's not the first time. Is that clear?" The gruff, commanding tone of his voice sends a sliver of desire through my body, and despite all my best efforts, I can't help automatically tense my thighs in response. Ryder's eyes flick to the movement, and his lip curls up in a sexy smirk that has the dimple I like so much appear.

I nod, then mutter, "Bossy bastard," under my breath. Why I thought it would escape his notice I don't know.

"Don't pretend you don't love it when I get all demanding and bossy. Don't think I didn't see the way your thighs clenched together just now. I bet your fucking soaked." he says, my eyes widening at his dirty talk. He crawls across the sofa towards me, prowling like a damn lion hunting its prey. "I bet if I was to slip inside those knickers of yours, your pussy would be dripping, ready for me to spread you out and feast on you like it's my last meal." I scoot further back, until I hit the corner of the sofa, now completely caged in as he reaches me. My breathing picks up, and if I didn't know the difference, I'd think I was having a panic attack.

All too aware of how close Ryder is, I reach out a hand to stop him, but end up running my fingers up his chest, to his neck, and feel his pulse racing there, just like his tongue did to mine earlier. His hooded eyes, heavy with desire, watch as I bite my bottom lip with a hunger matching his own.

"You can't hide from your demons, Cam, you have to embrace them. I see the darkness in your eyes, the way it turns you on when I take charge, the way your body responds," he whispers, his smooth velvety voice is replaced with a deep, devilish tone that has everything in me lit up. He leans forward, and the roughness of his five o'clock shadow grazes my cheek as he places a soft kiss to the spot behind my ear. My hand follows his movement, trailing up and winding into the nape of his neck, my nails biting into the skin there and causing him to groan.

"Don't tempt me, Cam. I'm hanging onto my restraint by a thread right now, and I'd love nothing more than to fuck you till you're hoarse from screaming my name," he grits out.

"Then why don't you—" I'm cut off as the elevator dings its arrival. "Fuck!" falls from my mouth before I can stop it, and Ryder laughs.

"Fuck is right," he grumbles. "Come on, dinner's here,

and I'm famished," he says, winking and pulling me up from the sofa as he rises to his full height.

Ryder dishes up the Chinese he ordered, while I lay the table. Not oblivious to how domesticated it all is, nor am I ignorant of the fact that since we had sex earlier, I've reverted to calling him Ryder, even if it is just in my head right now. I try not think too much into it, or that I was just about to tell him to fuck me on the sofa before we were interrupted. Instead, I take Jamie's advice and enjoy myself, get to know him and take a risk. How do you know if the risk is worth taking if you don't try, right?

Dinner is lovely. I haven't had a Chinese this delicious in ages. When I ask Ryder where it's from, he tells me it's a secret and maybe he'll take me one day. I'm not too surprised that he knows his way around the city, it's clear from this apartment that he lives here. Something tells me that this isn't his only home, so I'm not that shocked by his answer when I ask him.

"No, I also have a place outside London. Well, it's actually a house in Surrey. "

"No way!" I say excitedly, "I was born in Surrey." My smile drops slightly at the look on his face. "What, why are you looking at me like you just killed my dog or something?"

He fidgets in his seat, and that can't be a good sign, coughing into his closed fist before saying, "I know where you were born, Cam. I also know your real name, date of birth and your favourite colour." I sense the last part is tacked on to soften the blow of exactly how much he knows about me.

Feeling foolish for not realising he would know so much about me, I brush it off, "Of course you do." I can see he's not fooled, but I ignore it. "So, come on then, tell me something about you. I mean, I'm completely in the dark here." I swallow down the anxiety swirling in my gut and wait for him to answer.

"I'm really not that interesting," he states, a small frown furrows his brow. I raise my eyebrows at his reluctance to share. When it becomes clear that I'm not going to drop it, he starts talking.

I learn that his parents are still alive and living in Surrey. He talks fondly of his mum, Dawn, but I sense some animosity between him and his dad, Richard. He tells me about his brother Kyle who died at twenty-one, and I can see the pain and sorrow losing his sibling causes him. After the death of Kyle and the pain his parents went through losing their son, Ryder decided to leave the army and set up business with Rick.

Wanting to steer the conversation in a happier direction, we play twenty questions for the next hour or so. It's kind of hard to play with a moody arsehole not keen on sharing, but I'm hardly one to talk. Funnily enough the conversation never touches on relationships, marriage and children, and I'm glad, but a little surprised too.

Around 7pm, Ryder gets a call that he takes in the bedroom. Desperate to get out of my work clothes, I head to the room he showed me earlier. It's a simple room, a double bed with cream bedding, and a cream blind covers the floor to ceiling window in the room. There are two bedside tables, one with a lamp, a built-in wardrobe and a cream chest of drawers.

Digging through my bag I find my bikini, if you call two scraps of material a bikini. Jamie picked the most revealing one I own. One she bought, insisting that I could catch the eye of any guy in it. Oh, I don't doubt her on that. Pretty sure walking around almost naked, no matter your size, is enough to turn heads. Why would she even pack it? Then I remember the hot tub. Thinking back to our conversation earlier and my decision to take a risk, I quickly put it on before I can change my mind. I grab a towel from the en suite on my way out the door.

There's still no sign of Blue when I get back to the main room, so I go ahead and open the doors that lead to the balcony. The space is much bigger than I thought, and there are soft lights dotted through the tiles on the floor and set in the wall around the balcony. Glass panels with a handrail, allow a magnificent view of the Manchester skyline. I slowly walk to the hot tub taking in everything as I go, it's beautiful.

Once I figure out how to work the damn thing, I set the temperature and climb in, just as my teeth start to chatter from the chilly breeze that's blowing across the balcony. I sink into the heavenly warmth of the water, resting my back on the side and look at the night sky.

I find the brightest star in the sky, Venus, this year, and my thoughts drift to my daughter. She loved the stars, we would lay out in the garden in the summer, with a book on astronomy and try to identify as many stars and constellations as we could. I used to tell her I loved her to the moon and back, and she'd always giggle, then tell me she'd go there one day just so she could see just how far my love reached.

Suddenly, I sense I'm no longer alone, and as the sounds of soft music begin to play, I know I'm right. I can feel his presence behind me, and I wait for the moment that he reaches out to touch me, but he doesn't. I watch as his hands appear on the edge of the hot tub either side of me, then his voice whispers in my ear.

"I see you found the bikini I told Jamie to pack for you."

I can almost feel the smirk on his face, thinking he's clever but he's not.

Feeling brave, and more than a little turned on, I say, "Haven't you ever heard of skinny dipping, Ryder?" I can't see his face, but I hear his small intake of breath at the idea of me sitting here naked. "Are you coming in, or just going to stand there all night?"

"Oh, I'm coming in, don't you worry about that." I hear the rustle of clothing behind me, and my bravado takes a small nosedive when I realise it's him that's going to be skinny dipping. Oh, shit! I don't have any more time to panic as he tells me to slide forward. I do and then he's sliding in behind me, his legs outside of mine, and when he's settled, his arm wraps around my waist making me gasp as he pulls me back towards his chest.

Visions of another man behind me flit through my mind, and I'm reminded of the scars that mar my back. I shove them away, determined not to let them ruin this moment. I slowly relax into him and feel him do the same.

We sit in silence for several long minutes before I ask him if everything was okay with his call. He tells me that it was just work, and it's likely he'll need to go back to London for a day or two next week.

We chat about his work and where he's travelled to, and I tell him I've always wanted to visit Niagara Falls, New York and especially California so I can shop on Rodeo Drive. He laughs and asks if he should start calling me Vivienne, which earns him an elbow to the ribs. The movement has his hips thrusting forward, confirming my suspicions about his nakedness as his cock, his very hard cock, rubs against my lower back. The hand that's wrapped around my waist moves to splay across my belly, and I feel the exact moment he brushes across one of the scars there. Ryder's whole-body tenses.

"Don't. Don't ask, Ryder, not right now. Please." I hate the begging tone in my voice, but I just want to forget, enjoy his hands on me without questions. I hear a quiet 'Okay' before I feel his lips on my skin, where my neck and shoulder meet. I drop my head to the side, giving him better access. He doesn't waste a second at my invitation.

Ryder's other hand comes up, joining the one on my belly before both begin a trail up the side of my body, coming to a stop just below my breasts. I run my hands down his thighs, and as I reach his knees, his fingers edge under the bottom of my bikini top slowly lifting and pushing it up out of the way as my grip on his legs tightens in anticipation.

Continuing to trail kisses along my neck, his fingers scrape across my pebbled nipples before tweaking and pulling at them. A groan falls from my lips as my back arches, filling his hands with my heavy breasts before he squeezes to the point of pain, and I bask in the glorious darkness that clouds my vision at the feel of his rough hands on my body. Needing to put my hands on him, I spin around, kneeling on the seat in front of him, and he grabs my arse, yanking me forward before taking a nipple into his mouth. The warmth of his hot tongue against my chilled nipple sends a delicious shiver down my spine that has me gripping his shoulders and curling my fingers into his skin. As he continues to lave at my taut nipple, my hand slides into his hair, gripping tightly and holding his head in place. Ryder bites down, sending a spark of pleasure straight to my clit, and I cry out.

"Ahhh, harder." He happily obliges before switching to the other one as his hands work to undo the strings holding my bottoms in place, and as they fall away, I open my legs allowing him to skate his fingers through my folds before thrusting two fingers inside. Ryder pumps his fingers in and out while continuing his frenzied torment on my nipples. He suddenly pulls out and grabbing my hips, he forces me to stand.

"I need to taste you." Moving my feet to either side of him, he slides down in the water until his head rests on the edge, pulling me forward by my hips until my pussy rests over his mouth. His tongue flicks out, running the length of me, then again before he focuses his attention exactly where I need it. Within minutes my legs are trembling, my breathing choppy, the butterflies in my belly flutter desperately for escape as Ryder slams two fingers inside me, sucking and biting down hard on my clit, and I explode, screaming his name into the night sky.

"Fuck—Ryder, ahhh!" My body bucks and rocks, riding the waves of pleasure crashing over me, and as my body goes slack, knees giving out, I don't get a second to catch my breath before Ryder is pulling me down and slamming his hips up, ramming his cock into my still convulsing pussy. A growl escapes Ryder as he settles inside me, and then slowly I rise up his length before gliding back down, finding my rhythm and leaning forward to take his lips in a ferocious kiss. I can taste myself on him, and it sends my body wild. I speed up, his hands holding my hips in a bruising grip as he nears his release. Breaking the kiss, I nip along his jaw, down his neck, biting and sucking, marking him as mine, and then he howls out as I feel his hot cum releasing inside me.

He slides a hand up my back, grabbing a handful of my hair, and pulling my head back as he takes my nipple in his mouth, slowly he licks his way up my body, reaching my lips, I open for him, and as I slip my tongue inside I feel him getting hard again inside me. Pulling back, I raise an eyebrow at him, but all I get is a slap on my arse before he's on his feet with me in his arms, legs wrapped around him and heading for the bedroom.

SEVENTEEN

Blue

Laying here with Cam curled against me, I think about the scars on her body. After I took her a second time in the bedroom, she passed out instantly, her face flushed and lips swollen. I watch her sleep while scanning every inch of her and cataloguing every damn scratch that taints her beautiful body. Each mark, and there are many, makes my blood boil. I may know about the abuse, but I don't know everything, and that in itself is an issue.

I saw her face after I admitted that I knew her real name and where she was born, it barely touches the surface of what I actually know, but I'm not supposed to share the details of a job with the client. Fuck, I'm sure as shit not meant to sleep with one either.

This job, Sean Donovan, is personal, and I really can't afford to get distracted by a beautifully damaged woman, wrapped in a body of sin perfect for me to get lost in and quietens my own demons while I fuck her. Cam's different and that worries me. This woman has the potential to bring me to my knees.

As Cam begins to stir, I harden my resolve, putting my arsehole mask firmly back in place. Her hand rests on my chest, and as she wakes, she trails her fingers down my abs to the edge of the quilt that rests just above where my cock starts to rouse ready for round three. She slides her fingers underneath, but before she can reach what she's seeking, I grab her wrist stopping her.

"As much as I would love to fuck you again, we need to talk, Cam." She sighs, trying to pull her hand from my grip, but I tighten my hold. And when she tries to fight harder, I pull on her arm forcing her body on top of mine. I soon realise that was a bad idea, as her warm heat makes contact with my ever-hardening cock. And for all of a second, I forget about the conversation we are meant to have and imagine sinking my cock into her again and again.

Grabbing her face in my hands, I gently draw her to me, brushing her lips with mine. But she's not satisfied with that and using her hands for leverage, pushes herself closer, kissing me savagely and biting my bottom lip. Before I even catch my breath, she's straddling me with her hands on my chest as she begins to rock her hips. Her pussy is soaked with the remnants of her own orgasm and my cum, and it takes everything in me to grasp her hips and stop her movements.

"Cam," I implore, and as I look into her eyes, it's like looking in a fucking mirror. Her demons are riding her hard right now, she needs this. I'll give it to her, but she'll have to give me what I need too. "Start talking," I demand, my voice hard and leaving no room for her to argue. Rolling my hips, combined with the hold I have on her, allows enough friction so she gets the message of what the deal is.

"You're using sex to make—" I roll my hips again making her groan, "to get what you want. That's fucked up, you know?" she stutters out, and I just cock an eyebrow at her.

"Yeah, but we'll both be happy in the end," I say, with another roll of my hips that has her head falling back and eyes closing with pleasure.

"You're a fucking arsehole!" she breathes out, digging her fingernails into my chest. I welcome the bite of pain as my cock pulses beneath her. She's not wrong about me being an arsehole, but she'll give me what I need.

"Talk, Camryn. What happened today?" My hold is firm as she tries to move, and she huffs out a breath.

"I went to lunch, and when I returned there was a delivery on my desk," she pauses, taking a deep breath before continuing, "it was a bouquet of flowers," I roll my hips, encouraging her to continue, "of black lilies," she breathes out on a moan.

"Who were they from?" I ask her, she shakes her head. Initially, I take it to mean she doesn't know but I'm wrong.

"I didn't check if there was a card, I didn't need to. There's only one person that would send me those flowers." I grit my teeth as I realise what she's saying. Feeling that I'm losing her and needing to keep myself calm too, I slide her back and forth along my dick, almost bringing her to orgasm before stopping.

My voice is hoarse when I speak, and I'm not sure if it's from pleasure or anger. "Are you saying that Sean sent those flowers to you, Cam?" Clearly unable to speak, she nods, and that's it my restraint snaps. I lift her, just enough to be able to slide her back down on my cock, causing her to cry out, then I roll us over and pound into her like the devil is fucking chasing me.

When she screams out her orgasm, I pull out, flipping her over onto all fours before slamming back into her. Grabbing a handful of her hair, that has her arching her back, I lean forward whispering in her ear.

"What do they mean, Camryn?" Her stuttered reply has my own demon rearing its fucking head. The rage and pleasure mixing together has me driving into her faster as her sweet little cunt squeezes my cock and throws me over the edge into an abyss of pleasure bathed in darkness.

As awareness seeps back in, I become conscious of how rough I was, and a sliver of regret makes itself known. When I look to Cam, I see that I needn't have worried. With her head to the side and hair mussed, I can see the glazed look in her eyes. Pulling out and dropping down next to her, I roll to my side facing her and swipe her sweat slicked hair from her face before running a finger across her cheek and lifting her chin so her eyes meet mine. I search her eyes for even a hint of fear that my roughness may have caused, but I don't see any. Cam obviously senses the direction my thoughts have gone as her hand reaches out and runs down my cheek.

"I'm fine, Ryder. In fact, I'm better than fine," she tells me, as my hand comes up to rest on hers.

"He'll pay, Cam. I'll make him pay for it all," I vow, and no matter what else happens, I won't rest until he's dead.

"Ryder, he knows where I am." Her voice is strong, but I hear what she didn't say, and the fear behind her words. She knows as well as I do that he'll never stop and will keep coming for her, but what he doesn't know is that she's *mine*. And I protect what's mine, and I'm prepared to pay in blood to do it.

"Yeah. Yeah, he does." I can't lie, I may be lying to her about other things, but this? I won't lie to her about this.

I wrap her in my arms, and I can almost hear the fear whispering beneath her skin. She lays awake for a long time, and I know she's aware I'm awake too, though neither of us say a word.

And even when she finally slips into sleep, my brain refuses to rest. Cam's whispered reply about what the flowers meant had me wanting to find that fucker Sean and spend the whole night making him pay, watching the blood drain from his body as I cut into his flesh and relish his cries of pain, but instead, I buried myself deep inside what was once his.

I let my demons bathe in the darkness while I made Cam mine. And she is *mine*.

EIGHTEEN

Camryn

I wake to an empty bed, Ryder's side of the bed is cold, meaning he's been gone awhile. My body is deliciously sore, and a vision of the two of us from last night flashes through my mind. Throwing the covers back and sliding my legs out, feet to the floor, I rest there a minute and try to sort through my scrambled thoughts.

Ryder took advantage of my reluctance to talk, my attempt to use sex as a distraction, but I can't really be mad at him. If anything, I'm madder at myself. I just wanted to get lost in him, forget about the fact that my crazy ex is coming for me and knows where I am.

This morning there is no escaping the reality that he's found me and will destroy anyone that stands in his way, and that scares me more than anything else.

The bastard knew exactly what he was doing when he sent those flowers to me. They are one of my most favourite flowers, he knows this because he had some planted at the house for me. But they also signify death. More specifically my death.

Sean once told me that when I die, he would cover my coffin in black lilies, and no other flower would be permitted at my funeral. I remember thinking how sweet that was at the time. But when he covered our daughter's coffin in them and warned me that if I didn't produce an heir soon it would be me in the next coffin covered in black lilies, their beauty became just another way for Sean to hurt me.

Getting to my feet, I notice that my bag sits on the chair in the corner of the room. Desperately needing a shower, and hoping it will help to clear my mind, I riffle through till I find a pair of joggers and a tee before heading to Ryder's en suite.

Ryder's en suite is no ordinary bathroom. It's almost as big as the bedroom, and the centre piece is a cast iron free-standing bath. It's stunning.

In the centre of the far wall is a double walk-in shower, one has a rainfall shower head, and that's where I head to. Placing my clothes on the counter before walking in and using the touch controls to turn it on. As the water pours over me, I realise that the water temperature is preset, and it's bloody freezing. I laugh out loud at the thought of Ryder in here taking a cold shower, and then an image of him in here with water cascading down his ripped body and dick rock hard as he glides his hands up and down the shaft has my body heating with need. Damn. I'll need a cold shower myself in a minute. Quickly shaking the vision from my mind, I adjust the temp and step into the spray.

Once I've washed, I brush my teeth with the new tooth-brush I found in the cupboard below the sink. I couldn't find mine in the bag Jamie packed for me, but I did find my hairbrush. Just as I'm about to open the bedroom door, it flies open, and there stands Ryder. I know before he even opens his mouth that something is seriously wrong.

"What is it, what's happened?" I ask, as dread forms in my throat, and with his next words that ball of dread drops like a stone bringing me to my knees.

"It's Jamie."

NO, No, No. Please be okay. I fucking knew this would happen! Why wasn't anyone watching out for her? It's a question that's been plaguing me all the way to the hospital. I should have been there; it should have been me. And now, I'm sitting at the bedside of my only friend and praying to anyone that'll listen to please just let her be all right.

Ryder told me in the car on the way here that someone broke into the house and Jamie had disturbed them. Apparently, she finished her shift early, otherwise nobody would have been there.

Jamie sustained a significant head injury, has a broken wrist and several other smaller injuries. They had to put her into an induced coma to give her time to heal after an MRI scan revealed some swelling around her brain. Her right hand is in a cast, and her face is barely recognisable. I've been sat at her side, for god knows how long, with her good hand in mine as tears quietly slip down my face.

I hear the swoosh of the ICU doors and squeaky shoes on that dreadful hospital lino, and as the squeaky shoe owner draws nearer there's an audible gasp. I look up to find Jamie's parents have arrived. Jamie's mum, Louise, has her hands clamped over her mouth and tears stream from her eyes, the utter devastation at seeing her daughter this way is almost her undoing.

Dominic, Jamie's father stands behind Louise, one hand resting on her shoulder, his face is a mask. Not an ounce of emotion crosses that man's face, it must be a military thing. Jamie told me her dad was in the army, and it's the same expression I've seen Ryder wear. My dad was the same too.

I go to stand, but Louise rushes to my side, her hand on my shoulder stopping me. Dominic brings a chair for her, and she sits next to me, holding my hand in comfort while I hold her daughter's. The gesture brings a new form of torture to my heart. If she only knew that this is all my fault, she'd have me thrown out. I know I would. I know the unimaginable pain of losing a child, and I remember how I felt about the truck driver that took the most precious thing in the world to me.

If I could have had five minutes, just five minutes with that man, I would have made him suffer. I would have taken great pleasure in seeing the pain in his eyes as I broke him. I didn't even get to see him get the justice of going to prison. When the police finally tracked him down, he was dead. Sean told me that he hung himself, but I remember reading in the paper that he had a single gunshot wound to the head. Not sure why he would lie, but why does a psycho do anything they do.

I hear Ryder and Dominic talking, but I'm not really paying attention. I need to get out of this room. My guilt is slowly eating away at me, and I can feel my anxiety creeping closer every minute I sit here. A fraud. A liar. A curse. Death. Everyone I love dies. I'm like the man with the golden touch, except mine brings death and destruction.

I stand abruptly, the chair almost toppling over with the force, a muttered apology leaves my lips as I race for the door. I don't stop running until I burst through the exit. Bent at the waist, hands on my knees, I take in deep lung-ful's of air hoping to expel this soul deep pain and guilt inside of me. I hear Ryder call my name, but I don't think, I just run.

My legs carry me across the car park, but I'm not looking where I'm going, so I don't see the car until it's almost on top of me. I'm hit from behind, slamming into the ground with a thud and then rolled over, strong arms wrapped around me. I start fighting, my adrenaline taking over, kicking my legs, fists flying but hitting nothing but air.

"Cam—oomph, fuck! It's me, Cam, stop fucking fighting."

Slowly, Ryder's deep smooth voice penetrates my fried brain and I still. After a few minutes I say, "Let me up, Ryder." He doesn't let go. "Get the fuck off me!" I scream at him. He releases me, and I immediately scramble to my feet. "What the actual fuck?" I shout, spinning round to see him climbing to his feet too. I stomp towards him, thrusting my palms into his chest. "What the hell is wrong with you, why'd you do that?" He just fucking stands there, hands at his sides. I go at him again, this time managing to push him back a step, but as I go to slam him a third time, his hands come up catching my wrists.

"Stop! Just fucking calm down," he grits out. The grip on my wrists tightens, almost to the point of pain, and somehow, it's enough to calm me momentarily. But then I register what he said, why we are here, that my friend is laying in a hospital bed, and I see red.

Yanking my wrists from him, my eyes narrow, and I get right up in his face. "Calm down? Are you fucking insane? Calm down, huh. My friend almost died because of me and you want me to calm the fuck down. Pfft. Yeah, 'cause that's gonna help the situation, that's gonna turn back time so that I didn't bring all this shit to Jamie's door. That's going to change the fact that some fucked up, naive, weak, broken girl, who doesn't deserve to even be a-fucking-live didn't come in and fuck her life up too." Ryder's hands ball into fists at his side, what the fuck has he got to be so angry about?

"You don't get to stand there and tell me to calm down, you know fuck all about me, or how I feel. Do you have any idea what it's like to feel such overwhelming guilt, to look at your hands and see the blood of the people you love? No, I don't think you have the first fucking idea how I feel." I watch him for some reaction. His eyes harden as he watches me, waiting. So, I give him what he's obviously waiting for, I mean, I'm already showing my crazy, shouting and screaming in the street like a fucking escaped psychopath, why not go all the way, right?

"Why the hell wasn't there someone watching her? You can't tell me that the stick shoved so firmly up your arse didn't ensure you put security on her. I told you that he'd come after anyone to get to me. That should be me in that hospital bed, not her, Ryder. Not her!" I shout at him, and then heave a sigh, my shoulders slumping as the fight leaves me, replaced by the guilt and fear again.

I sink to the ground, my head in my hands, as the gravel pierces my knees like the pain that's stabbing through my heart. This position is where I belong, on my knees, wrecked and broken, heart in tatters. I don't deserve the kindness and love Jamie and her family bestowed upon me, or the safety and protection that Rick and Ryder have given me with nothing in return. This? This right here, is where I should be. And when Sean gets his property back, and he fucking will, I'll be six feet under, and if by some miracle I'm not, I'll wish I fucking was.

The utter despair, loss and guilt from Faye's death has returned tenfold for the pound of flesh my escape denied it of. The tears fall and I don't give a flying fuck as sobs wrack my body, tearing and ripping through the walls I tried to erect like a knife through butter. Just another reminder of how weak I really am. Another reminder of how completely and utterly worthless I really am.

"Are you finished with your little pity party for one?" Ryder asks, my head snaps up to see him standing there with his hands on his hips, hard eyes narrowed at me. I'm so shocked I just stare at him. "You talk about guilt like you own the fucking monopoly on it but let me tell you something. You fucking don't, Camryn. You think you can stand there and tell me I don't know how you feel, and that I don't have blood on my hands too. I have more than you'll ever have. I carry the guilt of my brother's death every day, I carry his blood on my hands because I should have been there, not fighting a war.

"During that war I nearly lost my whole squad on a mission. The only people to make it out alive were me, Sully and Seb. Seven men died because I made the wrong call, Camryn. Seven. Do I feel guilt, do I feel sad for those men's families? Every fucking day. But what is the point of letting that guilt eat away at me, drowning in the sorrow of their loss, there's no point. I refuse to allow their deaths to be in vain, so instead I get up every morning thankful I'm still alive, and then I go out there and do everything in my power to make sure more people don't suffer the same fate. I'm a survivor, I fight back, and that's what you are. You're a survivor too, Camryn." I shake my head at him. "Yes, you fucking are! You wouldn't have made it this far if you weren't. Tell me something, what makes you get up every day?"

I think about the answer to that, it's not all that hard, it's part of the reason I ran. "I want justice. I want vengeance. I want Sean to suffer like I have, I want to take away every-thing he loves, everyone he loves," I sneer, the anger at him returning, "I want all those things, but I don't want others to suffer for my own selfish desires. I don't want more people to die or get hurt getting what I want, that's not fair at all. I don't want to fucking play god with people's lives, Ryder."

"And what about Jamie? Do you think she'd want that to be you up there instead of her?"

"Yes...No, I don't know. What sort of a fucking question even is that? I lied to her, Ryder. I put her life in danger by not being honest with her or giving her the chance to decide whether she wanted me in her life or not." I hang my head again, as the guilt winds its way back in.

"Come on, Cam, do you honestly think Jamie didn't know what she was doing when she took you in? You need to give her more credit than that," he scoffs. "So, you didn't tell her everything, but you had your reasons. One being trust and the other because you thought you were protecting her, right?"

I nod. "But I didn't protect her, look what happened," I say, pointing back to the hospital, "A lie by omission, is still a lie," I state.

"Sometimes people lie or omit the truth not to be hurtful but because they think they are doing the right thing, not wanting to hurt the ones they love. I'm not saying it's right, but I can understand the motivation behind it." Then he just turns and walks away, leaving me kneeling on the pavement.

If I was thinking straight, I might have looked a little closer at that cryptic statement, instead I sit and wallow for several minutes before giving myself a swift kick up the arse and go back to the hospital.

When I return to the ICU, there's no sign of Ryder, so I take up my seat at Jamie's side with her parents.

While I was gone the doctor had been in, and he was confident that Jamie would wake in the next 24 hours. There is no sign of permanent brain damage and her broken wrist is a straightforward fracture that will heal nicely over the next six to eight weeks. She has a couple of broken ribs that will be painful but also heal on their own. Painful is an understatement, and one I can sympathise with.

Louise tries to get me to go home to get some sleep, but I refuse to leave Jamie's side. When she sees that I'm not going anywhere, she sends Dominic out for food and coffee.

I WAKE SLUMPED over Jamie's bed, where I obviously fell asleep, my hand still in hers. As I become more conscious, I feel eyes on me, but note the room is empty except for Jamie and me. Lifting my head, I'm met by the one eye of Jamie's that's not swollen shut.

"Hey, sleepy head, I wondered when you were gonna wake up," Jamie says, her voice hoarse from the ventilator tube and the attack as I note the bruises that mottle her neck.

"I'm so sorry, Jamie." I push the words passed the lump in my throat as tears begin to well in my eyes, blurring my vision. I drop my gaze to the bed, not able to look her in the eye.

"Cam." She pauses and when I lift my eyes back to hers, I see she was waiting for me to look at her, "This is not your fault, and I can still kick your arse if you even start thinking you're to blame," she says determinedly, squeezing my hand to cement her point further. I don't agree, but I tell her okay, now is not the time to argue with her. She's obviously suffering from concussion and not thinking clearly.

The nurse comes in to check her vitals, and I use the opportunity to find a bathroom and grab a tea. Entering the corridor, I see Ryder talking to Scott up near the elevator, but not wanting to talk with him right now, I turn and go the other way.

NINETEEN

Blue

I walk away from Cam as my own guilt about the secrets I'm keeping from her begin to raise their fucking heads. She's right, a lie by omission is still a lie, but does that mean that every lie is bad? I don't even know anymore. I have to believe that what I'm doing is the right thing, just like she thought keeping Jamie in the dark was right, to protect her, like I want to protect Cam. I will tell her, but when the time is right. I'll have to trust that when I do, she understands why.

Walking back into the hospital I find Scott there, and he tells me that Russ is here getting his hand stitched up. Filling him in on Jamie's injuries, I ask him what the fuck happened. Apparently, Jamie left early after she got a message about something wrong at the house, Scott doesn't know exactly what. As soon as Scott found out from one of the nurses, no doubt one he's been screwing, that Jamie left early he called Russ to let him know, but Russ said he was closer and he'd meet Scott there. When Scott arrived, the police were just arriving, and the paramedics were bringing Jamie out.

"What took you so long to get there?" I ask Scott, accusation clear in my tone.

"Some dickhead blocked my car in at the hotel, and I had to get reception to find the owner of the damn car before I could get out. The guy was as pissed as a newt when they finally found him, and I had to move the car myself. Turns out the guy wasn't even a guest at the hotel." I raise an eyebrow at that. "Yeah, coincidence? My thoughts too."

"What about at the house, did you find anything that can help identify this guy?"

"Nah, whoever did it knew what they were doing. The lock on the back door had been picked, at least it seems that way as there was no sign of forced entry. The one thing I don't get is the broken window in the back door, if the guy picked the lock, why break the window?" he muses, then shrugs. "Maybe it got broken during the struggle, I mean, most of the glass was on the outside, which indicates a window broken from inside. Once Jamie's awake, hopefully she'll be able to shed some light on it."

Before Scott leaves, I ask him to get Russ' statement, and then let me know when they are heading back out.

Not wanting to face Cam again after the way I left things, I head to the cafeteria. Grabbing a tea that's bound to taste like dirty dish water, I find a seat in the corner and call Sully to let him know the situation. As I finish my call with Sully, Jamie's father walks in, spotting me, he changes direction heading this way.

"Dom. How is she?" I ask, as he approaches the table.

"The doctor is hopeful that she'll wake in the next 24 hours, and there's no sign of permanent damage. Camryn is back in there with Louise, we tried to send her home, but she's stubborn and refuses to go anywhere." I give a nod to that assessment of Cam. "How worried should I be, Blue?"

I consider what I should tell him, he may be Jamie's father but he's a damn journo, and they'd sell their own mother for a good story. But I've known him for a few years, and he's a good man. "How much do you know about Cam?" I ask, feeling him out first.

He pulls a chair out, sitting down, he rubs a hand down his face. "I'm not stupid, I knew when Jamie told me about her that she was running from something...But, fuck, Sean Donovan, Blue. That's some serious trouble to be running from. She's a good girl, I gave her a job, works hard and keeps her head down, but—"

"I get it, Donovan is not a guy you want on your radar. I can't tell you too much, you know how it is, but we have something in the works to bring him down. I can have some extra guys brought in to watch Jamie, if you want?"

He shakes his head. "No, I have my own guys. When Jamie is released, she can come home with us, but what about Camryn, she's more than wel—"

"She's with me," I state, the territorial tone a dead give-away, and I wish I could have hidden it better. "It's my job to protect her, and that's what I'll do," I add, and it's the lamest attempt to cover up my true feelings, hiding behind my job. My fucking mask is sliding off my face like snow in an avalanche. Dom chuckles, which he tries to cover with a cough.

"How did you know it was Sean? Cam's been pretty tight lipped about him, barely even mentioning his name till recently."

"Jamie told me, said you mentioned the name Sean, and well, she's a smart girl, put two and two together. I wish you'd come to me first; you know I can get information. I could have helped. I still can if you need it." He seems genuine, I guess having your daughter in the sights of a man like Sean Donovan will do that to you.

"Thanks, Dom, and I'll call if there's anything," I say, with a head nod.

"Right, okay then, I best get back with this food and drink. You coming?" Rising from his chair and placing it back under the table.

"No, I have some calls to make, I'll catch up with you later." I wave my phone to emphasise my point. He spins back towards the food counter and joins the queue that's now formed.

Dom seemed a bit put out by my brush off of his offer to help, and whilst I believe he's being sincere, I can't afford for him to fuck this up by tipping the wrong person off while digging around for information. That man knows a lot of people, some of them worse than Donovan. But he could prove useful, so I won't write him off completely. Better to keep all options open.

I stay in the cafeteria, drink another disgusting cup of dish water and even manage something that just passes for a sandwich. Going over what Scott said it's likely that someone drew Jamie away from work intentionally, their motive obviously to cut Cam off, isolate her, fuck with her head. They did a pretty fucking good job of that if what went down between us earlier is any indication. I can't wait for the shit fit she's going to throw when I tell her that she's coming to stay with me.

With Jamie staying with her dad, maybe Sean will think his tactics are working, although, I've no doubt he knows I'm here. It's probably fucking with his head that I'm so close to his girl. That pleases the beast inside me, getting under his skin and bringing him down, has my beast purring like a damn cat.

My phone vibrates on the table, a message from Scott pops up on the screen. He's at the ICU waiting for me, I send a quick reply telling him I'm on my way. Scott is outside the lift when I step out, an envelope in his hand. Handing it to me, he tells me its Russ' statement, and he and Russ are heading back to the hotel. Scott's eyes flick over my shoulder quickly before coming back to me, a tingle running down my spine. I don't need to look to know it's Cam, I can fucking feel her. Obviously as keen as me to avoid each other, Scott tells me she went the other way. When I tell him that Cam will be moving in with me temporarily, the hard-faced bastard actually cracks a smile, which I wipe off his smug face in the next second.

"I have to go back to London for a day or two, I got a tip off about a new shipment coming in, and I need to check it out, so you and Russ are on babysitting duty." I don't even try to hide my smile. "One of you is to be with her at all times, you don't let her out of your sight. Seb is close by if you need him. I'll be leaving in the morning, so be at mine at 6am." He nods, getting in the lift just as it arrives.

Now I need to go find my startled little deer and break the news to her. This should be fucking fun. I'm not keen to leave Cam, but this is important. The tip off was anonymous, but with all the whispers Sully has heard recently it makes sense.

I head off in the direction Cam went, and as I round the corner, I see her slip inside a door on the left. I wait outside for her, and as the door begins to open, I quickly pull it open and shove her back inside closing and locking the door behind me.

"For fucks sake, Ryder, you scared the crap out of me!" I

stalk towards her, and she backs up as I invade her space. I watch as the shutters come down, and she lifts her chin with defiant eyes staring back at me.

"Shhh, Bambi," I whisper, putting a finger to my lips. Cam's eyes spark with fire, as I cage her in against the wall.

"You're a dick, do you know that? Normal people would just wait outside, not scare the living crap out of someone and lock them in a toilet with them."

"I've heard that once or twice before, and we both know that I'm far from normal, so let's skip the bitching. How's Jamie?" I ask, as I lean in, running my nose down her neck and taking in the sweet smell of vanilla that's always on her skin.

"She's awake, I left her with the nurse," she says, as a shiver runs across her skin, and that has my dick taking notice. Now is not the time, and certainly not in some skanky hospital toilet, no matter how much my dick tries to convince me otherwise.

"Good. Let's go talk to her, find out what she remembers." I say, taking her hand and pulling her behind me, down the corridor back to Jamie's room.

TWENTY

Camryn

This man infuriates me like no one else ever has. Scares the shit out me, sniffs me like a fucking dog, and then drags me behind him like a petulant child. I'm still angry with him for what happened outside, not because of what he said, we both know he was right about that. But more because he was *right*, and he called me out on it.

I hate liars but isn't that what I've been doing since the day I ran from Sean? Lying to everyone that knows me, lying about who I really am, and lying to myself. That one hurts more than anything else.

I don't know why I thought I could just up and leave, change my identity and live a normal life. I don't want to live a life where I'm always looking over my shoulder, never able to settle anywhere for too long for fear that Sean will find me.

I should have walked away from Jamie that morning on the streets, then none of this would have happened. But I didn't and I can't change that now. It wouldn't have saved Tyler, and if it wasn't Jamie it would have been someone else. There was always going to be a big red target on the back of anyone that came into my sphere. Did I intentionally set out to hurt Jamie? No fucking way. I need to stop blaming myself and realise that the person to blame for all this shit, is Sean-fucking-Donovan. Hindsight is a wonderful thing, it's just a shame it always comes too fucking late.

When we enter Jamie's room, there's no sign of her parents, but Jamie is sitting up, although a little awkwardly and in obvious pain. Jamie begins to laugh as she sees Ryder dragging me into the room, then winces as the pain from her broken ribs takes hold, stopping her instantly. Despite endeavouring not to blame myself, the guilt still tries to take the reins, and I'm unable to stop the memory that looking at her brings.

"YOU FUCKING STUPID BITCH! What have I told you before, huh? Keep your fucking stupid cunt of a mouth shut unless I speak to you. Dumb bitch!" He swiped his hand out, catching me across the cheek so hard my head whipped to the side. Before I even had a chance to recover, his fist landed in my stomach, buckling my knees and bringing me to the floor. With one hand on the floor and the other cradling my stomach, I tried to heave in the breath that my lungs screamed out for. His hand gripped my hair, yanking my head back. His eyes, normally a dark brown, were almost black as the rage consumed him, bored into mine. I smelt the whiskey on his breath, and it almost made me gag as he screamed in my face. The hold on my hair was so tight, my neck pulled back so far that I was sure he was going to break it. That would have been a blessing he'd never give me.

As he continued his assault on me, I drifted into my

special place, shutting out the pain, thinking of happier times, and my beautiful daughter. I don't know how long it lasted, time seemed to slow, it was almost like I was watching from outside of my body. I watched as he rained down hit after hit, and when I collapsed to the floor the kicking started. I remember my ribs were on fire, and my breaths shallow as I tried to get enough air into them. When he was spent, he spat on me before walking away and leaving me there.

His men never intervened, except when he asked them to hold me down, or touch me. The only one to ever show any emotion, other than hate or offer pain, was Tyler. It was him that came to me that night, cleaned me up, treated my wounds and dressed my broken ribs.

I COME BACK to the room as Ryder touches my cheek, and I flinch back from him. Confusion at my reaction swims in his eyes, I offer a small smile and a shake of my head that I hope tells him it was nothing. I reach for his hand as it drops back to his side, slipping my fingers between his, and before he can ask me what just happened, I pull him towards Jamie and ask her what the nurse said.

After Jamie fills us in on what the nurse said, Ryder doesn't waste a second getting to what he's here for. Jamie tells us how she left her shift early because she got a message from her neighbour to say there was a man loitering outside. Apparently, Jamie has herself a man I didn't know about, I give her quizzical look, then tell her I'll be getting all the details later. Thinking it was just her man arriving early, she didn't think anything more of it, but when she arrived home, there was nobody there. After showering, she came down to get some food and that's when she noticed the back door was open.

My sharp intake of breath, as them both spinning to face me. Shit! I realise that I never told anyone about my incident with the back door the other night. I wave it off for now, I tell Jamie to carry on. She does, but I can feel Ryder's eyes on me, burning the side of my face with their intensity, and I give his foot a kick to get him focused back on what Jamie is saying.

Jamie tells us that as she pulled the door closed, someone hit her from behind, and as she fell to the floor, they started dragging her backwards by her hair.

"He was dragging me; my vision was blurred. I started kicking and screaming, trying to loosen his hold on me, but it just made him angry, yanking my hair harder. As we neared the door from the utility, I grabbed the frame, and I tried to spin around so I could see him and maybe kick out at him, anything to get him to let go. He kicked my arm, I think that's how my wrist got broken, after that I couldn't hold on, he was too strong. I fought so hard, Cam." Her voice breaks, and I move closer, pulling her hand to mine.

"It's okay, Jamie, you're safe now," I say, but the words taste like another lie on my tongue.

"I started to look around for anything that I could use as a weapon, I still couldn't focus properly. As he pulled me down the hall, I saw one of your shoes, and I've never been so grateful for your laziness. Snatching it up, I swung my arm out, hitting him in the knee. It was enough for him to loosen his grip on me, and I scrambled away. Just as I got to my feet, I felt him at my back and ran. I ran for the back door, but he reached me before I could open it. Spinning me round and slamming my back against it, he lashed out, but I dodged it and he hit the window, smashing the glass. After that I don't remember much else, just his fists, and the kicks as he hit me over and over again. I'm sorry."

Those two words from my only friend, cause the tears that welled in my eyes as she told her story, to overflow and stream down my face. "What the hell, Jamie! You do not need to apologise. It's me that should be sorry. It's my fault this happened to you, and for that, I will never forgive myself." I drop my head, unable to look at her for a second.

Then I feel Ryder's hand on my back, remembering his words from earlier, I harden my resolve, and turn my guilt and pain into anger. And that anger has only one focus. Sean Donovan. Looking back up at Jamie, I say, "But, I promise you, Jamie, he won't get away with this. He will pay, I'll make sure of it. I will do whatever it takes." *Even if I have to pay with my life!* I won't allow him to hurt one more person I care about, and if that means I end up dead, then so fucking be it!

"Jamie, did you get a look at his face at all?" Ryder asks.

"No, he had a hood on, like the hoodie from a jumper and a scarf covering the lower half of his face. He didn't speak, and from what I saw his clothes were all plain and dark." Her brow creases for a second and then, "Hold on, he had a tattoo, on one of his forearms, I caught a glimpse when his sleeve was pushed up in the struggle, but I don't remember what it was of." She frowns, and I can see as she struggles to remember.

"That's great, Jamie. Every little thing you can remember will help. I imagine the police will want to speak to you at some point, just tell them everything you told me, but I have to ask you not to mention anything about Sean." Jamie agrees without question, and whilst I understand his reasons, I'm a little pissed he's asking my friend to lie to the police. Before I get a chance to say anything, the door opens, and Dominic and Louise enter carrying a bag for Jamie.

After a quick chat with Jamie's parents, Ryder ushers me out the door as I promise to come and see her tomorrow. As soon as we are in the car, Ryder turns from understanding, caring friend to overbearing arsehole.

"Start fucking talking, Cam!" He starts the car and peels out of the car park like his arse is on fire.

"Woah! Slow down, Ryder, for fucks sake," I say, as I'm slammed into my seat from the force. "I forgot about it because in case you haven't noticed, I've had other things on my mind. You know, like some grumpy," he looks at me from the corner of his eye, "sexy," I smirk at him, "arsehole that may have distracted me," I finish with a wink, trying to calm his rage-y beast some. He just looks at me with eyes that tell me to get on with it. "Okay, fine. Jamie was at work and I'd been in the garden. When I'd finished, I was dirty and went for a bath, but when I came back down the back door was open. I just assumed that I didn't close it properly when I came back in. That's it, nothing else to report, sir," I snark at him.

I let him rant and rave about my safety, and how I need to tell him of anything suspicious like that in the future. Had he have said all this before, then I may have thought he was overreacting, but given what happened to Jamie last night, I agree without argument.

It's dark when we pull up to the house, and as we turn into the drive, I see a flicker of light in the house across the road. Spinning in my seat to get a better look, there's nothing there. I search all the windows for any sign of movement but nothing.

"What's wrong?" Ryder asks, as he turns off the engine, turning to follow my line of sight.

"Nothing. I'm just tired." Despite our conversation just now, I honestly just think my brain is fried, and I need to sleep. "What are we doing here? Are we even allowed in? Shouldn't there be a cop here, you know to make sure the scene is secure?" I say, looking at the house and seeing the police tape. Ryder side eyes me, arching a brow.

"You watch too many crime shows." I tilt my head at him, raising my own brows. "Fine. Yes, and there is, but I have a friend on the force, so we're good. We're not staying, you're coming home with me, but I thought you'd like to collect some of your things."

I'm not even pissed at him telling me I'm coming with him, or for bribing a cop. If I'm honest, I don't want to even step foot inside the house right now, but Ryder's right, I could definitely do with some clothes and other bits and pieces. "Okay, let's get this over with then."

He seems surprised by my quick acquiescence. I may not appreciate his bossiness, but I'm not fucking stupid.

Getting out of the car, I realise I don't have my key, it's in my handbag at Ryder's apartment. As if he can read my mind, he pulls a key from his pocket, dangling it in front of me.

"Hey, how did you get that?" I ask, more than suspicious now.

"Jamie gave it to me," he replies, shrugging his shoulders nonchalantly. Why do I get the feeling he's not being totally honest?

"Ryder..." I say, drawing out the 'r'.

He drops his hand holding the key to his side. "Alright, fine. I took it from the key hook in the kitchen marked spare keys—" He realises the importance of that revelation just as I do. We both rush up the drive, ducking under the police tape and to the front door. Stepping into the house, eerie silence greats us, and my skin tingles as goosebumps cover my flesh. I stop as I see my shoe on the floor, spotting the drops of blood that dot the floor in the hall. Ryder has gone on ahead but stops when he sees I'm frozen in place.

"Cam?"

"I'm fine. Go, I'm right behind you." Pushing the fear aside, I lock down my emotions and follow Ryder to the kitchen.

When we get there, the smell of blood hits me, and as I take in the room, I see all the little markers from the crime scene investigators next to the blood that is splattered all over the floor.

"Breathe through your mouth, it will stop the smell."

I do as Ryder said and find it actually works. I begin to cautiously step towards where Ryder is waiting for me. When I reach him, I look to the key hooks, noting that where there should be two spare keys— there are now none.

"There were two spare keys here, if you have one, then that means..." Feeling the bile rise up my throat I dash to the sink, leaning over as I spew what little I have in my stomach into the sink. I turn the tap on rinsing the sink first then placing my mouth under the tap and spitting out a couple of times before taking a drink. Standing back up I swipe my mouth down the sleeve of my arm.

"Come on, let's get the fuck out of here," Ryder says, guiding me out of the kitchen towards the stairs. Once I have everything I need, we leave and it's not soon enough.

TWENTY-ONE

Camryn

When we get back to Ryder's, he tells me to order a takeaway, my choice, from the menus on the fridge, while he goes off to make a call. I pick pizza, not sure my stomach can handle much else right now.

After placing the order, I grab a beer from Ryder's fridge and walk to the windows to look out over the city. I love the view from here. The city lights look amazing and this far up it feels like all my troubles and worries are left down below. If only that were true. No, my troubles have become everyone else's, and that makes my blood boil so hot it's like lava flowing through my veins. A bit how that man in there makes me feel.

When I think back to how it was with Sean, even at the beginning when we first met, I never felt like this. I never felt like I'd stop breathing if he wasn't near, or the heart pounding desire I feel when I'm with Ryder. Not that I'd ever tell him that, the man has an ego the size of Everest. But I see underneath all that seriousness and bravado, I catch glimpses of the softer side of him when he's not looking. This is a man who when he loves, he loves hard. His loyalty goes above and beyond, and he'd give his last breath for the ones he loves.

I don't count myself in that circle yet, but I'm not going to lie and say I wouldn't like to be one day. I have no idea what we are doing, what this is between us, but Jamie's words about taking a risk echo in my mind.

I feel him the moment he enters the room, and that just solidifies my current thought process. I told myself earlier that I didn't want to live my life always looking over my shoulder, but I also don't want to live with any more regrets and what ifs. I spin around just as he reaches me. He quirks a brow in silent question, but I just laugh. He grabs my hips pushing me back against the glass. The cold even more marked on my heated skin.

"What's so funny, Bambi?" he asks, humour lacing his tone.

"Nothing, nothing at all," I reply, just as his fingers slip beneath the hem of my t-shirt, skimming up the sides of my body.

"Now, why is it that I don't believe you. Maybe I should *make* you tell me the truth," he says, as he buries his head in the side of my neck. The feeling sends a shiver of pleasure down my spine, and I can't help but moan at the feel of the rough stubble on his jaw as it grazes my cheek.

"And just how do you plan to do that," I ask breathlessly, unable to stop myself from showing him just how much his touch affects me. One particular method springs to mind as I remember last night.

"I think you know exactly how I work, and how very effective my methods are," he whispers, as he kisses along my jaw before taking my mouth. I wind my arms around his neck, the empty beer bottle dangles from my fingers, coming up on my tiptoes as though I want to literally crawl inside him. Before either of us get lost to the lust, the damn lift pings its arrival. Breaking the kiss, both of us panting and desperate for more of each other, he pulls back.

"Fucking lift," he mutters, as he walks away.

Yeah, I'm really starting to hate that lift. While Ryder grabs the food, I get myself another beer and one for him too and take them into the lounge. As Ryder comes in with the pizza boxes, I shamelessly ogle him, and although my stomach grumbles about the lack of food it's consumed recently, the rest of my body hungers for something else entirely. As if he can feel me watching him, he looks over to me as he places the boxes on the table, and I see my own desire mirrored in his eyes. Our eyes stay locked on each other as he comes to stand in front of me. I have to crane my neck, and as I do, he reaches out a hand cupping my chin, swiping a thumb across my bottom lip.

"These lips..." his eyes darken at whatever thought is running through his head, "I'd like nothing more than to see them wrapped around my dick right now." My eyes automatically flick to the bulge in his jeans, reaching out my hands, I run them up the side of his thighs before moving to his belt. Just as I start to undo it, Ryder moves back out of reach, and I frown at him, confused.

With my chin still cupped in his hand, he leans down, and his breath whispers across the shell of my ear as he speaks, "Food first, then I'm taking you to bed." He kisses me, nipping my bottom lip before standing back up, grabbing the pizza and dropping down in the seat next to me.

How the hell does he expect me to eat now, after that little show. My skins feels flushed, and I'm pretty sure I need some clean underwear. Urgh! Infuriating man.

I manage to eat a few slices of pizza and drink another

beer. With a full stomach and a slight buzz from the beer, I lay down on the sofa, while Ryder clears the pizza boxes and beer bottles away. I close my eyes and just allow my mind to wander. The light changes in the room, becoming duller, and when I open my eyes the whole ceiling is lit up like the night sky. It's stunning!

"Holy shit, Ryder, that's...wow." I'm blown away. Every major constellation is there, and even a few smaller ones.

"I had it put in a couple of years ago," he says coming back into the room. Instead of sitting, he lays down on the floor next to where I lay on the sofa. "When I was younger, my mum and I would go out as the sun set and watch for the first star to appear. My mum even paid to have a star named after me for my 10th birthday, the same year I got my first telescope," he says wistfully, full of emotion, and it's one I've not heard from him before.

"I used to do the same with—" Shit! What am I doing? "I used to do the same, but I haven't for a long time," I say, hoping he doesn't hear the quiver in my voice. I don't know if I can handle his questions right now. I will tell him about Faye, but I'm not ready, not yet. Thankfully, he doesn't call me out on my hesitation. Instead he throws a complete curve ball at me.

"So, I know the timing isn't great right now, not with what just happened to Jamie, but I have to go back to London in the morning."

I roll onto my side, leaning on my forearm as I look over the edge of the sofa at him. He has his hands behind his head, and his t-shirt has risen up, giving me a delicious glimpse of his abs and the line of hair running from his belly button down to his mouth-watering— I swallow and lick my lips at the sight. Trying to get my head out of the gutter and aware that he just told me he's going back to London, I run my eyes up his body. Before I reach his face, I spot another tattoo on the inside of his left bicep. It's extremely subtle, and probably why I've not noticed it before. I look to the ceiling until I find what I'm looking for, the constellation of Scorpio, just like Ryder's tattoo. My heart skips a beat when I think about the small constellation of Leo I have tattooed on the back of my neck. I don't know if Ryder has ever noticed it, he's never mentioned it, so I'm guessing not. Realising that I need to answer Ryder, I look back down at him, only to find his eyes on me.

"Sorry, I got lost in the stars. You're going back to London tomorrow? For how long?" I ask, trying not to let my disappointment and, let's be honest, fear at him not being here show too much. I know he told me he might have to go, but he was right, the timing is shit.

"It will just be for a day, two at the most. There's something I need to do," he says, being very vague, which instantly has me suspicious.

"Work?" I ask, then my mind races to another possibility, one that hadn't crossed my mind till now. "Girlfriend, wife?" I shoot up as I watch him wince at those words. "You're married? What the fuck, Ryder!" I shout, jumping up from the sofa and almost stamping on his leg as I stumble away from him.

"Fuck, no! Why would you think that?" he asks, climbing to his feet.

I start pacing, I knew he was a man-whore, that I should have stayed well away from him. How could I be so fucking stupid. I mentally slap myself for my idiocy. Again! "I'm just another on the job lay, right? When this job is over, you'll go back and play happy fucking families. Fuck!" I start searching the room for my bag. When I don't see it, I march to Ryder's room, assuming he put it in there. Huh, thinking he was getting laid again tonight. Well, that ain't fucking happening. I hear him following behind, telling me to stop and listen, but I don't want to listen. Don't want to hear anymore bullshit spew from his mouth.

I shove his bedroom door open, and it slams against the wall from the force. Seeing my bag on the floor beside the chair where my other bag still rests, I go over to pick it up, but as I bend down, I'm lifted off my feet. For a split second I'm transported back to another time when I was carried away, kicking and screaming, several in fact, but I push the memories away. I refuse to freak out, this is Ryder, not Sean. I might not know much about him, but I do know he'd never hurt me, physically at least. Emotionally? Yes. I already know that this man has more power over me than Sean ever did, and that freaks me the fuck out.

I'm tossed on the bed, and before I can even gather my breath, the bastard cages me in, his weight just enough to stop me escaping. I lash out at him, hitting his chest and trying to push him off, but he doesn't even flinch, just lets me rain all my anger down on him.

There was a time that this position would have had me spiralling into a full-blown panic attack, the fact I'm not speaks volumes.

I pour all my rage, guilt and everything else I feel into attacking him. It's like I'm goading him, pushing his buttons to see how far I can go before he snaps. He takes it all, until I'm just a hot, sweaty, emotional mess beneath him.

"Are you ready to listen now?" he asks, his voice firm, with an edge that speaks of his own anger. And once again, I become a bobble head, just nodding away. To be honest, even that's an effort after all the energy I just expended. "I don't have a girlfriend or a damn wife. I don't do relationships— and before you go getting all fucking mad at me again, just fucking listen. I don't do relationships, mainly because of the job I do and because I didn't want one. But I ain't no fucking cheater either. So, when I do have a relationship, you can bet your fucking arse there will be no one else. I may have fucked a lot of women, but they all knew the deal."

My anger, and I hate to admit, a streak of jealousy sparks inside me at those words. "And what is the deal, Ryder? Because I sure as shit don't remember any fucking deal being made before you fucked me against the wall." I ask, disdain drips from my words. He rolls his eyes at me, as the muscle in his jaw ticks, then the bastard rolls his hips. I close my eyes, as a moan rumbles up my chest, and I bite my lip to stop it breaking free, not wanting to give him the satisfaction.

"The deal is," another roll of his hips, "You. Are. Mine." Each of his words is punctuated with nips to my jaw and a roll of his hips. My body is on fire, as anger and pleasure swirl together making it impossible for my brain to grasp exactly what he means. I don't really care to figure it out either, all my body wants is more of this man. I want him naked, to explore every inch of his body, to mark him and claim him as mine, to bring him to the brink, then push him over the edge, and have him shuddering beneath me, calling out my name. I want to own him. I don't think on it anymore, I let my body have complete control.

When his lips finally meet mine, we become savages, ripping and tearing at each other's clothes until we are just a tangled web of naked limbs. My skin burns with his every touch. Yanking on his hair, I pull his head to the side at the same time as I push up, rolling us over so I'm on top. His eyes spark with a hungry desire and a hint of surprise.

Having Ryder beneath me like this rouses a dark piece

of my soul I never knew existed, spurred on by the feeling, I let the darkness have me and give in to my baser instincts.

With my hands on his chest, I lean down kissing his lips, along his jaw, down his neck, mirroring his actions from earlier. I continue my path, alternating kisses with nips that have Ryder growling, dragging my nails down his flesh as I go. I run my tongue over his nipple and take it into my mouth, scraping my teeth over it as it hardens. He grabs a fistful of my hair, and his hips buck at the bite of painful pleasure. Not allowing him to pull me away, I lick all the way down his happy trail as his hand falls to the side, releasing my hair.

His cock pulses as my breasts brush against it, I take him in my hand, and run my tongue around the rim before licking all the way down and back up. Looking up, as I crouch over him, his eyes darken to the colour of the sky before a storm. Keeping my eyes on him, I flick my tongue over the head of his cock, teasing and tasting before I slide my mouth over him, going all the way down till he touches the back of my throat. I watch from the corner of my eye as his hands curl into the sheet, clenching and twisting it up, and I groan deep in my throat at the sight of this man at my mercy.

I can taste him and myself, as arousal drips down my thighs, sliding my other hand down, I find my clit, dipping in and out of my pussy as I continue to take all of Ryder in my mouth. As my pleasure builds, I scrape my teeth along his length but before I can reach my climax, Ryder's hand is in my hair again, and this time there's no denying him. Yanking my head up, his cock leaves my mouth with a pop, and I'm dragged up his body, straddling him. Pulling my head down, our lips smashing together as I begin to circle my hips, rubbing my wet pussy along the hard length of him. A growl reverberates through his chest and up his throat, as I break the kiss, dropping my head into the crook of his neck as his scent surrounds me.

I sink my teeth into his neck as I pull forward enough to free his cock from between us before pushing back, angling my hips as I slowly slide down onto him. His grip on my hips tightens, and unable to restrain himself any longer, he thrusts up fiercely, and we both cry out as he fills me completely. Steadying myself on his chest, I rock back and forth, grinding myself on him, and as my orgasm builds my fingers curl into his skin, drawing blood.

The sight of his blood as it runs down his body in little rivulets, pushes me over the edge. My head falls back as my orgasm crashes into me with the force of a tsunami, and before I even take a breath, Ryder flips us taking back control. My heart pounds in my ears perfectly with every pump of Ryder's hips, and as he grips my arse, angling my hips up allowing him to go deeper, my toes curl as another orgasm builds in my belly.

"Fuck, Cam," he grinds out, as his control slips. My pussy clenches around him as my release slams into me, and no longer able to contain himself, Ryder follows me, my name a pained cry on his lips. "Fuck, baby! What are you doing to me?" he says, as he rolls us to our sides, planting a delicate kiss on the tip of my nose.

Tipping my head back so I can see his face, "I could ask you the same, Ryder Hawkins," I whisper, before letting my eyes fall shut and falling into a deep, restful sleep.

Ryder reaches for me twice more during the night, and I can't say I'm mad at the man for disturbing my sleep, not when he gives me orgasms like that.

After the second time, I lay with my head on his chest and trace the half-moon cuts I inflicted on him earlier, knowing that when I wake, he'll be gone. And I'll be stuck with 'too fucking happy' and 'not happy enough', in other words, Russell and Scott. They're the epitome of the 'good cop', 'bad cop' duo.

There's something about those two that has my alarm bells ringing, but I can't put my finger on what.

TWENTY-TWO

Blue

I drag myself from the bed and the warmth of the woman wrapped around me. A woman who is burrowing deeper under my skin every day. After a quick shower, I throw some clothes in my bag before grabbing a pen and paper to leave a message for Cam. I place the note on the pillow beside her, watching as her chest rises and falls with every breath. This has to be the soppiest shit I've ever done. Sully will rip me a new one and tell me that I'm pussy whipped if he ever finds out about this. I run a hand down my face, I'm so fucking screwed, and before I can change my mind, I lean over and plant a soft kiss to her head.

Stepping out of the lift, Scott and Russ are waiting for me. After a quick run through of their duties over the next 48 hours, I'm on my way.

Scott has been with us from the start, he's one of the best men we have, but he wears a permanent scowl, giving off a 'don't fuck' with me vibe that lesser men would run from.

Russ is newer, joining us three years ago. Him and Scott

are polar opposites, but equally good at what they do, and I know that Cam will be safe. As long as she does as she's told.

As I near London, I begin to feel on edge. Something doesn't feel right, but I can't figure out what it is. I brush it off as worry over Cam's safety, putting aside what is happening between us, she's still a job, her safety is my responsibility. And as I pull up to Sully's London home, I push my concerns away and focus on what I'm here for. The quicker I get this over with, the quicker I can get back. *To Cam.*

Like me, Sully has a couple of homes, one here, as most of our business is here, and his main home in Peterborough where he lives with Max, his son. After a quick catch up, we turn our focus to Jamie's attack.

Sully tells me that after Scott returned to the hotel there was no sign of the pissed owner of the car that blocked him in, no surprise at all, and no sign of the car either. As he wasn't a guest at the hotel, finding him is going to be difficult, but it goes some way to confirm our suspicions that he is linked to Jamie's attack. Sully is waiting for CCTV footage from the hotel and the car park, but I won't hold my breath. If this is Sean's work, like we suspect, then he's not stupid enough to leave even a crumb of evidence. Hence the reason this fucker has managed to avoid arrest for so long.

Sully managed to get a rush on the blood at the house and forensics confirmed that it was Jamie and Russ', no unknown DNA found. They are still working on the clothes they were both wearing and any fingerprints they managed to pull.

Jamie gave her statement to the police late yesterday, and it matches what she told me and Cam at the hospital.

It's pretty vague right now, which is to be expected after a head injury, but hopefully, in time, she'll remember more.

Russ says he was driving back from a bar a few streets away, when Scott called him, that's why he was so close by. No doubt getting his dick wet. When he arrived, he felt something was off and headed round the back to find the back door open and glass on the floor. When he entered the house, he found Jamie in the kitchen, covered in blood and unconscious. Rushing to get to her and slipping on the blood, he cut his hand as he landed, which is why there was so much of his blood on and around Jamie.

"Are you all set for tonight?" Sully asks, as he makes another cup of tea for us both.

"Yeah," I say, just as Sully turns, placing a cup on the counter in front of me.

"You don't sound so sure. What's the problem?" he asks, raising an eyebrow.

"I don't know." I shake my head, rubbing a hand over the scruff on my chin. "It's nothing. I hope it's nothing. Fuck!" I slam my hand on the counter, as that feeling in my gut returns. "Something isn't sitting right. I don't know if it's tonight or—"

"Or what, man?" Sully glares at me, searching my face, which I try to keep impassive, but this man knows me. Probably better than I do myself. "Shit, Ryder! You fucked her, didn't you?" I drop my head on a sigh. "I knew it. I knew it that first day at my house." He stands from his stool, swiping his hand out in frustration and pacing the kitchen. "I can't believe you'd be so fucking stupid. There are a million other women you could have had suck your dick, instead you pick a client. And not just any client, but an emotionally broken woman with more baggage than a fucking cruise liner. She's damaged, man, —"

I fly from my stool, rounding the counter and grabbing the front of Sully's shirt in my clenched fist, shoving him back against the cupboards behind him, my face an inch from his. "Shut your fucking mouth! Don't you dare fucking talk about her like that, you don't know a fucking thing about her." His eyes widen in shock at my outburst, hands up in surrender. "Cam's not broken, Sully, she's a fucking warrior. You've seen her file, don't be so fucking judgemental. Anyone that can survive what she has and still be standing, fighting, has bigger balls than you and me together." I let go of Sully, dropping my hands at my side. The rage at his words burns away turning to ash on my tongue. "I've seen her scars, Sully. The ones she wears on her skin are bad, but I can tell you they are nothing compared to the ones she carries inside. I've seen that haunted look behind her eyes before, seen the taint such a loss leaves on the soul. It might dim over time, but it never leaves, Sully," I tell him, rubbing a hand over the back of my neck.

"I'm sorry, Ry. I guess I just assumed she was another screw, but I couldn't have been more wrong, could I?" I hear the unspoken question. I know he's asking me the question I keep trying not to think about.

"You have no idea, Sully." I slump back onto my stool, running my finger over the rim of my cup. "This woman has crawled under my skin, wriggled into a heart I thought was iron clad, impenetrable. And now I have no fucking clue what I'm meant to do." I look up at him, "How do I tell her, Sully? She's going to fucking hate me, man."

"I wish I had the answers for you, I really do." He joins me back at the counter, hands braced on the top. "I think that you should hold off on telling her," I pin my eyes on him, frowning, he holds his hands up, "just hear me out. If you tell her now, she could freak out and run, we can't afford that when we've worked so hard on this job."

"Fuck the job, Sully!"

"No, Ryder. Right now, that's where your focus has to be, it's also what's going to keep her safe. If she runs, how long do you think it will be before he finds her, huh? You need to keep your head in the game, not think with you heart, or your dick," he mutters that last part, clearly not wanting to rile me up again.

I give a reluctant nod, knowing that what he's saying is true, but it doesn't stop that niggling guilt deep in my heart that this is all going to blow up when she finds out the truth. This conversation has done fuck all to relieve the unease rippling through me about this shipment either.

"Okay, so let's talk about tonight. Do you want me to call in Dean? He can be here in a couple of hours." He pulls his phone from his pocket ready to dial on my say so.

"Nah, leave him be. We need him where he is more than I need the help. Cam will be fine, she has Scott and Russ with her, and I told them to call Seb if there's any problems," I tell him, not sure who I'm trying to convince more.

We spend the next couple of hours going over the details of the meet and mapping out the best vantage point. Sully makes lunch, and we leave the work chat behind in favour of more personal matters. Sully tells me that Max is doing better at school now since he started seeing the counsellor.

When Max first started school, he began having nightmares and wetting the bed. According to the counsellor it can be related to anxiety and trauma, and in Max's case starting school brought forth questions about his mum. Sully has always made sure to talk about Sam to Max, ensuring that he knew who his mum was, but another boy in his class, whose mum knew Sam, was overheard by the boy talking about how Sam died after giving birth, and had asked Max about it. Max became withdrawn and that's when the nightmares and bed wetting started. The school spoke to the boy and his mother, and it was clear there wasn't anything malicious in it, just an inquisitive child.

Sully heads off to call Max around 4pm, and I make use of the time to check in with Scott. Scott tells me that he and Russ are at the hospital while Cam visits Jamie. Happy that everything is in hand, I drop a message to Seb giving him a heads-up that he may get a call. Needing to keep my mind busy and wanting to be as prepared as possible, I decide to go and do a drive-by of the container yard.

After driving past a couple of times, not wanting to risk looking too suspicious, I drive back to Sully's. When I arrive, the house is dark, and Sully's car is missing from the drive, so I let myself in. I'm only in the house for ten minutes when headlights flash through the front window, casting shadows on the dimly lit room.

"Blue, where you at man? I've got dinner," Sully calls, as he steps through the front door.

I head out and meet him as he's crossing the hall towards the kitchen. I don't need to ask what he bought, the smell permeates the air as he passes me, and I begin to salivate like one of Pavlov's dogs.

"Is that what I think it is?" I drool, as I follow behind him. He nods, placing the bag on the counter before grabbing a couple of plates. I waste no time in pulling out the cartons sporting the logo of my favourite Thai restaurant.

We eat in silence, and after we are done, I head off up to my room hoping that a full belly will help me get a couple of hours shut eye before I need to leave later. I plug my phone into the charger beside my bed and, rather optimistically, set my alarm for midnight before laying down.

After finally falling asleep, for what feels like only minutes, a persistent ringing pulls me from my dream, drawing me back into consciousness. Throwing a hand out and blindly searching for the culprit of the incessant noise. I latch onto my phone, and cracking one eye open, I turn the alarm off and am surprised to find I slept for so long.

Rolling over and dropping the phone beside me on the bed, I fold my arm across my eyes for a few seconds giving my brain time to catch up. Images of Cam riding me flick through my mind and explain the hard-on I'm sporting.

Rising from the bed, I head to the bathroom for a shower. A fucking ice cold one or I'll be jerking off like a hormonal teenager.

TWENTY-THREE

Camryn

Someone is holding my arms from behind, there are hands on my body, the pain is unbearable, then I'm on the floor with my arms held above my head. I'm thrashing and screaming; my legs are trapped, and I can't escape. My fists fly, but I can't seem to hit anything, then suddenly I'm falling.

Opening my eyes, it takes me a minute to figure out where I am. Slowly sitting up, I realise the sheet is wrapped tightly around my legs, and I'm on the floor of Ryder's bedroom. I start untangling my legs as the last vestiges of my nightmare ebb away. I haven't had a nightmare about that night for a long time but knowing that Sean is close is no doubt the reason.

Climbing to my feet, I grab the sheet from the floor and throw it onto the bed, and as I do a piece of paper flutters on the pillow next to mine. Reaching over I snatch it up, apprehension trickles through me as I unfold it, but relief floods my body when I see it's from Ryder.

Cam,

Stay out of trouble. Spend time with your friend. Go to work. Most importantly, do as your told! If you don't, be ready to have your backside tanned when I return.

Ryder

"Bossy bastard." But it brings a smile to my face, and my pussy pulses at the thought of Ryder spanking me, which is a complete surprise. Given what I've been through the idea of a man laying his hands on me that way shouldn't turn me on, it should repulse me. Actually, there are a lot of things that Ryder does that should have me running in the other direction, including the aura of danger that exudes from him, but I find myself drawn to him more and more. No accounting for craziness.

After I've showered and gotten dressed, I head to the kitchen for a cup of tea and hopefully something to eat, my stomach rumbling in agreement. I put the kettle on just as my phone vibrates in my back pocket, pulling it out I see a message from an unknown number.

Unknown: Cam, it's Scott. We are downstairs when you're ready to go to the hospital.

Short and to the point. Typical Scott, that man never says anything more than he needs to. I text him back to tell him I'll be down shortly, then finish making the tea and hunt for something to eat.

When I make it downstairs an hour later, Scott and Russ are standing like two sentinels outside the lift. Russ greats me warmly with a smile, asking how Jamie is. We fall in step alongside each other as we walk to the car, I tell him that Jamie will be fine thanks to him, and I'm sorry he got hurt looking out for my friend.

"Don't worry about it, Cam, it's my job. I'm just glad I

got there when I did," he says, giving my shoulder a quick squeeze as he steps forward to open the car door for me.

I slide into the back seat while Scott gets in the driver's side, and Russ hurries round to jump in the passenger side. Russ tells me about some girl he's been seeing, and in an effort to bring Scott into the conversation I ask him if he has a girlfriend.

"No," he grunts, from the front seat.

Leaning forward between the two fronts seats and turning to Russ I ask, "Is he always this grumpy?" Russ chuckles, and Scott side eyes me, his faced pinched in a scowl. I'm starting to wonder if this guy even knows how to smile.

"Nah, but with no girlfriend he's got blue balls." Russ replies, putting a hand up to hide his smile. Scott's only reaction is a small growl, and I can't help the laugh that bubbles up and spills from my lips. How the hell Russ works with this guy is beyond me.

"Well, I guess girls don't like the broody, silent type after all," I say, shrugging and sitting back in my seat. I catch Scott's gaze in the rear-view mirror, and he winks.

"Sure they do, you like the boss just fine." And I watch as his lip curls into an almost grin.

"Holy shit! He speaks," I gasp, clutching my chest before I burst out laughing.

When we pull up, Russ jumps out, opening my door for me, and we head inside while Scott goes to park the car. Russ' phone rings just as we exit the lift, pulling out his phone and checking who's calling before he motions for me to continue as he answers the call. As I walk away, I hear him say 'all good, boss' and then 'at the hospital', I roll my eyes at the fact it's probably Ryder checking up on me. I continue to

Jamie's new room on a ward on the second floor now she's awake.

As I push the door, it opens and I start to fall forward, but a hand reaches out grabbing my arm from behind and stopping me. I spin round, wrenching my arm free as my heart beats wildly in my chest and my breath hitches.

"Get your fuck—Scott." I heave in a deep breath, trying to calm my racing heart and stop the panic rising up. "I'm sorry. I didn't know it was you."

"I didn't mean to startle you." He gives me a quick nod before stepping back and taking up his position outside the door. I look to the nurse who opened the door apologetically, she offers me a small smile as she passes me.

"Jesus, Cam. You sure know how to make an entrance," Jamie exclaims from her place on the bed, as I stand inside the door. "Are you coming in or you just going to stand there all day?" She chuckles as I turn my gaze her way.

With my heart still beating double time, I stride towards her, looking her over as I make my way to the chair beside her bed. Glad to see that she's looking more herself today. Her left eye is still swollen shut, and the bruising on her face is more pronounced, but she looks more alert and in slightly less pain. Dropping my bag to the floor, I collapse into the seat. My nightmare has really done a number on me today, and I feel like I'm flying in the damn wind. Avoiding the elephant in the room, I ask her how she's feeling.

"I'm okay, Cam," she says, a hint of sorrow in her voice. "Don't look at me like that, and don't you dare start that apology shit with me again. I told you yesterday this is not your fault." I go to interrupt, to rebuke her for not hating me like she should for what I've put her through. "Stop. It's not up for discussion," she orders, pointing a finger at me. "Now, how about you give a girl something nice to talk about. Where's that sexy as sin man of yours?" Her face lights up at the thought of what gossip I might have for her, and what sort of friend would I be if I didn't give her what she wants.

"First off, he's not my man," Jamie just scoffs at that bullshit statement, "and secondly, he's in London for a couple of days, so I'm stuck with Tweedledee and Tweedledum out there." My nose scrunching in displeasure and pointing a thumb over my shoulder indicating to Scott and Russ. Jamie laughs but pulls up short when pain shoots through her ribs.

"Fuck! No more funny stuff, it hurts like a bitch to laugh," she says, with a grimace. I wince along with her.

"Yeah, I know it does," I say quietly. I keep my head down, not wanting to see pity in her eyes as I continue to talk. "The first time it happened I thought I was going to die every time I took a breath."

I let the words flow, and I don't stop until it's all out there. My heart feels ten times lighter, and the relief is indescribable. When I finally look at Jamie, I don't see pity, I just see the love of a good friend. She thanks me for trusting her with my truth, and as the tears well in my eyes, I climb onto her bed and hug her as best I can, while the tears fall.

When the nurse comes in a while later, I take that as my cue to step out to the bathroom. Scott is still where I left him earlier and follows me as I make my way to the toilet, the one Ryder cornered me in the other day.

I decide to nip down to the shop on the first floor in desperate need of junk food after the heavy conversation this morning. I tell Scott I'll be fine, but he just ignores me and continues to be my shadow. There's no sign of Russ, but before I get the chance to ask where he is, he comes barrelling round the corner and almost takes me out in the process. Russ offers a quick apology, and then I walk ahead of the two guys as they have a whispered conversation before leaving them at the entrance to the shop when I enter. Thank god for that. Five minutes without my shadows, it's bliss. I take my time in the shop and come out with a bag full of shit that will go straight on my hips, but I honestly don't care right now.

On our way back to the lift, we pass by a waiting area displaying the latest news report. The volume is down, but the subtitles talk about the body of an unidentified man discovered in a nearby hotel, along with a photo of the man and his car. Scott slows, watching the screen for a minute, his scowl remains in place, but there is a hint of what looks like recognition in his eyes. Russ carried on walking and is now waiting at the lift for us to catch up.

"Everything okay?" he asks, as we reach him. Scott gives a signature nod, and we enter the lift.

The clock in the lift shows it's almost 4pm, and I can't believe how late it is already. I know that visiting time will be over soon, and I'll have to return to an empty apartment. So, I plan on making the most of the time I have with Jamie.

Jamie helps me demolish the contents of my haul from the shop, I even bought her a couple of magazines for after I leave. I relax on the bed next to her, rubbing my bloated belly and thinking I'd escaped Jamie's interrogation about Ryder and me, but I was a complete fool.

"Come on, Cam, dish the dirt. There's no chance I'll be getting any dick anytime soon." She wriggles her eyebrows at me, and when I scowl at her, her bottom lip turns down and tilting her head, she offers me pleading, puppy dog eyes. Huffing out a sigh, I climb off the bed, feeling that I need to be walking for this conversation.

"What do you want to know, Jamie? Does he make my

fanny flutter?" I smirk at her. "Yes, every time he's in the room. Does he fuck like he looks? Duh, yep, hard and fast. Beyond that I don't have a fucking clue," I admit, as I spin on the spot and face her. Then I remember her slip about a guy she's been seeing. "And anyway, it sounds like you've been getting plenty of dick yourself?" I say, arching a brow and placing my hands on my hips.

"Nice try but this is not about me, besides, there's nothing to tell. I met a guy, we hooked up a few times, and that's it, just a booty call." In all fairness, Jamie having a booty call is not a surprise. She's never been one to shy away from the fact she likes sex and regularly hooks up with randoms. She shrugs before getting back to me. "Don't be dense, Cam." She waves a dismissive hand at me.

"I'm not being dense, Jamie. I'm being realistic," I say, defensively. "It's not as simple as boy meets girl, blah, blah, blah. And we all live happily ever fucking after. I'm not like you. I can't just go out and hook up, I've got baggage, I'm damaged goods, what man in his right mind would want me?" Finally admitting and voicing my real fears. "When I meet a man and finally fall in love, I don't want to live a lie. I want him to know me, all of me, the good, the bad and the ugly, Jamie. But how do I do that? How do I look at the man I love and tell him the horrors of my past without that changing how he sees me?" I shake my head in shame and defeat. My gut swirls with how revealing such truths will tarnish what we have. The woman who let a man beat her, debase her, a man she bore a child to, that was innocent and was cruelly ripped from this world in punishment for her failings as a woman and mother.

"I've told you before, and I'll tell you again and again until you understand. You are not broken or damaged, you're a fighter, Cam. Any man that can't see the beauty and strength needed to survive what you have, isn't a man worthy of your time. I think you need to give yourself more credit, and you definitely need to give more credit to a man like Blue. And I thought we'd already established that none of what happened is your fault, so there. Stop being so fucking stubborn and self-pitying, Cam. Dig deep, whip out those big arse balls I know you have and take the risk."

The anger at her words rises through my body, but I'm not angry at her or even what she said. I'm angry because she's right. "You're a bitch, you know that, right?"

"Hey, it's my most redeeming feature." She chuckles, "It's also why you love me. Now get back over here and give me something I can dream about later."

"Oh my god, Jamie, that's just all kinds of wrong." But I do as she asks, and for the next hour we chat and laugh like any other best friends. And that's what she is, my best friend.

It's almost dark by the time we arrive back at the apartment, but I'm glad I convinced the guys to stop and grab takeout on the way home. It's been an emotional day, filled with junk food, so may as well go the whole hog.

Scott and Russ leave me at the lift, with Scott telling me that one of them will be here all night if I need them. It's the most he's ever spoken to me, although, he seems distracted. Which is something I've never seen from him before. I'm not altogether sure why, but it has beads of worry settling in my belly.

I chuck the food on the counter, and rush to the bedroom for a quick shower, needing to wash the scent of the hospital from my skin. I throw on a comfy pair of PJs before leaving the room, grabbing my kebab on the way to the lounge and settle on the sofa. I flick through the channels searching for something light-hearted, while I stuff kebab in my mouth. My phone pings with a message, picking it up from the table I'm silently hoping it's Ryder. But it's not, and when I open it up, my heart sinks to the very depths of despair. On the screen is a newspaper article covering the car accident that killed my mum and Faye. What the actual fuck! Some sections have been highlighted, and I scan through them as my dinner threatens a hasty reappearance.

...POLICE ATTENDED the scene of an accident today, involving a woman and child. The child was pronounced dead at the scene, while the woman was taken to the local hospital, where she later died.

THAT'S NOT RIGHT. That can't be right. Sean told me they died instantly. How the fuck can this be true, and why haven't I seen this before? Why would he lie about it? My vision blurs as my brain tries to make sense of what I'm reading. I close my eyes and try to think back to that day, but my memories were hazy after the police told me our daughter was dead. I just remember pain, so much pain.

In the days that followed, Sean dealt with everything, while I drowned in unimaginable sorrow. I became the living dead; no care for myself or anything around me. As I continue to scan another section catches my eye, this one appears to be from an article a week after the first and triggers another memory.

THE DRIVER of a trunk that killed a grandmother and grandchild, has been found dead at his home. Police say that the 32-year-old man died of a single gunshot wound to his head and are asking anyone with any information to contact them on this number...

I REMEMBER READING THIS, but when I asked Sean, he said it wasn't the same man, that he hung himself. I thought it was strange then, but I didn't question it, why would I? Now, I'm questioning everything.

I search the internet for every article that mentions my mum, daughter and the accident. There is a dozen or so and all make claims that contradict each other and what I was told. I find a pad and pen in the drawer in the kitchen and make notes late into the night.

By the time I drag my arse to bed, my head is pounding, and my emotions are raw. I climb into Ryder's bed, curling into a ball and cry until my body is spent, and I finally fall asleep.

TWENTY-FOUR

Blue

I park a couple of streets away, walking the rest of the way to the yard. There's no one around at this time in the morning except low-life criminals, prostitutes and the homeless. As I near the yard, any light provided by the street lamps becomes almost non-existent, casting shadows perfect for hiding in. My footsteps are light as I slip through a gap in the fence, avoiding the camera over the wide-open gate. My heart rate picks up as adrenaline floods my system, but there's something else too. The same something that's been riding me all day; worry, fear, a bottom of the gut feeling that something isn't right. Pushing it to the back of my mind, I push on through the yard passing container after container and checking serial numbers as I go.

Tyres crunch on gravel behind me, slipping behind the nearest container just as headlights pass where I am. The car travels further up the makeshift track, and I follow using the containers as cover. Pausing as a car door slams shut, and low voices reach me through the silence of the early morning. I edge as close as I can without giving myself away, stretching my head and straining my ears in an effort to catch what is being said. Other than a few words here and there, I can't make out anything useful.

With all my attention focused on the two men ahead of me, I don't hear the person behind me until the last second. About to turn around, the snick of a gun has me halting as cool metal meets the back of my head.

"Don't fucking move, arsehole!" a gruff voice whispers to the left of me. "Boss is going to shit rainbows when I tell him that the great Ryder Hawkins is no more. Not only will you be dead and buried, no longer a thorn in his side, but he'll get his whore back too. I can't wait to watch that reunion. It won't be the first time I've watched him punish her or joined in the fun." His words are dripping with unrestrained desire, and my nostrils flare and my lip curls up in rage and disgust. I can't see the car from this position, but I become aware of an engine running before the car moves off and away. The pieces click in place; the car was a decoy to draw my attention. And I fell for it like a fucking rookie.

The dick behind me shoves the gun harder to my head and tells me to move. As I begin walking, he guides me with one-word directions and a knock to the back of my head every time, that has him snickering.

"She's a sweet little fuck ain't she. Don't be shy, we all know you've been screwing her, think there's even some footage of the two you floating around. Boss wasn't happy, obviously, but the rest of us wanked over that shit for hours."

I grind my teeth so fucking hard, I'm pretty sure I crack one. I store that little snippet of information away for later. I'm going to fucking rip this guy apart when I get my hands on him. They'll have to put him back together like a fucking jigsaw just to identify him, and I'll enjoy every fucking minute of it.

I keep walking, tuning him out so I don't lose my shit too soon. I should have listened to my gut; I knew something felt off about this. I fucking knew it. When I spot the car up a head, I know I don't have long to make my move. But the moron with a gun to my head is actually cleverer than I gave him credit for. As we approach, the driver's side door opens and out steps dead man walking number two.

"In the back, and mind your head," he mocks, and then slams my head on the roof as I go to slide in. My vision darkens for a second, but he'll have to hit me harder than that to knock me out. Prick! He shoves me the rest of the way in, climbing in after me. The driver gets back in, starting the engine as corpse numero uno grabs a roll of duct tape from the footwell and begins to tape my hands together. God, these guys are amateurs.

As we pull out of the yard, we turn left heading towards Barking Power Station, but we turn off the road onto an industrial estate just before it. Pulling up outside a warehouse, numero uno steps out shutting the door before walking round to meet the driver as he climbs out too. The door locks click into place, and keeping my eyes on the two men, I lower my hands at the same time as lifting my left leg and pull out the compact spring assisted knife I keep there. The guys are still talking, and the driver looks pissed about something, waving his hands around animatedly. I close my fist around the knife just as the driver opens my door, shoving a hand inside and pulling me from the car.

I allow him to drag me into the warehouse, and as the light is flicked on, dust motes float in the air disturbed by our feet. The warehouse is empty except a single chair and several large crates stacked in one corner of the room.

I'm pushed onto the lone chair as numero uno stands to the right of me, his gun pointed at my temple. I wait them out, let's see what these fucking clowns have up their sleeves. The driver stands in front of me, a wiry guy with slicked back black hair and arms covered in tattoos.

"Boss wants his whore back, and you dead, but we thought we'd have a little fun with you first," he says, stepping forward and landing a punch to the left side of my jaw. My head whips to the side as the metallic tang of blood fills my mouth, and I spit it on the floor before turning back to him with a small smile on my lips.

"That all you got?" I ask, goading him on. "I know girls that hit harder than you," I scoff at him. His eyes spark with fury, his lip twitching as the anger at my mocking bubbles up inside him. He steps forward again, this time landing one on my nose and blood shoots out, filling the back of my throat and cutting off my air for a second.

I don't get time to provoke him further, as the hits keep coming; another to my jaw, to my ribs and finally an uppercut that has my teeth clashing together and my brain rattling. Catching my breath at last, I let out a roaring laugh that echoes through the empty warehouse. From the corner of my eye I watch numero uno lift the gun ready to pistol whip me as I continue to laugh, and at the last second I raise my arms, swinging to the right and knocking the gun from his hand. Caught off guard, I flick the knife out as I leap from the chair, swiping out and catching his cheek. He screeches, grabbing his face in his hand as blood seeps between his fingers, dripping down his neck and body. Within seconds his t-shirt is soaked through.

Turing quickly, I see the driver stepping back, his face ashen white. I spin the knife round and cut through the duct tape holding my hands as I stalk towards him. The moment the tape drops to the floor, the driver bolts for the door, but he's not quick enough. I grab his neck from behind, squeezing the pressure point I know is there.

"Fuck you, man. Boss is gonna make you fucking pay for this," he shouts out, as I drag him back to the chair and his friend, who has passed out on the floor. Guess I must have cut him deeper than I thought. Oops.

"Now, it's my turn to have some fun," I tell him, as I throw him to the floor, and the beast inside licks his lips at the blood that's going to run tonight.

WIPING the blood from my hands, I pull out my phone and call Sully. I don't give a shit that it's almost 5am. It only rings a couple of times before he answers.

"Sully, I need a clean up crew at the industrial estate near the power station. I'll text you the address," I tell him, my voice an octave higher than normal from the adrenaline pumping in my veins. I haven't felt this wired since my last tour in the army five years ago, and the night I lost six men.

"What the fuck, Blue?" he grumbles. "This was supposed to be recon, observation only. What the hell happened?" His voice is muffled slightly, no doubt from him dressing as he talks.

"It was a fucking set-up. Just get your arse down here." I end the call before he can ask any more questions. He's going to go postal on my arse when he sees the mess I just made of these two pricks.

I send the address to Sully, then a message to Seb, telling him to sweep my apartment and Jamie's house. That bastard's been watching us the whole fucking time, but the more important question is how?

Half an hour later Sully comes storming through the

warehouse door like his arse is on fire, coming to a grinding halt when he sees me.

"Fuck me!" he mutters, as his eyes rove over the scene in front of him before coming to rest on me. I'm sat on the chair, naked from the waist up, with blood splatter covering every inch of my skin. "If you wanted a part in a horror movie, you should have said, I could've hooked you up," he quips, taking measured steps towards me and avoiding the blood covering the floor. "So, you want to tell me what happened?"

"Later. We have more important things to worry about," I declare, rising from my chair and shoving a phone into his hand as I pass him. "You need to watch that. I need a fucking shower, then we'll talk." I exit the warehouse just as the crew arrives, and by the time I make it to Sully's car he's bursting out the door after me.

"How is this possible, Blue? How the fuck does he have footage of you and Cam screwing?" he asks, as he reaches me.

"Simple, Sully. We have a fucking mole," I grit out, before getting in the car.

BACK AT SULLY'S, I have the fucking hottest shower possible without scolding myself so badly I'll need a trip to A&E, then dress in some spare clothes I always keep here. What the fuck was I thinking? Oh, yeah, I wasn't, again. My head is fucked right now. I don't regret slicing those fuckers up, especially numero uno after all the shit he spouted about Cam, and when I found that footage of us at my apartment on his phone, I thought I was going to explode with the need for vengeance. He was already dead, but I took great pleasure in going back, cutting his dick off and shoving it down his throat. Since leaving the army I've worked hard at keeping my demons locked up, but there wasn't anything in this world that could have stopped me tonight.

I find Sully in the lounge, a file sitting on the coffee table, alongside two cups of tea and a plate of bacon sandwiches. Taking the seat opposite him, I grab my tea and a sandwich. Knowing I need the food despite my stomach roiling as soon as the smell hit me on the way down the stairs.

"Before we go into what went down at the warehouse, I also have something to tell you. You're not going to like it, but I had my reasons, which won't mean much right no—"

"Just fucking spit, it out, Sully," I growl at him around a mouthful of sandwich.

"I got a call this afternoon," I go to stand but Sully waves his hand gesturing for me stay sitting, and I see in his eyes that Cam is fine, "from a cop in Manchester. They identified the guy from the hotel, found him dead at his house. That's the file there, nothing much to go on; lives on his own, not married and no kids, likes to gamble, a little too much, so that could be something to look at. He's bound to owe someone money, which means he'd be desperate enough to work off his debt or do a job for a decent amount of money."

"For fuck sakes. Every time we get a lead they disappear or turn up dead. He's always one step ahead. He has to have someone on the inside, especially to get that footage of me and Cam."

"I agree, and last night, setting you up, there's only a few that knew about your movements." I nod, quickly running the names through my head and not liking any of it. "So, what happened tonight? Although, I can have a pretty good guess."

I run Sully through what went down at the yard and warehouse, we go over the dead guy's file and set one of the guys on possible leads. Then we discuss our leak and put a plan together to catch them. After that, I head upstairs to try and get some shut eye before I drive back to Manchester this afternoon.

TWENTY-FIVE

Camryn

Light pours in through the open blinds, and I scrunch my eyes shut as I search for my phone to check the time. Finding it, I bring it to my face and crack a single eye open. When I can finally focus enough to see what the time is, I throw the covers off and run for the shower. I overslept, no surprise there after staying up half the night, and then crying myself to sleep.

The shower does fuck all to lighten my mood or make me feel any way near to being human. I dress in the first thing I pull from my bag. The simple black trousers and white blouse are in desperate need of an iron, but I don't give a shit. I make a quick cup of tea before blow drying my hair and slapping some make up on my face, but it does nothing to hide the dark circles under my eyes. I gulp down my tea, grabbing my handbag and attempt to put my shoes on as I rush for the lift.

As the lift comes to a halt and the doors open, my stomach pitches and saliva pools in my mouth, I slam a hand over my mouth as I make a dash for the nearest bathroom. I crash into the cubicle, making it just in time, and no longer able to hold back the contents of my stomach as it's ejected into the toilet.

What a shitty Monday! After a quick clean up, I dart back to the lobby, only to run into Scott as I exit the bathroom.

"Oomph! Shit, sorry," I shriek, as Scott grabs my arm to stop me falling. He frowns down at me, as I crane my neck to look at him.

"Are you okay?" he demands. His gruff tone belies the concern in his eyes. And I thought Ryder was hard to read, this guy wins the medal for how to keep a girl guessing.

"Yes. I'm fine, thank you," I say, pulling my arm free of his grasp. Stepping round him to avoid answering any more questions. I don't need him calling Ryder because there's no way I can handle his interrogation tactics, no matter how deliciously torturous they are. It's not like I can talk to him about what's going on. No, that's just another bomb waiting to explode in my face, and until then it's silent ticking is a constant reminder of all the secrets I hide.

Scott trails behind me, opening the car door when we reach it, but the mask stays firmly in place. If I didn't know better, I'd think he was some kind of AI robot for all the emotion he shows. Slipping into the back, I rest my head on the headrest, closing my eyes and willing my stomach to settle. Thank god the drive to the office isn't too far, otherwise I might be paying for a valet service.

I'm busy, which is great for keeping my mind occupied, but it's like I'm crawling through molasses. My head hurts, and my eyes feel like someone threw sand in them. By lunch time I'm about ready to collapse. I still haven't eaten anything and have only managed to drink a bottle of water.

I have no idea where to go or what to do with the

information someone kindly dropped in my lap last night. The only person I can possibly talk to about this is Jamie, but even that plan goes out the window when around 3pm she calls telling me she's been discharged. Not wanting to go back to the house, not that I blame her, neither do I, she's going to stay at her parent's house for a while.

I finally pack up to leave around 5pm, with my head about ready to explode and throbbing like there's a steel band inside my brain. I rub my temples as I wait for my computer to log off. Once it's done, I switch the light off as I leave.

Scott is alone when I reach the lobby, and I don't have the capacity to care or even ask where Russ is as I follow him to the car.

"Are we going to the hospital, Camryn?" Scott asks, as he starts the car, and pulls away from the curb.

"No, not today. Jamie's been discharged and has gone to her parent's house to recover," I reply, a little dejectedly, but then feel guilty for my bitterness. I'm not even sure why I'm so sad, I should be happy she's okay, and I am, but...I don't fucking know. I just want to crawl into bed and forget this day ever happened, but I won't. I'm not going back to that place, I'm going to uncover what it is this person obviously wanted me to know, and then I'm going to do whatever it takes to get justice for my mum and daughter. I close my eyes to block out the light and hope it eases the drumming in my head.

I must drift off, coming awake with a start and surprised to see we are still on the road. Looking around, I have no idea where we are, and the fact it's almost dark outside is no help. We seem to be on a small country lane, street lamps are few and far between, and the road is made darker by the tall trees that line the roadside. Wherever we are, we are not in the city anymore.

My mind begins running possible reasons as to why we aren't back at Ryder's. None of them are good and all involve Sean. I slide up in my seat as my heart begins to race at the idea Scott is taking me to Sean, but I tell myself not to panic yet. Scott catches my eye in the rear-view mirror before quickly flicking past me to the road behind. I'm just about to ask Scott where we're going when headlights blare through the back window, lighting the car up from behind. I spin in my seat, but it's too bright. Turning back round, a muttered 'Fuck' comes from Scott.

"What's going on, Scott? Where are we?" There's an edge of fear in my voice, and when Scott doesn't answer, that fear unfurls, burrowing and taking root deep inside. Instead of letting it take control, I channel it into anger. "Scott, what the fuck is going on?" I bark at him. "Now is not the time for stoicism or keeping me in the dark as some twisted form of protection, that's bullshit. So, start fucking talking," I demand, reaching out a hand to the seat in front, steadying myself as Scott takes a sharp turn.

"We're going to Seb's," he states. His tone is matter of fact as his eyes flick up to the rear-view mirror, and for the first time, I can read what he's not saying perfectly. His next words confirm that things are not good. Not good at all. "I thought I lost this fucker," he snarls, as his lip curls, baring his teeth.

Well, I wanted more emotion, I certainly got it. I was thinking more along the lines of a smile maybe, not a 'shit yourself and run for your life' inducing snarl, but beggars can't be choosers. Scott's cell lights up, then a deep gravelly voice comes over the speaker.

"Scott. How far out are you?"

"About fifteen minutes. Thought I'd lost him, but the fucker is tenacious I'll give him that."

"Okay, keep on the route I gave you. I'm leaving now. Stay safe, both of you." That last part is delivered with a thinly veiled warning, but I don't have time to think on it too much as we are bumped from behind. Scott keeps us steady, hitting the accelerator and taking turns like a rally driver.

We manage to stay ahead, but as we reach a crossroads, the car behind speeds up. Scott spins the wheel to take a left, the clang of metal meeting metal rings out as the car behind smashes into the left rear end, sending us spiralling out of control. Dust flies up as we careen across the road, breaks pierce the unnaturally quiet night sky, and the smell of burning rubber assaults my nose as we skid on the tarmac.

Time seems to slow, spinning, spinning, and then the road falls away below us as the car begins to roll. My head smashes against the window, and something wet and warm trickles down my face and into my eye. The sound of glass shattering and metal crunching penetrates the fog in my mind, and pain explodes in my leg as we come to a grinding halt. Screaming. Someone's screaming.

I hear my name being called, but I can't focus on anything but the burning pain that's tearing up my leg.

"Camryn. Camryn. Listen to me, you need to be quiet." Scott's groggy voice prods at the edge of my consciousness, and I try to latch on to it, letting it draw me back as I block out the pain. "Stay still, Camryn. Focus on me, just breathe, I'll get you out. Stay with me, you're fine." Scott's voice is lower now, and I wonder if I'm losing consciousness.

I hear tyres crunching on gravel and the low hum of an engine as light flashes through the window. The sound of a car door closing echoes through the air before muffled footsteps and twigs snapping underfoot reaches me. My heart pounds in my ears, as I reach for the seat belt button, pushing down on it, but it holds firm. I begin frantically pushing it again and again until it finally clicks, releasing me. I can't hear Scott anymore, and when I look over to him, he's slumped over the wheel. Fuck!

"Scott. Scott, wake up, someone's coming," I hiss, reaching forward to shake his shoulder. I grit my teeth as pain flares in my leg. I ignore it, grabbing his seat and using it to pull myself forward. "Scott, fucking wake up," I rasp, as more pain assaults me.

Movement outside the car draws my attention as the silhouette of a man stalks through the trees. I try waking Scott one more time with no luck before dropping back into my seat. I begin searching for something I can use as a weapon but come up empty. There's no way I can run as I look down at the shard of glass sticking out of my leg, and if I'm right and this is Sean taking back his property, then I know whomever is out there won't kill me. I just hope they don't hurt Scott. Sagging back in my seat, I try to slow my breathing and hope that the darkness hides any evidence of the pain I'm in.

I wait for what feels like a lifetime before the sound of the car door being wrenched open comes. I keep completely still, then I feel the seat beside me dip as someone leans in. When their breath whispers over my cheek, it takes every ounce of restraint not to cringe and move away. Their scent invades my senses, and I freeze instantly as cold dread rolls through me. *Lewis.*

"Sweet, sweet, Kasey," he mocks, as a hand fists the front of my top, dragging me across the seats. I can't help the cry that bursts from me at the movement. "Tut, tut, tut, thinking you can fool me. You might have changed your name but you're still the same stupid bitch you always were," he snickers, as I'm pulled from the car, crashing to the ground when he lets me go.

"Fuck you, Lewis!" I spit at him; I'm almost certain he can't kill me. He's already hurt me in every way possible in the past, so screw cowering to him or anyone else anymore. He lets out a full belly laugh, then he fists my hair in his hand as he starts hauling me through the trees towards his car. "Aaargh!" I shriek, "You sick piece of shit. Getting off on hurting woman makes you a fucking coward." Ignoring the throbbing in my leg, I start kicking and thrashing about. If he thinks I'm going to come quietly, he couldn't be more fucking wrong. I scream out, over and over until my voice is hoarse, but I don't give up.

Suddenly the hold on my hair is gone, and I'm dropped to the ground, only to receive a boot to the ribs as I try to catch my breath. My side aches, but I scramble backwards, kicking out with my good leg, catching him in the knee and causing him to stumble. Slamming into a tree, I grip the base, shimmying my hands up and getting to my feet just in time to dodge the fist flying towards my face. The action causes me to lose my balance slightly, but I hobble upright, turning to try and make a run for it when the snick of a gun sounds behind me.

"I'll blow your fucking brains out, cunt, if you so much as twitch." The threat clear as the barrel pushes into the back of my head.

I freeze, I'm prepared to fight, but I'm not stupid. I heave out a sigh, my hot breath coming out in a cloud as it meets the cold night air. "You can't kill me, Lewis, it would be more than your life's worth and you know it," I state, hoping to buy some time while I search for a way out.

"Maybe, maybe not," he wagers. "Do you think I couldn't make it look like an accident? Believe me, I've had plenty of practice getting rid of whores that cause problems. Sean likes his bitches to be submissive, compliant and do as their fucking told. Disposing of sluts that become more trouble than they are worth is a piece of piss, especially, interfering mothers and their whinging daughter," he jibes.

His words hit their mark as I suck in a breath as catches in my throat. My chest aches, my heart breaking apart thinking about my mum and daughter, but then something about what he said has me pausing. Forgetting about the gun to my head, I go to spin round just as a deafening crack echoes through the night.

I'm falling and then everything goes black.

TWENTY-SIX

Blue

I woke around 11am, only managing a few hours of decent sleep. That thread of worry hasn't left me, in fact, if anything it's worse today. I called Scott around lunchtime to check on Cam, he told me she overslept, but otherwise, everything was fine. I let him know that I'll be leaving at 4pm and depending on traffic, I should be home around 8pm tonight.

I spend a couple of hours in the gym, hoping to work out some of the left-over aggression from last night and shake off this feeling that something is wrong.

When I come downstairs after my shower, Sully is just coming in the front door.

"Hey, man. Did you manage to get some sleep?" he asks, meeting me at the bottom of the stairs. "Ooh, nice bruises. I don't need to ask how the other guys look," he says, laughing.

"Yeah, a few hours anyway. What you got there?" I say, pointing to the folder in his hands. He waves it in the air, beckoning for me to follow him as he strides away towards his office. Inside he rounds the desk, sitting down and motioning for me to sit too. That's never a good sign.

"What's going on? 'Cause I got to tell you, something is seriously fucking with my head. I think we are missing something," I tell him, dropping into the seat and resting my elbows on my knees, eager to hear what he has to say.

"So, this morning someone sent me these." He slides the folder across the desk to me. "We already knew that there was something suspicious about the accident that killed Faye and Lorraine, but this..." he gestures to the papers I'm currently flicking through, "proves we were right."

The folder contains a dozen or more articles covering the accident, some have highlighted sections. But the one thing that has my attention is the last document. It's an autopsy report of Cam's mum, Lorraine, stating cause of death as asphyxiation.

"How is this possible? The autopsy report we have states she died of internal bleeding, so how can this be?" The question is completely rhetorical because we already know how. What we still don't fully understand is the why. Sean's a fucking psycho, but I'm not sure he's crazy enough to kill his own daughter. I guess it's something I couldn't possibly comprehend.

"It gets worse, whoever sent these to me also sent the newspaper articles to Cam," he tells me, eyebrows raised in question.

"Fuck! Cam must be freaking the fuck out. Scott said she overslept this morning, and I bet this is why." I wave the stack of papers at him.

"No doubt. Does she know you know about Faye? Has she mentioned her at all?" His questions are tentative knowing it's a sore subject. I just shake my head at him, running a hand through my hair. "Ry, you need to tell her.

If you really care about her." My gaze snaps to his. "I'm not questioning it, I'm just saying that it needs to come from you, man."

I throw the articles down on the desk, leaning back in my chair. "She blows my mind, Sully. I used to think that everything we saw and went through on tour was bad, but this crazy, beautiful, strong woman has suffered more pain than even the strongest of men could endure. She calms my demons, but raises the beast in me, ready to fight to the death for her. If she feels even half of what I feel for her, it's going to break her heart when she finds out just how much I know. I don't want to be responsible for that, man."

"I get it, Ry, I really do, but that's not reason enough to hold back. You said yourself she's strong, she'll deal with it, but if you want her, to keep her after this is done, then she's going to need to know she can trust you. Trust me, nothing good will come from hiding the truth, even when you think you're protecting the people you love." Sadness laces his words, and I'm all too aware where his mind just went.

"You've changed your tune from the last time we spoke about her, so what gives?" I leave the question to hang there, but when he doesn't reply and just gives me raised brows, I continue as though I hadn't asked. "I'll tell her, soon. Now, what are we going to do about this?" I ask, glancing at my watch and seeing it's almost four.

"Leave it with me, I'll do some more digging. Sean's not the only one who has a coroner in his pocket. As for Cam, maybe she'll open up on her own after getting sent this shit. Sure is going to leave her questioning everything she thought she knew," he tells me, as I rise to my feet. "Drive safe and I'll call when I have anything."

"Will do, thanks, Sully. Give Max a big hug for me,

catch you later." I hurry up the stairs, grabbing my phone and jacket, then I'm out the door.

The fucking M25 is jammed, nothing unusual there. Finally turning off onto the M40, I relax a little knowing I'll be back with Cam soon. After driving for a little over an hour, I see a sign for services up ahead and desperate for a piss, I change lanes ready to turn off.

After a quick dash to the toilet, I grab a coffee, and get back on the road. I hit traffic around Birmingham, then it eases up as I pass Wolverhampton, and I make up the time I lost earlier. My phone rings, and as it lights up from its cradle, I see it's Seb calling. Shit. As the call connects, that unease that's been sitting heavy in my gut rears its fucking head full force.

"Seb?"

"Yeah, man, it's me. Listen, so Scott said he tried calling but you weren't answering, everything okay?" he asks, his voice light and easy, but I know Seb.

"Yeah, but I have the distinct impression that's about to change. What's going on?" My skins prickles as I wait for him to answer.

"Scott had a tail after he left Cam's work. He didn't want to go back to the apartment with no Russ, so—"

"Hold on, where the fuck is Russ?" I roar, as red begins to invade my vision.

"Fuck knows, Scott said something about food poisoning. Look, he's on his way to mine, okay. Should be here in about twenty. How about you, where you at?"

"A couple hours away tops. Is Cam alright? Scott lose the tail, yeah?

"She's fine, man, chill. Anybody would think you're in looooove with the chick." He chuckles down the line. "Just meet us at mine, see you in a few lover-boy." I hear kissing noises over the speaker before he hangs up on a laugh.

I shake my head at the idiot. Who said anything about love? As I check the rear-view mirror, I catch the small smile on my face and let out a laugh. Yeah, I'm royally screwed.

I'm not entirely happy with Scott on his own and having a tail, so I notch up the speed. However, knowing they will be with Seb soon keeps me from completely gunning it home.

Two hours later, I'm pulling down Seb's driveway, ready to see Cam and enjoy a cold beer with the wise-cracking jerk that makes up our trio. But as I round the bend there's no sign of Scott's car, only Seb's and one other I recognise instantly. Alarm slams into me as I slam the breaks on, skidding to a stop alongside Seb's Audi. I shove the car door open and race for the front door. Bursting inside, I'm met with raised voices and a high-pitched scream from upstairs. I don't waste a second, taking the stairs two at a time and calling out Cam's name.

As I reach the top of the stairs, Seb emerges from a room on the right, pulling the door closed behind him and muffling the cries of pain coming from inside. He's covered in blood, and my heart drops like a fucking stone.

TWENTY-SEVEN

Camryn

Pain. Voices. Pain. I can't move. I'm trapped, my legs are trapped. I try to pull them free and searing pain fires up my leg. Wet. Cold. So cold. My head throbs. Voices shouting, they sound so far away. Footsteps, running. Someone groaning. More pain. Shouting again, right here next to me. Where am I? Talking now, but it's muffled and gurgly like I'm underwater. Hands on me. Pulling at me. It's him, he's here. I pull away. Need to run, to get away. Can't let him catch me. I try to move, get up, to run, but someone is holding me down. Hands touch my face. "Get off me, I won't go. I'll die first," I shout at them. Well, I think I do.

"Camryn, it's Seb, Blue's friend. Can you hear me? I'm not here to hurt you."

I don't know this voice, but he sounds nice. It could be a trap. But he said Blue, that's Ryder, I know him. He's the bright star in my dark sky. He's safe.

"S...Seb, Ry...Ryder?" My voice is croaky, throat scratchy and sore. I try to open my eyes. Light shines above me as I slowly open my eyes, bright, blinding light that makes my *head throb. "Ryder, where's Ryder?" I say, as my eyes open, and I stare at the face above me. The face of an angel. Eyes of molten caramel, flecks of gold flicker in the light. My eyes fall shut again.*

"Camryn?" the angel says, as a hand touches my face. "Camryn, can you open your eyes again for me?" His voice is clearer now as I open my eyes again. "There she is," he says, a smile lighting up his face.

"You're pretty," I say, and someone laughs. I try to turn my head that way, but a stabbing pain shoots through my head and dots dance in my eyes.

"She must have bumped her head real hard to be calling you pretty." A gruff voice states, then laughs.

"Don't try to move for now. You banged your head pretty hard when you fell," says the guy with the caramel eyes. He must be Seb.

"What happened?" I ask, as images flash through my mind. A car following us. A crash. Scott and Lewis. "Scott, where's Scott?" Panic rises in my chest. "Lewis was going to kill me. A gunshot. Have I been shot?" My brain scrambles for answers. Trying to remember what happened.

"Lewis is gone, and Scott is right here. You're safe, we just need to get you home. I'm going to carry you, okay. Can you put your arms around my neck for me, darling," Seb asks, I don't try to nod but raise my arms instead, latching on to him as he slides an arm under my legs and one under my back. As he lifts me the pain in my leg flares, I scrunch my eyes shut and bite my lip, but a groan still manages to escape.

THE NEXT TIME I open my eyes, I'm in a plush bed, messing it up with all my blood and dirt and shit. My mind is a little clearer, my head is still throbbing, but it's nothing compared to the throbbing in my leg.

Looking down, I see that the glass has been removed, and a bandage is wrapped round the top of my thigh, but it's almost soaked through with blood.

The door opens and in walks the angel, Seb, followed by another man carrying what looks to be a medical bag.

The doctor places the bag down on the bottom of the bed. He's around my height, greying hair and beard, with glasses that hang low on his nose, and he's dressed in a suit. That's something you don't see every day.

"Camryn, it's good to see you awake. I hope you still think I'm pretty," Seb says with a wink and a cheeky grin. "This is Dr. Mike Wallis, he's going to check you over and sort that leg out for you, okay, darling." I offer a small nod, and worry has me biting my lip. The doctor moves around to my right side, and I pin my gaze on him. There's something familiar about him, and I'm sure I've seen him before. My mind is still a little fuzzy, so I just put it down to that.

"Hello, Camryn. It's good to see you, just unfortunate it had to be under these circumstances," he greets, offering me his hand to shake. I reach out, placing my hand in his. It's warm and soft, and as his fingers close around my hand, he turns it over, resting his other hand on top. When I look up, his light blue eyes sparkle with kindness, and I relax a little. He pats my hand a couple of times before letting go.

"So, Seb tells me you bumped your head rather hard. Can you tell me how it feels now? Any spots in your vision, any blurriness, a headache, or anything else?" he asks, reaching over to his bag.

"Yeah, I have a slight headache, but no spots or blurriness now. It hurts to move my head too quickly though, like a stabbing pain. And I feel nauseous." He nods along with my answers, then checks my eyes with his little light, checks the bump on the back of my head and concludes that I have minor concussion. I didn't really need a doctor to tell me that. "It's not my first rodeo," I tell him, bitterness and anger lacing my words. He just nods, no surprise or judgement on his face.

When he moves on to my leg, that's a completely different kettle of fish. That shit hurts. Once the bandage is removed, I can finally see the damage. That's going to leave one hell of a scar. Just another one to add to the collection. It's going to need suturing, again not my first time, I tell him this too, and that I don't want any anaesthetic, that shit doesn't agree with me.

As the doctor sets up his equipment, I watch Seb as he stands in the corner of the room. He has his arms crossed over his broad chest, both arms are sleeved in tattoos, and as he turns his head to look out the window, I spot a tattoo that goes from his neck down below the collar of his t-shirt. I narrow my eyes trying to decipher it better, it looks like wings, and then recognition hits. And so, does the doctor.

I let out a high-pitched scream as Dr. Wallis begins cleaning my leg. He pokes around, ensuring there are no smaller pieces of glass. Through the fog of pain, I can hear someone calling my name, but I can't focus on it right now. I close my eyes, taking slow deep breaths, as the Doc starts suturing. Then I hear him.

"Where the fuck is she?" Ryder shouts, and I open my eyes to see that Seb is no longer in here. I can hear Seb trying to calm him down, but he's fuming.

"Move out of my fucking way, Seb, now!" The door flies open as Ryder stomps into the room, stopping the moment his eyes land on me. His face is red, I'm not sure if it's from rage or exertion, and his nostrils flare wildly with each breath he takes. His hands are at his sides, clenched tight, and as my eyes scan his face, I see the tic in his jaw and several bruises marking his beautiful face. Ryder's eyes are a swirling, stormy blue that look like they could fire bolts of lightning, striking anything in his way. The doctor hits a particularly sore spot, and I cry out.

"Argh, fuck!" My cry is drowned out by the growl that rips from Ryder's throat as his eyes fly to the Doctor. I see Seb seize Ryder's arm stopping his advance. Scared for the Doc's life if I make another noise, I bite my tongue. Ryder watches me for several more minutes, then without a damn word he storms from the room. Seb offers me a sad smile before he races after him.

"Well, that was interesting, wouldn't you say," the Doc says, his amusement clear. "Almost done, Camryn. You're going to need to keep this dry for at least 48 hours and change the dressing every day for the first week, but let me guess, you already know that." There's no judgement there, he's simply stating what I've already told him. I know the drill.

When he's done, he packs away and wishes me well. He leaves his card on the bedside table, telling me to call if I have any concerns. As the door clicks closed, I huff out a huge breath, leaning my head on the headboard. I realise that I don't know what happened to Scott or if he's okay. I vaguely remember Seb saying that he was, and I'm certain I heard Scott's voice when we were back at the crash site.

A bone-weary tiredness crashes over me, but before I allow it to swallow me, pulling me into the darkness, I need to clean up. My trousers have already been removed, I'm guessing cut to shreds, but I'm still wearing what's left of my once white blouse. I slowly push myself in to a sitting posi-tion, shuffling to the edge of the bed. The pain as eased since the Doc gave me some painkillers, leaving a bottle next to the bed for me to take regularly.

A wave of nausea washes over me as I get to my feet, and I pause a second till it passes. There's another door in the room that I'm praying is a bathroom. It is and after a lot of manoeuvring, I finally manage to clean up and wash my hair. I catch a glimpse of myself in the mirror above the sink. My skin is sallow, and there are bruises just beginning to bloom on my face. My usually bright brown eyes are dulled, and there's a cut above my right eye where I banged it on the window during the crash. To be fair, I've looked much worse before.

Turning away, I exit the bathroom to find a pile of clean clothes on the freshly made bed. Quickly dressing in what is most definitely a man's t-shirt and joggers, I climb back under the covers and sleep.

My sleep is fitful, but sometime during the night I wake crying, only to be swept up in safe arms that hold me until I fall back to sleep.

TWENTY-EIGHT

Camryn

As consciousness beckons, I can almost pretend that last night never happened, but as I stretch, every ache and pain makes itself known. My leg twinges as the muscle contracts with the movement, and the sutures pinch. My head feels sore, but there's no longer an annoying little miner in there hammering away. Whilst I'm aware of the rest of my body, it feels more like I had a hard workout rather than a car crash and a fight with...Lewis. Shit. I need to find out what happened to him. As Sean's second, he'll be missed, and Sean will want payback if he's dead. Not that I give a flying fuck, I hope he's dead and wild animals have ravaged every part of his body. I only wish I could have been there to see him suffer. I'm seriously starting to worry about my penchant for brutality and death.

I'm on my way to the bathroom, wincing with each step, when there's a knock on the bedroom door, and then it opens and in steps Seb carrying a tray. Seeing the bed empty has panic flashing in his eyes, then he spots me, and a relieved smile crosses his face.

"Hey. I brought you some breakfast and thought you could do with a dose of this handsome, no, sorry that's not right. What was it you said? Oh yeah, pretty was what you said. So, have your fill of this pretty face." He puts one hand on under his chin, tilting his head slightly and wagging his eyebrows at me.

I let out a little laugh, it's impossible not to. "I see you're the *pretty,* cocky, joker of the trio," I say, stepping into the bathroom and shutting the door.

"That laugh tells me you love me already," he calls through the door.

Five minutes later when I step out of the bathroom, he's sitting on the other side of the bed, one foot on the floor and eating what I'm assuming is the toast he made for me. I shake my head as I hobble back to the bed.

"Rude much." I point at the toast halfway to his mouth, not in the least bit bothered he stuffs it into his mouth. Sitting down, I shuffle back and gingerly bring my left leg up onto the bed. "You better not leave crumbs in my bed," I tell him around a smile that I try my best to hide but fail miserably.

"Your bed, huh? Well, for a start, it's my bed," I raise an eyebrow at that, "and second, it's not the crumbs you need to worry about but the giant anaconda that lurks here 'cause he eats injured woman for breakfast."

I don't even try to hold in the burst of laughter that leaves me at that. "Really? More like eats the injured woman's breakfast." I deadpan, but I can't keep a straight face. "Does that shit really work for you?"

Seb holds a hand to his chest feigning hurt, "My poor wounded heart," he says, before dropping the act. "Of course it does. The ladies lap it up, what with my *pretty* face and charming conversation."

"Well, the conversation part remains to be seen, so excuse me if I don't take your word for it." I fidget, trying to get comfortable. Once I'm settled, a cup appears in front of me, thanking Seb as I take it. Then he holds out the toast in offering, but I shake my head.

"You need to eat. Don't want that banging body wasting away. A man likes to have something to grab onto when he's —" He doesn't get to finish as a growl sounds from the doorway. We both turn at the sound to see Ryder there, arms folded across his chest, a scowl on his face and hard, cold eyes narrowed on Seb.

"I think that's my cue to leave," Seb whispers through the side of his mouth, but keeping his eyes trained on the predator by the door. "Enjoy your breakfast, Camryn." he says, then quickly leans forward grabbing my face and planting a kiss on my cheek, pulling back with a wink before leaping from the bed as Ryder charges into the room. I stifle a laugh at the gall of the guy but also that he knows it's pissing off Ryder and he doesn't care.

"You better run, motherfucker," rings out from Ryder, as he reaches my side of the bed. Seb makes a dash for the door, pausing long enough to blow me another kiss then scampering away down the hall.

The air in the room shifts, tension weighs heavily between us, and I'm not sure how to deal with it. I'm still confused over Ryder's reaction last night, he was livid but at who, about what? If he wasn't angry at me, then why the hell did he storm out?

I watch him from the corner of my eye as he shuffles his feet seemingly unsure of himself, and more than a little awkward. Who'd have thought that Ryder Hawkins would ever be awkward or unsure. The man exudes confidence, demands respect, and offers no apologies. You know what, screw this. I've done fuck all wrong, and I won't let him make feel otherwise.

"Are you going to stick around for a conversation this time, or are you going to stomp off like a fucking toddler again?" I demand, looking at him fully for the first time. I see the bruises I noticed briefly last night more clearly today, and I can see a small cut to his lower lip too. They are a rainbow of colours, and I want so badly to reach out and kiss them better, to know what happened and if he's okay. But I'm mad at him right now. He's close enough to me that I see him bristle at my accusation, and I'm glad to see I hit home with my comment.

Moving to the end of the bed, he sits facing me, and when his eyes finally lock onto mine, I see guilt and what looks like hurt too. It's not enough to dampen my ire at him, but it does have me questioning his reasons. I place my still full cup on the bedside table, not sure I won't spill it as my temper rises.

"It's not what you think, Cam," he states.

"No? So, what is it then? 'Cause I'm a little confused, you came racing in here like the devil was chasing you, took one look at me, and poof, you're fucking gone. I'm not a mind reader, Ryder, and even if I was, I'm pretty sure I'd fail at reading yours. You're like a damn fortress." I wait for him to say something, but he just hangs his head. My disappointment hums through me. "You know what, just forget it," I say dismissively. "How's Scott, is he okay?" I ask, feeling like this is safer territory.

He seems shocked at my switch of topic but doesn't comment. "He's fine, a few cuts and scrapes and a nasty bump to his head, but he'll live," he tells me, the gruff and commanding tone is back. That's fine by me, I can't, and I won't do this back and forth shit with him.

"What about Lewis? Is he dead?" I ask, my voice quivers when I say his name and a shiver runs up my spine.

Ryder watches my face, no doubt assessing if I can handle the truth. Obviously deciding that I can, he tells me that Seb shot him.

"Sean will come looking for him, you know that don't you?" I caution. Ryder arches a brow at me then nods his agreement. "So, what happens now?"

"We'll stay here for a couple of days. You and Scott need time to recover, then we can head back to the city. I'll talk to Sully, put some extra security in place for when we return."

"I can't stay here. I have work, Sean knows where I am, and I need to figure out..." I trail off as I realise what I was just about to say. Ryder frowns at me, his eyes boring into mine, searching for answers I'm still not ready to give. Then I think back to our previous conversations and all the things he said he knows about me. He knew Tyler, so it's not a stretch to think he also knows I have—had—a daughter. I can't believe I didn't think about it before. I narrow my eyes at him. "Exactly how much—"

I don't get to finish what I was about to say as a knock comes at the door. Part of me is relieved and the other part is freaking the fuck out, with a healthy dose of anger mixed in for good measure. The door opens, and Scott is there. Casting his eyes quickly over the scene before he turns to Ryder telling him that Rick is here.

"I have to go. Get some rest." He gets to his feet, I feel his eyes on me, but I don't look at him. Then he walks away. I look up when I hear him moving down the hall, Scott is still there, watching me. I begin to feel a little uncomfortable under his scrutiny, pulling at the covers awkwardly.

"Good to see you're okay, Camryn."

"You too, Scott. I'm sorry you got hurt and that your car is wrecked."

"Just doing my job." And with that he leaves, pulling the door closed behind him.

Job. That one word slaps me in the face so hard I see stars. I silently thank Scott for reminding me that I'm just another job.

These guys aren't my friends, Ryder isn't my boyfriend, he's just a guy I've been screwing. And I'm just another client and notch on his post, despite what he tells me. With that thought, I harden my heart and my resolve, vowing not to let him in anymore. Any more than he already is, anyway.

I need a phone, or my phone more precisely, although I'm guessing I'll never see it again. As I move to the edge of the bed, my leg throbs, reminding me that I need to take some painkillers. Snatching the bottle up, I shake out two and then down them with my cold tea.

I don't have any shoes, but I find a pair of warm socks in one of the drawers. Getting them on would be hilarious if I were watching someone else doing it and not feeling like a red-hot poker was searing my skin with every movement. With the socks finally on my feet, I shuffle into the hall, pulling the door closed behind me.

This place is fucking huge. The hallway is long with doors lining both sides, and if it wasn't for the light, modern decor, I'd be forgiven for thinking I'd booked into the hotel from *The Shining*.

Turning right, I make my way towards the staircase at the end of the hall. Taking in the stairs and then looking at my leg, I can see this is going to be a barrel of laughs. Gripping the handrail on my left and taking a deep breath, I ease myself down the stairs. When I reach the bottom, my heart is hammering inside my chest, my breathing is rapid and sweat beads on my forehead. Using the bottom of the t-shirt I'm wearing, I swipe it across my head, and then take a look around.

The entrance is vast with a high ceiling, and there's a stunning chandelier hanging from the ceiling that casts a rainbow on the walls as the light coming through the glass windows either side of the front door hits it. The room to my left appears to be a lounge, I head in that direction when I hear voices coming from one of the rooms on the other side of the hall.

Inside, the focal point of the room is a magnificent fireplace set in a wall of exposed brick with an oak beam mantle piece. Two black leather L-shape sofas are in front, creating an almost square seating area with a matching oak coffee table. There doesn't appear to be a television, but to the left are floor to ceiling windows with doors in the centre that lead to a small patio and acres of garden and woodland beyond. I'm glad I put socks on as the floor is slate grey flagstone, and I can feel the cold seeping through.

I'm looking out the window, watching the sun's light breaking through the trees in the distance, when I hear someone enter the room behind me. I know it's not Ryder, but I'm surprised to find Rick there when I turn around.

"Rick," I exclaim, surprised as he strides towards me, eating up the distance within seconds and wrapping me up his arms. I stiffen before relaxing in his warm embrace. Realising this is what I needed but from someone else, not Rick. "I'm glad someone is pleased to see me," I mutter, my face squashed against his broad chest.

Pulling back and holding my shoulders, a confused expression on his face. "Ah, you're talking about the Neanderthal in the other room, I take it." He teases, a smile pulling up the corner of his lips. "Yeah, well, Blue's never been good with expressing his feelings." He guides me to the sofa, groaning as I lower myself into the chair, and he takes the seat next to me. "You scared him, and he doesn't know what to do with that feeling."

"Don't try and defend him. He might be your friend, but he's being a dick," I point out, arching a brow at him. "Besides, you give great hugs, and it was actually just what I needed, so thanks."

"Happy to be of service. So, how are you?"

"I'm okay. A little bit sore in places, but I'll live." *I've had worse.* I don't say that out loud, though. "Ryder mentioned that we are staying here for a day or two, if that's the case then I really need to call work and sort out a few days off. And Jamie, I need to check she's okay. I could really do with my phone; do you know what happened to it?"

Rick rubs his hands up and down his thighs. "Seb went back early this morning and collected your belongings. I'll have someone bring them to you, but you don't need to worry about work." I look at him, my eyes wide and brows raised. "Ryder called them this morning and told them you needed some time off." His voice remains firm, giving nothing away, but the flexing of his jaw tells me that he's not entirely happy.

"Are you fucking kidding me? No, of course you're not." I huff, dropping back in the sofa. "I might have a psycho ex out for my blood, Rick, but I'm not a child. I don't need him acting like my fucking father," I snap at him.

"Look, I know you don't and that's not his intention either, trust me. He's..." he rubs a hand over his face. "He's a good guy, Camryn. It's not my place to say, but he carries his own demons and guilt, so don't be too hard on him, okay."

"You're talking about his brother, aren't you?"

Rick gasps, "He told you about Kyle?" The surprise is clear on his face, so I'm guessing Kyle is something he doesn't talk about much.

"Yeah, a little. And about how you lost your men on your last tour." Feeling that Rick is uncomfortable with the direction of the conversation, I try to lighten the mood. "We don't just fuck, you know. We talk too, sometimes." I smirk at him.

Rick roars out a laugh. "I can see why he likes you," he says, shaking his head. "I need to get going, I've got to be back in Peterborough this afternoon for Max. I'll see you soon." He gets to his feet, and I go to get up too, but he stops me, leaning down and kissing my cheek. Picking up a control from the coffee table, he pushes a button, and a TV extends from the wall above the fireplace. "Knock yourself out with some trash daytime telly."

"Thanks, Rick," I tell him, a little choked at the realisation that without him, Seb and Ryder, I'd probably be dead right now, or begging for death to come and claim me.

"No thanks needed. Take care, Camryn." I watch as he leaves the room, and then I let the tears fall. Tears that started to build when he mentioned his son.

TWENTY-NINE

Blue

I burst into the office, eyes scanning the room like the hunter seeking his prey. Locking onto Seb, who is the other side of his desk, no doubt thinking that will save his arse but it fucking won't. "You son of bitch! Stay the fuck away from her," I roar, marching towards him only for Sully to step in front of me, stopping me with a hand to my chest.

"Hey, hey, what the fuck is this all about?" Sully demands. Shooting looks between Seb and me, waiting for one of us to enlighten him. I shove his hand off and turn away from them both.

"Ask that arsehole," I shout, waving my hand in Seb's direction.

"Fuck you, Blue. What's the matter, can't you handle a little healthy competition?" He smirks, and my fists flex. The cuts on my knuckles from hitting the wall last night split open making me hiss. The pain is good, grounding me, and saving Seb from a serious arse kicking.

"All right, that's enough you two. Save your pissing contest for later," Sully scolds. "I think we have more important things to talk about than who wins the girl. How is she?" He looks to me, frowning when it's Seb that answers.

"She's fine." They both look to me when I growl at that, muttering under my breath about how she's not fucking fine. "She has a small cut above her right eye, a bump to her head from falling when I shot that prick Lewis, a nasty gash to her right thigh, that Mike stitched up and a few bumps and bruises."

"Okay, good." I lurch forward, ready to rip Sully apart. "Sit the fuck down. Now. Or you can get the hell out," Sully barks at me, and I take the seat furthest away from the desk. I hang my head in my hands and grip my hair so tight I almost scalp myself. "If you can't do your job, Blue, then I'll put someone else with her."

"The hell you will," I say, snapping my head up.

"Then get your head in the game. We have too much going on for you to be going all fucking caveman on us. I take it the body has been dealt with?" Seb and I nod our agreement. Turning to Seb, Sully asks, "What did you get from Blue's apartment and Jamie's house?"

"Jamie's was clean, but there was a small recording device in the bedroom and one in between the kitchen and lounge. There was no audio but more than one recording of Blue and Camryn together." His eyes flick to mine, the inference clear as mud. "I haven't been able to trace where the recordings were sent yet. The IP address is in the States, so they're obviously using a VPN to disguise their true address. The same with Camryn's phone and the newspaper articles she was sent. But I have someone working on it. I also sent a guy to your house in London too, just to be safe."

"Good, chase them up. I want some answers like yesterday. Where's Russ, and why wasn't he with Scott and Camryn?"

"Scott told me Russ messaged saying he had food poisoning, shitting and puking all over the shop. I've spoken to Russ this morning, he's okay, but thinks it was the burger he got from some dive place up from the hotel. Must have been bad, he usually has the constitution of an ox."

"Right, well I need to get going if I want to make it back home for Max later. I have a few leads to chase up on the dead hotel guy and also the problem of our mole, but nothing concrete, yet, and I'm still waiting to hear about the autopsy on Lorraine. I'll check in on Camryn before I go."

"She's in the lounge," Seb casually states, pointing a finger to one of the monitors on the far wall. I stand, moving close to the screen as I watch her limp over to the windows and take in the view outside.

"I'll see you both later, and no fucking fighting. Seb, lay off, okay?" I hear Sully's footsteps as he walks across the hall to the lounge. I watch as Sully embraces her, and the small smile as Sully says something to her while pointing in our direction. Jealousy rises in me, and I can't help the growl that escapes.

"Bet you want to go in there and smash his fucking face in, don't you?" Seb mocks. "Never thought I'd see the day that you'd be pussy whipped, but I'll tell you what. It's the funniest shit I've seen in ages. You look like your head is about ready to pop right off your shoulders. Who knew that green would be your shade?" He roars with laughter, smacking his thigh with his hand.

"Fuck off."

"Aww, hey now. I'm only messing with you. Seriously, though, what the fuck is going on with you two?"

I turn away from the screen as Sully bends down kissing

her on the cheek, it makes my blood boil. I sit back in my chair, crossing one foot over my knee and fiddling with the laces of my boots.

"I don't know, it's complicated," I mutter, dropping my laces, moving instead to pick invisible fluff off my trouser leg.

"No shit, Sherlock. If a woman is involved, then it's always complicated. Do you want to know what I think?"

"Not really. The only thing you know about women is how loud they can scream your name, but I'm sure you're going to try and impart your limited knowledge upon me anyway," I say, with a roll of my eyes.

"They love to scream my name and loud too," he retorts, with a wag of his eyebrows. "But that's all smoke and mirrors, just sex, no substance. The woman that drives you crazy with jealousy every time another man so much as glances her way, has your heart thumping so loud you think the whole world can hear it, leaves your skin alive with an invisible electric current every time she's near, that right there. That's a woman you want to hold onto with everything you have."

There's a note of wistfulness to his words, despite them being for me, I know it's what he hopes for one day too. "It's not that simple and you know it, Seb. I'm not a good man, I have a darkness that lives in me, one that she should never see. She's seen enough."

"Man, you are so wrong. That woman in there has her own fucking demons, ones that I know call to your own. Like seeks like, Ry. Besides, I've seen the footage of you two, that shit is hot." I let out a low growl in warning. "Quit the growling. All I'm saying is I've seen you fuck other women, I ain't ever seen you like that. We all have demons, but they deserve to find their other half too." He rises from his chair, coming around the desk to stand next to me. "And when they do, I pity the poor, unfortunate soul that unleashes the wrath of your demons." He slaps me on the shoulder as he leaves.

I stay there thinking about what Seb said as I watch him retrieve Cam's bag and phone, then take it to her in the lounge where she's watching TV. She smiles when she sees him, but it grows when he gives her the bag. I know how happy she'll be to get her phone back so she can call and check on Jamie, but I also know there's something more important on that phone.

I've seen the search history. I know she's looking for answers about her mum and Faye, but I know those answers are going to destroy her.

How do I help her find them and watch the woman I lo —I care about fall apart in front of me? Regardless of how much it's going to hurt us both, I promise to talk to her about Faye when we get back to the apartment.

THIRTY

Camryn

After Seb returned my phone, I called Jamie straight away, there were already some missed calls from her, and I knew she'd be worried. We spent an hour or more catching each other up.

Apparently, her mum and dad are driving her insane, between Louise's constant fussing and her parent's arguing, she can't wait to go home. She's concerned about what's going on with them, claiming she's never seen them row so much, but I tell her I'm sure it's nothing to worry about.

She tells me about her nightmares, and I give her some tips that might help. I know only too well what effect nightmares can have if you don't deal with them. When we say goodbye, I promise to come and see her as soon as we are back in the city, in a few days hopefully.

I don't see Ryder until the evening, when he brings dinner up to my room and changes my dressing with barely a word, and then he's gone again, claiming to have work to do.

When I finally fall asleep, the nightmares are there to

greet me, and it's not long before I'm screaming and crying in my sleep. Then, like the night before, arms wrap around me that help keep the demons at bay, but they are gone by the morning.

The next two days pass in the same manner. Ryder visits only to bring me food and change my dressing. I refuse to let him see how much it hurts that he's distancing himself from me.

Seb often comes and sits with me in the evenings, and we watch reruns of The Young Ones and Only Fools and Horses, both of us laughing until our sides hurt.

On Friday morning, Dr. Wallis returns to check my wound. It's healing nicely, and I should be able to have the stitches removed in a week or so, providing I stay off it as much as possible.

Then after lunch we pack up and say our goodbyes. Seb promises to come and visit soon, and when I give him a hug, I spot the tattoo on his neck again, and it brings back the memory of my interview. He's the guy from the lobby, I'm sure of it. But what was he doing there? I'm not concerned, I find I like and trust Seb, but I make a note to ask Ryder later, if he'll talk to me.

I hear a low rumbling growl from Ryder as Seb embraces me, and just to piss him off, when I pull back, I quickly lean in and give Seb a small kiss on the corner of his mouth. The growl turns to a roar as Ryder calls out. "Get in the fucking car, Camryn." I wink at Seb as I step away.

"You're naughty and a little crazy poking the bear like that. Although, with all that growling, he's more like a wolf, or a mangy mutt." Seb steps back several steps as feet pound the ground behind me. I spin just as Ryder reaches me, then I'm thrown over his shoulder and carried to the car.

"If I'd have known I'd get this sort of reaction, I would

have kissed your friend sooner." I say it loud enough for Seb to hear, looking up to see him doubled over with laughter, just as a hand smacks me on the arse making me yelp.

"You kiss another guy again and I'll make your arse shine so bright the sun will be jealous," Ryder says, the words rumble through his chest causing arousal to flood through me.

"Wow. For a guy that's barely said two words to me, you sure are possessive of a woman that doesn't belong to no fucking man." I bark at him, my words falling slightly short of the venom intended as I bounce on his shoulder.

I'm lowered to the ground as we reach the car, and his hands linger on my hips a little longer than necessary. "Get in," Ryder demands, opening the car door.

"And if I say no, then what? You gonna spank my arse like a naughty child," I sass, folding my arms across my chest and jutting out my hip. Ryder steps forward, his nose almost touching mine as his scent surrounds me.

"Get in the damn car, Camryn. I can guarantee you don't want to see what will happen if you don't," he whispers, his jaw clenching.

I lick my lips, watching as his eyes track the movement. I consider doing what he asked, but this will be more fun, so I poke the wolf a little more. Pushing up onto my toes, I graze his cheek then whisper in his ear, "You might make my panties wet, Ryder, but don't ever mistake my attraction to you as submission or ownership." As I pull back, I swoop in and nip his bottom lip, drawing blood. He doesn't even flinch, but I watch completely mesmerised as he swipes a thumb across his lip, catching the drop of blood before cupping my chin and smearing it across my own lips. I gasp before running my tongue over my bottom lip, and as I taste his blood a small whimper leaves me. The grip on my chin tightens just as Ryder's lips meet mine, and everything around me disappears. And just as I lose myself in the feeling, his lips are gone.

"Get in the car, Camryn," he demands again, his voice low and dangerous. His eyes are hooded, and I can see the burn of lust and desire coursing through him, just like it is me. A shout of "get a room" comes from behind us. Ryder raises his hand over his shoulder giving Seb the finger, and as his laughter rings out it's joined by another. Taking a peek over Ryder's shoulder, I see Scott has joined Seb. It's the first time I've ever seen anything other than a scowl on Scott's face.

"I had no idea that Tweedledee there, even knew how to laugh," I mutter, lowering myself into the car. Ryder lets out a snort. "What? Him and Russ are like the giant equivalent of the dwarfs Happy and Grumpy. It's comical," I say, clicking my seatbelt in place. A flicker of anxiety creeps in at being in a car again, but I tamp it down. Besides, there's too much sexual tension rolling around in me for the anxiety to have much of an effect. I'm almost certain that there's a damp patch the size of Lake Windermere in my underwear, and my vagina is currently screaming about the lack of orgasms. Join the club.

The drive back to the city isn't long but it felt it. On the way, Ryder called Russ telling him to meet us at the apartment in an hour. That was the only conversation the whole way.

Scott's scowl had returned before he even got in the car, and Ryder went back to ignoring me, apart from his furtive glances every now and then in the rear-view mirror.

I flicked through my phone, checking the news and messaging Jamie to let her know we were on our way back.

When we pull up outside Ryder's, I damn near leap from the car, well, as best as my leg will allow.

When I enter the lobby, Russ is already there talking to the security guard at his desk. He's wearing a t-shirt today, with a jacket slung over his arm, and it's the first time I get a proper look at the tattoo I spied at the edge of his cuff that first day. It's an unusual piece, tribal but around the edge, which traces the line of his wrist, is a Celtic band. I'm a little surprised to see it there as it is usually a sign of Celtic heritage, but it's a popular tattoo nowadays. I walk to the lift as Ryder veers off towards Russ with Scott.

By the time the lift arrives, the three men have joined me, and we enter the lift together. As they normally stay downstairs, I assume Ryder wants to chat with them, so when we arrive at the apartment I take off in the direction of the bedroom. But when I near Ryder's room I hesitate, unsure of where I'm supposed to go.

That decision is quickly made as Ryder comes up behind me, a gentle hand on my back steers me into his room as he closes the door behind him. My protest dies on my tongue when I'm spun around and pinned to the door.

"You sleep in here, with me," he states, orders, demands, whatever you want to call it, but his tone offers no room for arguing. And it pisses me off.

"Maybe I don't want to share a room with you," I sneer, as I shove him back away from me. Of course, he doesn't move far, and as I try to slip past him my stupid fucked up leg slows me down, allowing him to pen me in.

"Stay," he whispers. And that one word has me melting like ice on a hot summer's day. All my indignation at his demands is forgotten as my libido perks her greedy little head up.

"Okay," falls from my lips unbidden. Ryder kisses me on

the head, then leaves adjusting the bulge in his pants as he goes.

Grrrr! I want to scream. I don't like how easy I give into his demands, but I'm powerless to stop it.

I snatch my bag up from where Ryder dropped it and fire a text to Jamie venting my frustration at the fact my vag has taken control of my senses, and I desperately need an intervention. I should have known Jamie would be no help whatsoever, and I roll my eyes as I look at the picture that Jamie sent back of tumble weed with the headline **Your future**. I throw my phone onto the bed, and then myself, face first. My tired body relaxes into the comfy mattress, although Seb's bed was lovely, this is heaven. I must fall asleep, all the nightmares I've been having taking their toll.

I wake sometime later, and the position of the sun tells me it's late afternoon. I'm still laying on my belly like a starfish, and as I attempt to rise up on my knees my right leg screams in protest. Groaning, I roll to my back and stare at the ceiling while I wait for the discomfort to ease. I slept really well, but I don't want to think too much about the reason why.

While we were at Seb's, Ryder slept in another room, but when my nightmares hit, he was always there. I would sleep better once he was there. Again, I don't want to look too closely as to the reason why.

I'm still wearing borrowed clothes, but the ones I'm currently wearing belong to Ryder. I know because I can smell him, and I heard him moaning about me wearing another man's clothes. Stupid possessive alphahole. I still have no idea what's going with us. Demanding I stay in here makes me think there's more to it than a job or sex, but when he goes cold on me? I'm confused again.

I understand what Rick was saying, but I carry my own

demons too. Demons that are becoming a little harder to quiet lately.

My mind has been running wild with thoughts of my mum and Faye recently. I always felt something was off with their death, but I could barely get out of bed let alone think.

Revenge. A little voice whispers.

There has to be more going on than just my safety. How does Tyler play into all of this? What did he want on Sean's computer? These are questions I should have given more thought to. I thought I had more time to put the pieces together, but now Sean knows where I am, my time is running out. I need answers, and I know exactly where to start.

I have a quick shower then finally dress in my own clothes before going in search of Ryder. I find him on the balcony sitting on the rattan daybed and swirling the amber liquid in the glass that dangles from his hand.

It's raining and the afternoon sky becomes a slate grey as more clouds roll in. His eyes lift as I close in on him, he's wearing a small frown, but his eyes are alight with a hunger I haven't seen in a couple of days. When I finally reach him, he hooks a finger as his eyes pass over the space beside him. I hesitate for a split second knowing what will happen if I do. I have a billion questions I need answers to, but at the moment, I need this more.

Ignoring the pain in my leg, I climb onto the daybed and watch as Ryder's blue eyes darken with desire. He knocks back the last of his drink, and his legs open as I crawl between them. He's wearing joggers and nothing else, his sculpted upper body on full display, and I lick my lips at the thought of running my tongue up his body and tasting him.

His scent reaches me on the soft breeze that's blowing,

and my heart beats a little faster as I kneel up and run my hands up his thighs. His muscles tense beneath my fingers, and that dark part of me lights at his reaction to me.

Pulling my hands away, I reach for the hem of my top, peeling it up and off before throwing it and any doubts to the side, baring myself to him.

My breasts are heavy with arousal and aching for his touch. I slide my hands up my body, cupping my breasts and tweaking my nipples until they're hard as bullets, reaching out to him, calling to him. My head drops back, eyes closing as I chase the pleasure, knowing he's watching me. Releasing one breast, I run my fingertips down my torso, dipping my hand below my waistband and seeking the warmth of my throbbing pussy.

As I graze my finger over my clit, a firm grip on my wrist stops me, and opening my eyes I see Ryder leaning up on one arm as his eyes burn a path across my body. Pushing himself all the way up, he pushes down on my wrist, forcing my hand lower, and as my fingers glide into the slickness there, it coats them. A moan leaves me as I pump my fingers in and out, and my eyes fall closed again.

"Eyes on me, Cam." Ryder's deep voice has my eyes snapping open, looking into his blues. I love the way they become like a stormy sky when he's turned on, with flecks of silvery grey lining the edge of the iris. His nostrils flare as his grip on my wrist tightens before pulling my hand free and bringing my fingers to his lips. His tongue swipes out as he slips my fingers into the warmth of his mouth, sucking and licking them clean. Releasing my fingers with a pop, his hand glides to the back of my head, gripping my neck fiercely and pulling me forward to meet his mouth. My skin heats as his tongue delves into my mouth tasting myself there, and he swallows the groan that escapes.

I reach out needing to touch him and latching onto his hips, I feel the shiver that rolls through him causing goose-bumps to the surface of his skin.

When I reach to free him from his joggers, needing to feel him, his hand is already wrapped firmly around his rock-hard cock. I look down to watch as his hand glides up and down the shaft, the head of his dick is red and engorged, and a drop of precum glistens there. My breath falters at the sight of him pleasuring himself.

"Fuck! That's sexy as hell, Ryder," I pant out, as he latches his mouth around my nipple, grinding his teeth and causing sparks of pain and pleasure to shoot straight to my clit.

His hand still gripping my neck, snatches up a fistful of hair and yanks my head back exposing my throat. The move arches my back and thrusts my pelvis forward allowing me to feel him as he continues to pump his cock. Ryder switches his attention to my other breast and keeping his one hand in my hair, his other one comes up taking my throat in his grasp. A flicker of fear skitters down my spine at the aggressive hold, but then he bites down hard on my nipple, and I cry out. My thighs begin to shake as the plea-sure rises, feeling like I could come just from this alone as beads of sweat roll down my back despite the cool evening air.

Suddenly Ryder releases me, and before I can take a breath, I'm lifted and laid out on my back. Ryder quickly removes my shorts then buries his face in my pussy, eating me out like it's his last meal. I writhe beneath him, hands searching for purchase as I fight between wanting to get closer and moving away as the pleasure becomes almost painful.

A hand comes down on my stomach restraining me as

Ryder drives two fingers into my pussy, curling them up to hit that sweet spot and sending me spiralling into an orgasm that has my hips bucking. Both hands grip his hair, holding him there, while I grind my pussy into his face as I ride out my release.

"Ryder. Fuck, Ryder." His name falls from my lips like a prayer as I slowly come down. Ryder lifts his head, and seeing my juices dripping from his chin and glistening on his lips has my pussy clenching and pulsing with need. A smirk pulls at the corner of his lips, forcing his dimple to appear, and then he dips his head and licks up my folds, skimming over my too sensitive clit as a tremor tracks from my feet to my head. I push his head away with a laugh. Sitting back on his haunches, he licks his lips and groans before rising and pushing his joggers off completely.

Running my eyes the length of him, my body thrums in anticipation. Ryder drops to his knees on the bed before falling forward, caging me in and bringing his lips to mine. As our tongues war with each other, I grip his hips pulling him down as he slams home, and my nails bite into his skin. A scream tears from my throat as he pulls back slowly and thrusts forward again.

Pushing up on to one arm, his other hand closes around my throat, squeezing enough to hurt, but not enough to cut off my air supply, then he begins a brutal and punishing rhythm. I suck in air as dots begin to dance in front of my eyes, my orgasm builds as his hips pound forward over and over again, and just when I think I'm about to pass out, Ryder releases his hold on my throat as we crash over the edge together.

THIRTY-ONE

Camryn

As my breathing levels out and my heartbeat returns to a normal rhythm, my skin tingles as the cold air blows over my hot, sweat slicked body. Ryder lifts his head, eyes meeting mine as his fingers brush my hair back from my face and tucking it behind my ear. He kisses me before pulling back, and as I move my leg, I become aware of the dull ache there.

Ryder reaches up pulling the canopy over us and grabbing the blanket that rests at the back of the bed before laying down next to me and covering us over with it. He pulls me into his side, and I rest my head on his chest while throwing a leg over his hips and brushing against his still semi hard cock. I know he'd be ready for round two given half the chance, but instead I bask in the post-coital bliss, happy to just be held.

I absentmindedly run my fingers over Ryder's chest, down to his belly button and back again while my mind tries to make sense of how I enjoy rough sex with this man. A man that carries darkness so much like my own, and I see vengeance and retribution swirling in his beautiful blue eyes sometimes too.

Then as if a light bulb has gone off, I remember our conversation about his brother. How he got in with the wrong crowd and was killed. Ryder knows a lot about Sean for a guy that runs a private security company. The cogs start whirring, and then I start to question Rick and Ryder's willingness to help me. How does Tyler fit into this? Ryder said they knew Tyler, but how? Suddenly I don't feel so blissed out anymore.

Pushing up on Ryder's chest so I can look at him, I ask, "How did you know Tyler?" A look of surprise crosses his face, and then he frowns.

"I told you, we were friends with him." He tries to pull me back down into him, but I lock my arms.

"Yeah, but you never said how you knew him. I mean the guy didn't exactly keep the best company, did he?" I raise an eyebrow and wait for him to answer. His body tenses beneath me, and I already know whatever he says next will be either a lie or not good. He rubs at his jaw, something I've noticed he does when he's uncomfortable or anxious.

"He was a friend, Cam, but then things changed. What's this all about anyway?" He slides out from under me, snatching his joggers and yanking them on. I wrap the blanket around me, covering my nakedness. I know he's not being completely honest, but I don't push the matter.

"Nothing. Forget it," I tell him, and flop back down on the bed, throwing an arm over my eyes. I know he's lying to me, but I can't bring myself to ask the question that's really bothering me. Why is he helping me? That tells me that Ryder means more to me than I'm ready to admit, and I'm scared of his answer.

I hear him sigh, and I bet he's rubbing his jaw again. I lift my arm a fraction, and there he stands rubbing his jaw, then running a hand through his hair. He's going to walk away any second, and I don't care to stop him. I continue to watch from under my arm, his slight hesitation, as if he wants to say something, but then he drops his head and strides away.

I lay there for a few minutes just listening to the rain and the sounds of the city below. I could have told him about Faye, maybe then he wouldn't have walked away, but then again, maybe that would have been the end of whatever this is. At the very least it would have led to more questions, ones I'm not ready to talk about. Will I ever be ready? I can feel he's keeping things from me, and that infuriates me, but I'm also not being honest.

This whole situation is a complete fuck up, and I have no clue how to navigate through it.

A crash comes from the kitchen as the aromas of garlic and onion make my mouth water and my stomach grumble as they reach me. I search around for my top, and I'm surprised to see Ryder's glass smashed on the floor. It's very telling at how lost in the moment I was to not have even heard it.

Finally locating my tee, I pull it over my head, then find my shorts and pull those on too. Approaching the door and seeing Ryder has his back to me, I quickly tip toe down the hall to the bathroom to clean up.

Returning to the kitchen, I realise I was gone longer than I thought as there is no sign of Ryder, but a plate of spaghetti bolognese is on the counter for me. Assuming Ryder is in his office, I sit down to eat alone, then rinse my plate before putting it in the dishwasher. I hunt round the kitchen for a dustpan then go and sweep up the broken glass on the balcony.

It's still early and not wanting to go to bed, I put the telly on and settle on the sofa. At some point I must fall asleep, and I become aware of being carried but sleep drags me back under.

The apartment is empty when I wake, no Ryder and no note this time either. Brushing my disappointment aside, I shower and dress before deciding to message Jamie and see if she's up for a visitor.

I'm beginning to feel like the only time me and Ryder have any real connection is when we're fucking. I don't know if it's because that's all we actually have, or because we're both keeping secrets.

When Jamie's message comes through more disappointment washes over me as I open it. Things are bad with her mum and dad and she doesn't think now is a good time. I message her back telling her to call me if she needs anything and we'll catch up soon.

Another message comes through, I think it's Jamie, but it's from an unknown number. Clicking on it, a document fills the screen, and as I zoom in to read it, I can see it's from a medical examiner. Scanning it quickly a name jumps out at me that has me sucking in air so fast I nearly choke.

Lorraine Eleanor Smith.

It's an autopsy report that states my mum's cause of death as asphyxiation, but that's not possible. The police and hospital said she died of her injuries at the scene.

I'M SAT on the sofa hearing but not listening to the movement and voices around me. I can see Sean talking to a man I've never seen before. I don't know what they're saying, all I can hear are the words the policeman told me two hours ago. 'Miss Kasey Smith, there's been an accident, and I'm very sorry to inform you that Lorraine Smith and Faye Donovan were pronounced dead at the scene.' *They run through my head over and over again, and each time, I pray that I misheard him. That he's wrong, that this news is meant for someone else, and that they should be the ones living this nightmare, this hell. Sean hands the man something then they shake hands, and he leaves.*

When Sean turns around, his eyes land on me. Black soulless eyes that warn of danger, telling you to keep away, to run away and don't look back. He doesn't seem upset, just so angry, at me mostly, and I don't understand why. Maybe he blames me and wishes it was me instead. I wish it had been me, him, anyone else but our daughter.

AS THAT MEMORY fades another one from a few weeks later slams into me.

I GAVE the nurse my usual spiel about how I fell down the stairs, again. Anyone with half a brain knows that's bullshit, and considering I've seen this nurse a couple of times before, I know she didn't believe a word of it. As she placed the sling around my neck, she told me how sorry she was about my mother and daughter. That she was here that day, and how nice it was that Mr Donovan was here with my mum.

AT THE TIME, I wasn't really thinking straight. I was in so much pain from Sean's latest beating, and still raw from the loss of my mum and daughter, that I hadn't really paid attention to her words. I was just going through the motions. Now I latch onto the memory, trying to remember everything she said to me that day.

I close my eyes, picturing her in her nurses' uniform, her black hair tied back in a ponytail and the name badge pinned to her tunic. I see it now, Evelyn Gallow. That's it. I close the message and open my browser typing in her name. The first hit at the top of the page is for an artist that lives in America, but the next entry is a link to a newspaper article. Clicking it, the page opens, and there's a picture of Evelyn with her parents at her graduation from nursing school. The article details the murder of Evelyn Gallow, a 24-year-old nurse from London who was found murdered in her flat on the 12th July 2019. I slam my hand over my mouth as I realise that this can't be a coincidence.

I spend the morning scouring the internet for any information on her murder, and I even do a search on Sean. I don't find much else on Evelyn, no one was ever caught for her murder, but there are pages and pages of articles and reports about Sean and his links to drugs, sex trafficking, murder and gangs.

I feel sick, dirty, disgusting, and my skin is crawling like it's alive with a million insects running beneath it. How could I have been so blind and not seen or known any of this about him. Then the anger comes.

Anger at myself, anger at him, anger at my dad for leaving me, and anger at my mum for not warning me about men like that. But it's wrong to blame my parents. They had a fantastic relationship, and I read the paper and watch the news. I can't pretend I'm not smart enough to know there's bad in this world. I had my suspicions about Sean's dealings, but I chose not to listen, not to believe that a man I loved could be involved in such heinous crimes.

All those feelings of guilt rush back in, but this time, I know it's not my fault. Oh, I know I'm guilty of falling for his charms, being swept up in the excitement of it all, blinded by the money and the fairy tale every girl dreams of. For falling in love with the wrong man. But all the rest? There's just one person who's to blame for that. Sean Donovan.

Shoving to my feet, I pace the bedroom. Then I decide to do something that could ruin any chance of a relationship with Ryder.

Standing outside his office door, I take a deep breath before turning the handle and praying it's locked, but it isn't. The door swings open revealing a modern office that wouldn't look out of place in Canary Wharf. To the right there is a small seating area and in the centre of the room is a large desk with several stacks of papers, but no computer or laptop. Over on the left there's a tall filing cabinet, with several drawers, including a bottom one that has a lock on it. I step towards the filing cabinet just as the sound of the lift arriving stops me. Quickly retreating, I pull the door closed, part of me relieved I was interrupted and walk out into the kitchen.

Ryder emerges two seconds later deep in concentration at something on his phone. My anger simmers under the surface, and before my brain has a chance to catch up, my mouth opens, and the question pours from it freely.

"Why didn't you tell me?" Ryder stops at the sound of my voice. I watch as confusion crosses his face, but in an instant it's replaced with defeat. Putting his phone in his pocket he walks toward me, but I step back.

"Cam, I wanted to talk to you about her, but then—"

"Hold on. *Her?* What are you talking about?" My brain scrambles to understand what he's talking about. He told me that there's no wife or girlfriend, so who the fuck is he talking about? I frown at him, chewing the inside of my cheek as anxiety ripples through me.

"Come and sit down, Cam." Ryder edges towards me and gestures to the stools at the breakfast bar. I can see the pleading in his eyes.

"I don't want to sit down. Talk, Ryder," I demand, crossing my arms over my chest. I try to connect the dots and just as Ryder goes to speak, the only possible answer hits me. I feel my mouth drop open, and the blood drains from my face as I realise he's talking about Faye. He knows about my daughter. "Faye." Her name is a whisper on my lips, and the pain of her loss fractures my heart, along with the pain at his deception.

"Cam." I hold a hand up, then wave my finger at him as I try to get the words out. Ryder's eyes are heavy with sorrow, but it does nothing to quiet my anger.

"You...you knew, all this time and you never said anything. Why?" I ask, my voice and body shaking. A rage I've not known before comes over me, and I see red. Despite my logical half pushing to take control, I don't let it. I let the rage free.

"Yes, I knew, but I also knew how painful that loss would have been for you. I didn't want to cause you pain, Cam. I believed you would talk to me about her when you were ready. When I told you about Kyle, I thought you would have told me then. Realised that I understood your pain."

"No, no, no!" A derisive laugh leaves me. "Don't you dare. There is no pain like the loss of a child, Ryder. None."

"Don't you think I know that, Cam, huh? I watched what Kyle's death did to my parents. It fucking ruined them. I'm not trying to compare for fucks sake. Is that how little you think of me?" His voice rises as his own anger begins to show.

I know what he's saying, but it's too late for me to stop the destructive fury coursing through me. This news with the message I just received has blinded me to all reason.

Gripping my hair, I let out the scream that's been building. When my voice is hoarse, I lash out at the stools before me, and they crash to the floor with a clang. Picking up the vase from the counter, I spin and throw it directly at Ryder, he ducks, and it shatters in a shower of glass behind him. I roar out my frustration at missing him before dropping to my knees and hanging my head.

Knees appear on the floor in front of mine as hands grip my face lifting my head until my gaze locks with Ryder's. My face is a wet mess, a mixture of tears and snot and hair plastered to my cheeks. Ryder's thumbs brush away the tears on my cheeks, and then he brings his lips to mine in a gentle caress.

"Cam, I'm so fucking sorry." His blue eyes bore into my watery browns. I see the sincerity he's so desperately trying to convey and despite how hurt I am by his deception, my hands fist in his shirt, and my pain slowly turns to desire.

Desire for this man, the need to feel his body against mine, and a want so powerful it eclipses everything. I crawl into his lap, straddling his hips and gripping his shoulders as I grind my pelvis against his. His arms snake around me as his lips crash against mine, teeth and tongues clashing together in a blinding battle of control.

I fist his hair, ripping his head back as I nip his jaw, down his throat to the crease of his neck and sinking my teeth in and forcing him to cry out. I do it again, trailing from one side of his neck to the other as his hands slide up my back gripping the neck of my tee and ripping it clean in two.

I release his hair, pulling my top away from my body as his hands find my breasts, twisting and tweaking my nipples between his finger and thumb and pulling on them violently. My hips buck forward at the spike of pleasure that rushes to my core making my clit pulse and my core throb, begging for something to fill the emptiness and clench down on.

Desperate to have Ryder inside me, I grind against him as he continues his assault on my nipples. Sliding back and giving me space to reach the waistband of his joggers, I yank on them, freeing his cock. It throbs as I take it in my hand, squeezing and pumping it hard as Ryder groans while he bites and sucks at my neck. I run my thumb over the crown of his cock, coating him in the precum there before lifting my thumb to my mouth. Ryder lifts his head, watching me as I suck my thumb into my mouth, sucking it clean before pushing it into his mouth. His eyes glisten with unadulterated desire, and I let out a growl at how fucking hot it is seeing how much he wants me.

Sliding my arse to the floor so I can remove my shorts, I'm pushed back so I'm resting on my elbows as Ryder takes over, stripping me down within seconds.

I flip over, rising to my knees, raising my arse in the air as I drop my upper body to the floor. With my pussy on full display, I hear Ryder's whispered "Fuck!" just before his hands slide along the cheeks of my arse, pulling them open further.

"You been fucked here, Cam?" he grits out, as his thumb circles my tight hole. I moan, pushing down the memories and instead focusing on the pleasure Ryder is drawing from me.

"Yes," I whimper, as he eases his thumb inside before pulling back and pushing all the way in. His other hand reaches for my clit, circling it as he pumps in and out of my arse. I feel my climax building, but I want to come around Ryder's cock.

As though he can read my mind, he leans forward brushing his lips over the shell of my ear, "I'm going to take this arse, but not today. Today you're going to cream all over my cock." He circles my clit once more, then lines himself up at my entrance and pushes in agonisingly slow, and when he's fully seated he lets out a groan that rumbles through his whole body, gripping my hips so tight I can feel the bones grinding together.

I drop my head to the cold floor tiles, but he grips my hair in his fist, arching my back as he pulls back and thrust forward, his hips slamming into mine. My breath is expelled from my lungs in a grunt, and then he finds the perfect rhythm that has my body screaming in ecstasy as my climax builds again.

Hand still wrapped in my hair, a sharp slap stings my arse cheek as he thrusts forward, again and again, and I explode with an earth-shattering orgasm that leaves me winded. As Ryder reaches his own release, shooting his hot cum inside and coating the walls of my cervix, my pussy contracts around him prolonging my own climax.

Collapsing in a heap on the floor, Ryder rolls to the side so as not to crush me, pulling me against his chest. "You're so fucking perfect, Cam." My heart smiles at his words, but my mind takes a different direction, wincing internally when I think of all the awful, disgusting things that have been done to me. If he knew, he'd never think of me as perfect.

THIRTY-TWO

Camryn

Ryder carries me to the bedroom, where he takes me again, but this time is different. It's slow and sensual, not our usual hard, angry fucking. This is not fucking at all. This is making love. And in that moment I know that I'm falling in love with him, and I know deep in my heart when this ends, which it will, and he hurts me intentionally or not, it will be the end of me. My heart will shatter into tiny pieces of myself that will forever be fractured. Yes, I'll glue them back together, but they'll never heal. It will be like papering over the cracks.

I know he feels it too, and when we crash over the edge together, those three words hang in the air between us like pollen on a hot summer's day. Never spoken but carried away on the wind. Ryder tucks me under his arm, and I feel the change, the moment he's going to ask.

"Tell me about her, Cam. Tell me about your daughter." I hear the hitch in his voice, and swallowing the lump in my own throat, I do as he asks.

"She...was the best thing I ever did, and so, so beautiful.

And smart, like blow your mind smart." I let out a little laugh. "She certainly didn't get that from me. I like to think that was all my dad. She had this cheeky little grin, and even when she was being mischievous, which was a lot of the time, it would melt the hardest of hearts." I let the tears fall as I picture her smiling and laughing as my mum chased her around the garden. "The day...that day was the most excruciating pain I've ever felt, and I've felt pain." I mentally slap myself for that slip. "I lost everything that day, my baby, my heart, my soul. I was broken. I'm still broken. There is an emptiness inside, a deep, dark space that used to be filled with the very essence of her, and that will never be full again." My voice cracks as I relive the pain of that day, then I feel a finger beneath my chin as Ryder lifts my head.

"Cam." I see the glint of unshed tears in his eyes, and as another tear slips down my face whatever Ryder was going to say dies on his lips. He leans down kissing me on the nose. Then he squeezes me tight, and I relax back into him.

I know there's a sea of secrets between us, some that should stay buried, but Faye is not one of them. I feel relieved that Ryder knows, and I no longer need to hide her from him.

There is one more secret that I could share with him about Faye and my mum. The question is do I trust him enough.

"Ryder, there's something that doesn't add up about their accident," I say, testing the water. If Ryder and Rick know so much about Sean maybe they can help or know something themselves. If I wasn't so close and looking for it, I would never have noticed the slight tensing in Ryder's body at my words.

"What do you mean?" he asks tentatively.

"Well, I always believed that my mum and...that they

both died at the scene, but I found something that says otherwise. Several things actually, and I don't know what's the truth anymore." I shift so that I can see his face before I continue, "Those first months after are a blur, I don't remember much, but someone sent documents to me that have me remembering things I had forgotten or blocked out." I wait for him to react, and he does, but not the way I would have expected. He doesn't jump up demanding to know who sent them to me or how. He remains reasonably calm, simply telling me that he'll look into it if I share what I have with him.

After the way he reacted when I received the flowers from Sean, I was expecting a similar response. Maybe it's because of the conversation we just had, or maybe it's because he already knows. Whatever the reason, I don't like it, and I vow to reconstruct that wall around my heart that he so easily managed to break down.

I GO BACK to work on Monday, with Scott and Russ back to chauffeur duty. Russ is as happy as ever, and Scott has recovered and back to his grumpy self. Happy days. Ryder and I, well, I don't know about us. I sleep in his bed with him every night, giving him my body, but I lock my heart in the vault. I feel him pulling away from me, as I am him.

While I'm at work I try to do a little digging into the autopsy report, and I print off the articles and report giving them to Ryder. I tell him about the nurse from the hospital too, so he can see what he can find.

ON WEDNESDAY, Scott drives me to see Jamie after work. I'm so happy to see my friend that I choke back a few tears as I hug her. She looks better now the bruising has started to fade. Her ribs are still hurting like a bitch, and I remember the arnica cream I put in my bag for her.

While we talk, I notice how tired she looks and the dark circles under her eyes. Jamie tells me that's she not been sleeping well, what with the constant arguments and tension between her mum and dad and the nightmares of the attack, she's struggling to get more than a few hours. She still has no idea what's going on with her parents, but she's remembered some little things about the attack.

"There just silly little things, I'm sure they're useless," she tells me.

"You need to let the police know. Even if it's small, it could be important." I remind her of what Ryder and the police told her.

"Yeah, I will. It's funny, I remember this smell, like sweets, maybe bananas or something, but I can't quite figure out what it is. Oh, well, I'm sure it will come back if it's important. So, tell me what's been going on with you?"

I give her the cliff notes version of the accident and skirt around the subject of me and Ryder. When I mention Seb, she perks up, and then she peppers me with questions about him, most of which I can't answer. I tell her that when I see Seb on Friday I'll try and sneak a picture of him and send it to her. She thanks me in advance for the spank bank material.

When I say goodbye, I tell her to call me if she remembers anything else and to take care.

When I arrive back at the apartment Ryder isn't there, so after a quick bite to eat and a shower I crawl into bed. I try not to think about where Ryder is, or who he's with as I fall asleep.

I don't see Ryder at all on Thursday either. He's gone

when I wake up, if he even came home, and he's out when I get back from work. Resigning myself to the fact that whatever we had is obviously over, I order a takeout, watch movies and drown my sorrows in a tub of cookie dough ice cream before finally dragging my sorry arse to bed around midnight.

Friday morning is like ground hog day, no Ryder again. But he's been home because there is a note on the pillow beside me reminding me of our dinner date with Seb tonight. Apparently, he's going to meet me there. Well that's just fucking grand. Maybe I won't bother turning up at all. Screw him!

There's no sign of Scott when I exit the lift downstairs, instead I'm stuck with an alternate version of Russ. In fact, I could be forgiven for thinking that Scott and Russ have switched personae. Somebody definitely got out of bed the wrong side this morning.

After a quiet and slightly awkward drive, in what I discover to be Russ' car, I jump out like my arse is on fire as Russ shouts to me that he'll pick me up at five. The plan is for me to go home first to change, and then Russ will drive me to the restaurant to meet Seb and Ryder.

My day goes from shit to shittier. First my computer malfunctions, a virus apparently, then around lunch I get a migraine that has me wincing every time I move. The light from the computer screen sends a blinding pain through my skull, and my lunch makes an unscheduled return. After taking some tablets and surreptitiously dozing at my desk for an hour the pain starts to ease.

By the time five rolls around I'm ready to collapse in my bed and fall into a deep sleep that even Sleeping Beauty would be jealous of.

There's still no sign of Scott, and when I ask Russ where

he is, he just tells me that he's on another job. Sensing that's all I'm going to get, I fall into the back seat and shut my eyes for the twenty-minute drive back to Ryder's.

I run a bath, I don't really have time for, but I've decided I don't give a shit. After a nice relaxing soak in the tub, I search the small wardrobe space that Ryder cleared for me looking for something to wear. I don't have much, most of my clothes are back at Jamie's house, but I do have a simple, but classy, black dress. It's the staple of every woman's wardrobe. I drag it out, pulling it over my head and smoothing it down as it hugs my body. It sits just above the knee with a sweetheart neckline that shows just the right amount of cleavage.

I half blow dry my hair, letting it fall in soft waves down my back before applying my makeup. Once I'm ready, I grab a pair of cream heels and a small clutch bag big enough to carry my phone.

Outside there's a chill in the air, sending a shiver through my body that has me wishing I had grabbed my small jacket. Russ opens the door for me and it's nice to see his mood hasn't improved since this morning.

I'm sat behind the passenger seat, and I can see the grim look on Russ' face as he climbs in the car, turning the engine on. He reaches behind him for the seatbelt, and once he's settled, we pull away into the early evening traffic.

As we drive, uneasiness creeps over me. This whole day has been a shit show from the start, and now that has transformed into anxiety. I feel my face heat, and my heart rate kicks up a notch. Resting my head back on the seat, I start to take some slow, deep breaths in and out. I catch Russ' eye in the rear-view mirror, and he asks if I'm okay. Before I can answer him, he leans across the passenger seat opening the glove box, just as my phone starts ringing in my bag.

Shifting my attention to my phone, I pull it out as Jamie's name flashes across the screen.

"Hey, what's up?" I answer, as I look back up at the road ahead, only I'm met by Russ' hand holding out a small paper bag to me. I lean forward to see what's in it as Jamie starts frantically talking down the phone at me.

"Cam, I remembered what that smell is," I dig my hand in the bag pulling out a... *"pear drops. I can't believe I didn't get it straight away, I loved those as a kid."* I see Russ watching me in the mirror, and I school my features, offering him a nod of thanks. *"Anyway, I also remembered the tattoo on the guys arm,"* As he pulls his arm back, I see the tattoo on his wrist, and I know what Jamie's going to say before she says it. *"It was some tribal piece but there was something different, like a Celtic knot or something."*

With no other option, I shove the sweet in my mouth as I feel Russ' eyes on me again.

"That's great, Jamie. I bet your so happy now that's sorted." I plaster a smile on my face. "So, I'm just about to arrive at the restaurant, and I promise to send you that picture of Seb. Can we talk about this tomorrow?" *Please just say yes, please say yes.*

"You okay, Cam, you sound weird?"

"Put the phone down, Camryn," Russ demands from the front, his eyes meeting mine again, and I know I'm busted. Without another word to Jamie, I end the call. Russ holds a hand out for my phone. I know that if I pass it over, I'll have no chance to let Ryder know what's happening, but I don't have much choice, smacking the phone down into his hand before sitting back in my seat.

THIRTY-THREE

Camryn

I try not to freak out, locking my anxiety away. Ryder knows that I'm with Russ, and when I don't turn up, he'll come looking for me. Won't he? It's been fifteen minutes since Jamie called, and we should have been arriving at the restaurant by now.

Wherever Russ is taking me can't be good, so I need to find a way to stop us from getting there. Preferably with Russ dead.

As I don't have any weapons, I stealthily search the car for something I can use to hit him over the head. Coming up empty, I decide to get as much information from him as I can while I pray for a damn miracle.

"Where are we going?" I venture, watching the cruel smirk that lifts the corner of Russ' lips.

"You'll find out soon enough, and by the end of the night I'm going to be balls deep inside you, just like Sean promised me," he says, chuckling, and it has goosebumps breaking out all over my flesh.

My nose wrinkles in disgust, "You sold me out so you

could screw me? Wow. That's disgusting and pathetically sad." I hope my face doesn't convey the fear running through the rest of my body.

"Shut your fucking mouth!" Russ barks, taking one hand off the wheel to try and grab my leg, but I move to the left just out of reach. "I'm going to enjoy fucking you, especially, as I missed out fucking that sweet little friend of yours. She passed out, and I prefer my women to have a bit of fight while I make them scream."

Bile rises in my throat, and I turn away to look out the window. We pass a signpost, but with the car going so fast I only manage to see the last part; something Country Park.

My anxiety is banging against the box I locked it in, but I know if I let it out, it will consume me. Then I'll be as good as dead. My fear of Scan may not have gone away completely but this time away from him as helped me gain back some of the strength he took away from me. My backbone is ramrod straight, and I won't go down without a fight this time. After all, isn't this what I wanted, revenge and justice for my mum and Faye. Not only to make him pay for what he did to me, but I'm almost certain he had a hand in their death too.

A phone rings in the car, and it sounds like mine and is coming from the passenger seat. Maybe it's Ryder, or maybe it's Jamie? She never called back after I put the phone down on her, which is odd. I try not to let that thought develop and take root because I have more pressing issues to think about. A laugh brings me out of my thoughts.

"Aww, would you look at that. Poor little Ry, Ry, calling to check on you. Such a shame he'll never see you again. I sure would love to see his face while Sean punishes you. Maybe he can record it and send it to him as a goodbye gift." The ringing stops and is replaced by Russ' twisted laughter.

Then it starts again, only it's not the same phone. Russ digs around in his pocket, pulling it free before answering it. His eyes meet mine in the mirror, sparkling with a devilish intent.

"Hey, boss." I can't hear the voice on the other end, but I bet my last breath it's not Ryder. "Yeah, all good, we're almost there." He ends the call, throwing the phone on the seat next to mine. "Well, looks like boss man is starting the party before the guest of honour arrives. The screaming is like music to my ears and makes my dick hard," he says, grabbing his crotch, squeezing and groaning as his eyes roll back in his head.

We pull off at the next slip road, and my heart starts beating ten to the dozen, it's so loud I'm surprised Russ can't hear it. Travelling a little further on this road before we exit onto a dirt track, and then into a long driveway as I catch sight of a building up ahead. There is nothing but trees and fields out here, and I doubt there's another house for miles.

Thinking this might be my only chance to escape, I slip off my shoes, and as Russ pulls up and exits the car, I lean down and grab one. I tuck it under my bag as best I can and hope he doesn't see it. Russ comes round, opening my door.

"Get out," he demands, then grabs my upper arm trying to yank me from the car. As I get out, I tighten my grip on the shoe, ready to make my move, and when I'm fully on my feet I swing, heel pointing out, catching Russ on the side of his head. I don't waste time, I run. I run as Russ' cries of pain pierce the night air, and the gravel cuts into my bare feet.

Feet pound the dirt behind me, but I daren't look back. I keep my focus on the tree line up ahead, just a little bit further. *If I can just reach the trees.* I push my legs harder just as a shout rings out behind me, and I'm almost there when I hear the sound of several more feet on the ground. Lots of smaller, little feet and much faster, I'm not left guessing for long as a growl reaches me. Dogs. Fuck. I can't outrun dogs.

Refusing to give up even though my legs are screaming, I crash through the tree line aware that Russ is still close behind me, and I immediately veer to the left. Branches and twigs slap me in the face and dig into my feet, but I can hardly feel them as adrenaline pumps through my veins. My heart feels like it's about ready to burst from my chest it's beating so hard, and I feel a stitch coming as it burns up my side.

A screech rings out, followed by several snarls as some-thing heavy hits the ground. I keep going certain that the dogs have Russ, but I don't have time to look, or give a shit right now. That bastard deserves everything he gets.

I see a break in the trees and run right for it, but I'm so focused on it, that I don't see the shadow coming right for me on the left till it's too late.

I hit the ground with a bone crushing thud as a heavy weight lands on top of me, and all the air bursts from my lungs from the force. I desperately try to draw breath as the man above pins me to the hard ground, pushing my face into the dirt with his big meaty hand.

With my one free hand, I blindly strike out behind me several times before I get lucky and connect with the guy's face enough for a grunt to leave him. His slight movement allows me to get my other hand free, and I'm able to twist to the side, hitting out with both hands. Punching, slapping, scratching and thrashing my legs in a bid to be free, but he's too heavy.

Snatching one of my wrists, he twists it causing a scream to break free as pain ricochets up my arm. I lash out, scratching down the side of his face. I feel his skin tear beneath my nails, and as the dim light from the moon peeks through the canopy of trees, I see blood trail down his cheek. I smile internally at the win, but my celebration doesn't last long as his fist swings towards my face, landing the blow on my temple.

My eyes roll, and my vision blurs from the force as pain pulses through my head, rippling out across my cheek and face. In the split second I'm distracted, he grabs my other wrist and squeezing them together in the fierce grip of one hand, he strikes me again. I desperately try to hold on to consciousness, but my eyes fall shut and darkness invades.

As consciousness creeps over me, so does the pounding in my head. My lips are dry, and as I peel my eyes open the bright light burns my retinas causing me to screw my eyes shut away from the pain. When I try to bring a hand to my head, my shoulder protests the movement as a dull ache blooms.

Lifting my head and through slitted eyes, I see I'm strung from the ceiling by my arms. Each wrist is shackled with a leather cuff that hangs from rope attached to cara-biners in the wooden beams. My legs are free, but only the tips of my torn and bloody feet reach the floor.

Fear rushes through me now the adrenaline from earlier has worn off, and this is a position I have been in many times before. I know what comes from being here like this, and my stomach twists in revolt as the memories play in my mind's eye. Closing my eyes, I force the visions away, knowing that if I allow them in, I won't stand a chance of escaping, or surviving.

I open my eyes again, and as they adjust to the light, I begin to take in the room around me. It looks like an old church hall, with a high beamed ceiling and old pews pushed against the walls either side of the room. How very apt that the devil should do his work in the house of God. There are several chairs lined up in front of where I hang ready for Sean and his audience no doubt.

I'm still wearing my dress, which is covered in dirt and broken leaves and twigs.

A noise from behind me has me spinning around, but I'm jolted to a halt as my shackles lock into place. Footsteps echo around the vast room, several more follow, along with the sound of whimpering. Then a voice that turns my blood to ice calls out.

"Kasey. My darling, darling, Kasey." His voice is loaded with venom all covered in a sickly-sweet tone. If I didn't know him as well as I do, then I wouldn't have a clue as to the rage simmering below the calm exterior.

Coming to stop in front of me, his hand reaches out to touch my face, and I turn away on instinct. Bad mistake. In a lightning fast move, he slaps me across the cheek before catching my chin in a brutal grip between his thumb and forefinger. Squeezing my face so tight my lips pout, and my teeth grind together. I don't make a sound, instead I stare defiantly into the pools of blackness that masquerade as his eyes.

"Is that any way to greet your fiancé?" he hisses in my ear, before letting go and turning to address the crowd that has gathered in front of us. "Gentleman, and whores," he adds, gesturing to me and the woman on the floor beside me. "It would appear, that my once loving and adoring fiancée has forgotten her place whilst she's been whoring herself out in Manchester. So, I have arranged this little soiree in celebration of her return." He spins on the heels of his feet to face me, "It wouldn't be a Donovan party without a little bloodshed and debauchery now would it." A cruel smirk lifts at the corner of his lips.

The woman on the floor next to me begins to sob, and I will her to be quiet, but she doesn't. Sean marches towards her, grabbing a fistful of her hair in his hand and yanking her head back at an awkward angle. She lets out a pained cry, her arms lurch forward as she tries to stay on her knees. Sean's eyes lift to meet mine as he pulls her head back further, forcing her back to bow.

"This pitiful creature here is Tammy, and she's been kind enough to warm my bed while you've been gone." I don't miss the spark of arousal his words bring to his eyes, or the wistful hope of even a small amount of jealousy from me. I mask my emotions as best I can, and the only thing I feel for Tammy is pity. When he doesn't see what he was hoping for, his other hand wraps round Tammy's slender neck. He begins to squeeze as she begs him to stop, but if anything, it just makes him squeeze harder. I learnt the hard way that begging for mercy does nothing but bring more pain to you and more pleasure to Sean.

I can't believe that I ever loved this man. Sean's not a man. He's worse than the devil himself.

I hear groaning over to the left of me, turning my head a fraction, I see Russ. His clothes are torn and dishevelled, hair matted with blood from a gash on his head, and he appears to have a dog bite to his leg. I cast my eyes over the rest of the room, but quickly turn back to Sean as Tammy lets out a wailing cry.

He's let go of her hair but is still holding her throat, and he has torn open her dress revealing her nakedness to the room. Tammy's body is almost completely covered in bruises and among them are small scars and recent slashes to her skin that still weep blood. Sean leans forward whispering in Tammy's ear, and her eyes widen in fear and shock at whatever he said.

Not able to watch anymore I look away, scanning the faces in the room. Some of the men I recognise, but a few I've never seen before. Standing at the back of room, arms folded and leaning back against the wall is Lewis' brother, Lincoln, his signature toothpick hanging from the corner of his mouth. His eyes primed on me and burning with pure hatred.

A shiver of fear cascades down my back at what he will do to me if Sean allows him to get his hands on me. Lincoln will be out for my blood in vengeance of his brother's death. He pulls the toothpick free from his mouth then points it directly at me in a clear threat. Dropping my gaze from him, I see Sean throwing Tammy to the floor with a kick to the ribs before walking back to me.

Sean must have removed his belt at some point, and now folded in half, it hangs from his fingers as he approaches. Taking the other end in his hand he pulls sharply, snapping the two halves together and causing a crack to splinter the air.

Sean walks around me before stopping at my back, and I can feel his breath on my neck as he speaks.

"Russ, come forward," he calls out, and I watch Russ as he awkwardly climbs to his feet before stepping forward a few paces. "Tell me, Russ, how many times has Kasey allowed herself to be fucked by Ryder fucking Hawkins? The fucking thorn in my side for so pissing long." He spits Ryder's name, and a frown creases my brow at Sean's barb at Ryder being a thorn in his side. What the hell does he mean by that?

"I've lost count, boss," Russ replies, chuckling while his

eyes remain on me. He licks his lips, and the bulge, in what's left of his trousers, is clear.

"That many you can't even remember, wow. That's impressive work for only a few weeks, hey, Kasey?" A hand trails up my back, gripping my neck. "You made me wait longer than you've known that cunt Hawkins." The whoosh of the belt as it flies through the air is the only warning I get before it strikes the back of my legs. My body lurches forward, and my legs lift from the ground putting pressure on my shoulders, that causes more pain to ripple through me. I scream internally, grinding my teeth together to keep from letting it break free. "But no matter, I've heard he has a taste for whores, seen it myself. Does he know you're a whore, Kasey?" He strikes me again with the belt, in the same fucking place, and it burns. Oh, my god, it burns. Sweat beads on the back of my neck as I try to control the pain. "Answer me, cunt!" he roars, striking me a third time.

"I'm not a whore," I grit out between panting breaths.

"Wrong. Fucking. Answer." Each word is punctuated with another strike, this time to my back. Sean has released my neck, and with each hit my back arches, pulling at my wrists and shoulders. "You are a whore. You're my whore and guess what?" he whispers in my ear. "He knows all about it." He roars with laughter as he lands another blow to my back.

My heart sinks. Sean must be lying because there's no way Ryder knows. I scramble to understand how that could be true as my body and brain drown in pain from Sean's blows. That last strike split the skin as blood begins to run down my back beneath my dress, and as if he knows, Sean tears the back of my dress open. I hear him hum out his satisfaction at his work, and the tiny beads of sweat that formed on my neck, roll down my back. As they reach the welts in my skin, mixing with the blood there, they sting like a bitch.

"What's the matter, Kasey, don't you believe me?" he sings, loving what he's doing to me. "Lincoln, would you do the honours, please."

Raising my head, I watch Lincoln fiddle with a phone as he walks closer to me. Then Ryder's voice fills the room.

"Cam's broken, Sully, she's a fucking whore. You've seen her file. Fuck, she's just a job."

THIRTY-FOUR

Camryn

The pain on my back fades to nothingness as Ryder's words play out. Time seems to standstill, and his words are all I can hear as the room and everyone in it continue around me in slow motion. I can hear laughter, but it sounds far away.

I drop my head to my chest as the first tear begins to fall, and I curse myself for opening my heart to another man.

My body becomes limp, and I don't even flinch as Sean takes up lashing my back again. I'm numb. I'm broken.

Lincoln plays the recording on repeat, but I don't need it. It's etched into my brain.

Men begin to move around the room, and I can faintly hear screaming. A hand brushes up my arm, but I barely feel it, continuing its path to my shoulder. I think it's Sean, but I don't know. The hand moves to my breast, squeezing painfully as another hand trails up my thigh.

"Cam's broken, Sully, she's a fucking whore. You've seen her file. Fuck, she's just a job."

"Cam's broken, Sully, she's a fucking whore. You've seen her file. Fuck, she's just a job."

Over and over, Ryder's voice fills the room, drowning out the laughter, the chatter, the screams and grunts and groans of pleasure. It would normally make me sick, but I don't think anything can make me feel sicker than I already do. How could he?

I always knew that my past would stop any man from loving me. Sean was right all along, I'm nothing but a whore. He'll make me his wife, only in name and on paper, then he'll turn me into his incubator, and he won't stop till I give him the heir he so desperately wants.

As Ryder's words continue to play, I notice the slight pause between some of the words, and as I listen harder, I notice a small, barely audible click after some of the words too. It could be nothing but during my journalism degree we had a guy on the course that could edit recordings, and I remember him mentioning this as a sign of an edited recording. Poorly edited at that. If Sean has been listening into Ryder's conversations, and he's gone to these lengths, which I don't doubt for a second knowing what I do about him now, then he must be worried.

Sean's goal has always been to break me, isolate me from others, friends and family, and if he knows I care about Ryder then he would do anything to make me believe that I'm nothing but a fuck to him.

Bolstered by the notion that this is Sean's way of breaking me, I snap out of it as the hand trailing my thigh reaches the edge of my knickers. My stomach turns over as fingers reach beneath my underwear, and I let out a snarl as anger overrides any other emotion right now. I wish I had my hands free so I could pound my fists into Sean's face.

Sean steps back, cracking me across the face. My head

whips to the side, and as I turn back to face him, the coppery tang of blood fills my mouth. Reaching up, Sean begins to undo the wrist cuffs. As he undoes the last one, my legs give way beneath me, and I collapse into his arms.

The scent that once made my heart flutter, now has me heaving as bile rises up my throat. My arms hang limp at my side, pins and needles prick at my skin as the blood rushes back into them, and my shoulders throb their relief.

"Me and you are going to have some fun in private," he murmurs in my ear, as he begins to carry me away. Fear skitters over me, but I turn it to rage, focusing every drop onto Sean.

We pass Tammy, who is laying on the floor while a man pounds into her prone body from above. She isn't moving anymore, and I don't know if she's passed out, or if she's dead. There's blood on the floor next to her head, and I pray that she's just knocked out. Given what she's no doubt been through, I wonder if she would prefer to never wake up. If I hadn't had Faye I would have wished for the same, and for a long time after her death, that's exactly what I prayed for.

Sean pulls me through the door at the back of the room, and my eyes catch on Russ watching us with a look of hunger before the door closes behind me.

I was right about this being a church as the hall we are going down has several smaller prayer rooms leading off it. Sean pulls me into a room on the left at the end of the hall, throwing me to the floor and slamming the door shut.

I scramble back to the far wall, and when the cold, rough brick makes contact with the raw skin of my back, white-hot pain radiates down my spine. I bite my lip to keep the scream contained and more blood fills my mouth.

Sean stands in front of the door, his eyes are black, soulless pits that burn with the fires of hell, and a cruel smirk crosses his face at my obvious pain.

"I love to see the pain in your eyes, it makes my dick so hard. Hmmm." He stalks towards me. "I'm going to wipe the memory of that cunt Hawkins from your mind and body."

"What happened to you?" I ask, hoping to distract him. It's something I've never asked him, and if I make it out of this alive, I feel like I need to understand what went wrong.

"This is me, Kasey. It's always been me. You were just too stupidly in love with me, and that's exactly how it was meant to be. Things would have been different if you had done as you were told, and I would never have had to teach you a lesson. Of course, giving me a daughter instead of the son I deserved pissed me off immensely."

"How the fuck is that my fault? You don't get to pick and choose the sex of a baby, Sean," I snap back at him. My anger at his ridiculous notion I had a say in the sex of our child has my nostrils flaring, and my fists clenching at my sides.

"Of course it fucking is!" he bellows, as he begins pacing the floor. "What the fuck was I meant to do with another whore, whining and moaning and making my life a misery. I can't even fuck her. Well, I could have, I guess. Who knows what might have happened as she got older," he says, with a shrug, like what he just said isn't the sickest thing ever. A visible shudder runs through me, heart breaking as I thank the stars that Faye is not here, and he can't hurt her. Internally I fall apart, but outwardly I keep it together as best I can.

"I wanted to kill you when you told me, to slit you open and cut out that bitch growing inside you. I remember beating you that night, it was heaven until I realised that you and *she* had survived. But then Douglas showed me a better way. He made me an offer that would secure my position when he retired and Daniel took over. A mutually satisfactory joining of our two families. Daniel likes them young, it never really interested me, but each to their own, and Douglas told me Daniel took a liking to our Faye. When Faye turned sixteen, she was to become his wife, and I would become Daniel's second, while you, in the meantime, were to provide me with an heir. But that never happened did it, Kasey?"

Oh, shit. He knows about the implant.

After Faye was born, I vowed I would never bring another child into that life. At first, I was able to sneak a prescription of the pill, but Sean almost found them one day, after that I couldn't take the risk. Then when Tyler came and I started to trust him, he and mum were able to get me to a doctor who gave me the implant. Holy shit. Mike, Dr Wallis, is the doctor, but that means—my thoughts are cut off as Sean starts talking again.

"You can't pull the wool over my eyes, Kasey. I know all about your little trip to the doctor behind my back. I always knew I should have gotten rid of your mother sooner. Another sneaky, interfering fucking whore. When I discovered what you'd done, I decided to find my heir elsewhere and get rid of you at the same time. It was meant to be so perfect. I would get my heir, and you and your mother would be long gone because I knew you'd cause trouble over Faye's marriage. Then you went and fucked that up too. Destroying all my perfectly laid plans."

I'm so shocked that I don't see him move till the last minute, landing a hit to my head. The action causes me to fall to the side, my back scrapes along the wall, and combined with the painful hit forces a scream to burst from my lungs.

"It was you? Oh my god, oh my god. It was you." I push myself upright, then use the wall to steady me as I climb to my feet. I know I've torn my back up even more, but I don't fucking care. "You killed my mum and your own daughter. For what? Money and power?" I surge forward, poking my finger in his chest as a rage so savage consumes me. Sean's eyes widen as I get up his face. "You sick fucking bastard!" I spit, then I fly at him. Caught off guard, I manage to land a couple of blows to his head and face that has his nose spurting blood. A few droplets land on me, and the demon I've kept caged for so long is let loose.

I reign blow after blow down on the man that has destroyed my life. Beaten me, raped mc and allowed his friends to watch or join in, isolated me from everyone I know and taken the most precious thing I had left away from me too. Ripped my heart and soul out by murdering my mum and daughter all for money and power.

We grapple for a couple of minutes, but once Sean's shock wears off, he overpowers me. Tackling me to the ground, I land awkwardly shoulder first and hear a pop, and then blinding pain. I already know I've dislocated my shoulder, again. After the first time the nurse warned me it can happen easier a second time, she wasn't fucking wrong, but it's a fucking shame the same can't be said about the pain.

Sean rolls me so I'm on my back and with only one arm, it's not difficult for him to subdue me. Realising I'm at a disadvantage brings a smile to his face. A wicked, cruel smile. Using his weight and one hand to restrain me, he pulls a blade from the sheath on his leg. It's his favourite, and the one responsible for the scars I wear on my body. The white bone handled hunting knife used to be his father's and became Sean's after his father was murdered. The day he told me that story I should have known the type of man I was in love with.

He places the blade against the jack hammering pulse in my neck and pushes just enough to prick the skin. Blood still drips from his nose, and it makes me smile. I let him see it too because I have nothing to lose now. He's going to kill me anyway.

"What the fuck are you smiling about, bitch?" I let out a laugh. "You think you can attack me, run away from me, fuck someone else. And not just some random bloke, oh no, you had to pick the fucker that has caused me no end of problems over the last three years," he sneers, teeth gritted as his eyes blaze with rage.

I don't understand where Sean's hatred for Ryder comes from, and Sean must see the confusion on my face.

"You don't know, do you?" He lets out a crazed chuckle. "Oh, this is just priceless. Your precious fuck buddy and his friends have been trying to put me away for the last three years. Even managed to plant one of their own in my ranks." I raise my brows at that, and Sean continues like this is the best story he's ever told. "That's right, Kasey. Your little friend Tyler, the devious fucker, squealed like a fucking pig while I gutted him. It was almost as good as when you scream, but not quite, and I've missed those sounds." He leans forward licking up the side of my face, and as I try to turn my head the knife digs in further. I feel a warm trickle of blood as it tracks down my neck. I close my eyes, blocking out the smell of his foul breath and instead fill my mind with thoughts of my mum, Faye, Jamie and even Ryder.

Despite the pain in my heart, I still want him, but that can never happen now. I know the recording of him was likely edited so it appeared he said those things, but he must have said those words at some point just in a different context. And he knows everything. Shame washes over me at that thought and tears prick at the corner of my eyes, but I won't give Sean the satisfaction.

Swallowing back the pain, the tears and shame for another time, I spit in Sean's face. "You make me sick." I watch as my saliva runs down his face before mixing with the blood from his nose, and his face turns red as the vein at his temple pulses with anger. "What kind of man kills his own daughter? You're not a man, you're a fucking joke. A pathetic excuse for a human being and people like you should be drowned at birth." The fire in my gut, and the hatred for this man rushes forward.

Shouting and hollering comes from outside the door distracting Sean, and in that split second, I take the only chance I'm going to get. Ignoring the pain, I buck my hips just as the door to the room flies open. It's enough to knock Sean off balance and in turn releasing my good arm. With my now free hand, I grip his hand holding the knife, and with every ounce of pain, anger, fear and shame, I twist his hand round and shove upwards as he looks towards the door. As if in slow motion, the knife plunges into his neck.

Instantly, his other hand comes up to the knife now sticking out of his neck, and his head swings back to me. Blood gushes from the wound, and a horrid gurgling sound rises up from Sean's throat as his eyes settle on me. When he tries to talk, blood spurts from his mouth spraying me in tiny droplets as his throat fills with blood, and he begins to choke. Drowning in his own blood.

The black of his eyes begins to clear, and I'm met with the dark brown ones I fell in love with all those years ago. As his skin begins to pale, he falls backwards. I pull my legs clear, and then he drops to his side as blood pools beneath him.

Movement at the door has me lifting my head, and there stands Ryder with blood splattering his face and clothes. His hands are clenched tight, and his nostrils flare as he takes in the sight before him.

A rasping from the floor in front of me has me looking back to Sean, and the pool of blood on the floor creeps across the tiles like the evil that lived in him is searching for a new host. I watch as Sean's breathing becomes shallow, and his eyes glaze over before the light in them fades altogether as he takes his last breath. Lifeless eyes now stare back at me, and I release the breath I didn't even know I was holding.

Relief. Such beautiful relief surges through me knowing he can never harm me again. Knowing that he can never hurt another person. That I got justice for my mum and Faye. I killed him, and I don't feel even the tiniest bit of remorse for his loss of life. I have no idea what that says about me, and I'm sure a psychologist would have a field day with that knowledge.

Someone crouches down in front of me, and as a hand comes out to stroke my cheek, I flinch and scramble backwards away from the touch. I pull my knees up to my chest, wrapping my one good arm round them.

"Cam, it's me, Ryder. It's okay, you're safe now." His deep voice washes over me, calming my raw nerves and slowing my frantically beating heart. I know it's him, my body knows it's him, but my mind struggles to catch up with the rest of me. I have never feared this man, never worried that he would lay a hand on me in anger, only with passion, but my heart is fractured at his deception.

I look up at him, his beautiful blue eyes are a swirling

storm that speak of his restrained anger, but I can see pain too. And I don't understand that.

He drops to his knees, resting his hands in his lap so I can see them. My body is screaming at me. Pain. Fear. Shame and guilt, but the overriding emotion is the need to crawl into his lap and let him hold me and bathe in his warmth and love. It may not be real, or true but it's what I need to feel right now, and I give in to it. Scrambling to my knees, I shuffle towards him as his eyes track me wearily, and I cautiously climb into his lap when I reach him. Ryder's arms hesitantly wrap around me, and I relax into him.

After a few seconds, Ryder's fingers brush over my cheek, pushing back hair from my face. "Cam. We need to get you to a hospital." I wince as his hand glances across the slashes on my back and every injured part of me makes itself known as the adrenaline wears off.

Keeping my head buried in his chest and my eyes away from his penetrating gaze, I give the gentlest of nods.

Careful to avoid my shoulder and back as much as possible, Ryder scoops me up into his arms, stepping past Sean's body on the floor as we leave the room.

THIRTY-FIVE

Blue

When we crash through the doors of the small church hall, the team takes down the men that are still here, while I scan the room for Cam. Not seeing her anywhere, my chest hurts at the thought we are too late.

The sound of my voice breaks through the shouting of the men as they are restrained, and my heart sinks when I hear the words that I know Cam will have heard. I don't doubt that she would have believed them too. Fuck. I fucked up not telling her I knew what she'd been through, and what that fucker Sean had done to her. But I can't worry about it now, I need to find her first.

Just as I go to move through the room, I catch movement out of the corner of my eye and dodge the fist that flies towards my face. It's Lincoln, Lewis' brother.

"You motherfucker, you murdered my brother!" he bellows, as he comes for me again.

"Not me, prick, though I wish it had been," I spit out, just as he reaches me with his fists swinging. I duck, then land a blow to his gut that knocks all the air from his lungs.

Following up with a jab to the kidneys before finishing him off with an uppercut that has his jaw rattling and eyes rolling in his head. He hits the deck, cracking his head on the wood floor, out cold.

The phone he was holding, still playing my voice, lays on the floor next to him, and I snatch it up. Turning it off, I shove it in my pocket for later.

I see Seb take down two other guys over on the left as I stride down the hall. I catch a glimpse of Russ as he limps through a door at the back of the room. No way, arsehole. Rushing forward, I pass a girl, of no more than twenty, in a pool of blood, and my heart rate skyrockets.

I push through the door cautiously, knowing Russ can fight with the best of them, but I needn't have worried. He hasn't got far, the injury to his leg slowing him down as he reaches a door at the end of the hallway.

"You're a dead man walking, Russ," I shout, as I charge at him. He doesn't even try to fight back as I smash my fist into his face, and he lands on his back. I grab the front of his shirt, lifting his face to mine. "I would kill you, but instead I've arranged a nice welcoming party in prison for you." I punch him again, letting him drop to the floor unconscious.

I hear Cam's voice in the room next to me, and I burst through the door, coming to a dead stop when I catch sight of the woman I'm in love with. Her face is contorted with pain, eyes wild, looking almost feral. She's beautiful. I watch with pure admiration as she rams the knife into Sean's neck, with a snarl on her face. Blood sprays all over her as Sean tries to talk but chokes on his own blood. Good. As he falls back, she shifts her legs away from him, no longer trapped. I see that her left arm hangs limply at her side and her dress is torn at the back, but I can't see anything else from this angle. Cam's eyes meet mine, and I try the best I can to rein in my fury so I don't scare her.

Cam looks back at Sean, and I watch her watching him as he breathes his last breath. I move very slowly towards her, then crouch down in front of her. I reach out a hand to touch her cheek, but she instantly flinches away. I'm not going to lie and say it didn't fucking hurt. It cuts like a knife. She scrambles back from me, out of reach, so I stay where I am and wait.

When her eyes meet mine again, I drop to my knees in front of her, and I watch a myriad of emotions cross her face as she stares out at the room. Then she's in my lap. I wrap my arms around her, feeling the wetness of blood on her back, and I grind my teeth, looking back at Sean and wishing I could kill him all over again. She buries her head in my chest, and I give her a couple of minutes hoping that she can feel my love for her.

As her breathing evens out and she relaxes in my hold, I brush the hair from her face, seeing her split lip and bruises. It slays me to see this beautiful woman marked in such a way. A woman that I love. I tried to deny it, but I can't any longer. No woman has ever made me feel the way Cam does. I know she's going to be mad at me, she's going to have questions, but I just hope the answers I give are enough.

Telling her she needs to go to the hospital, she gives a small imperceptible nod, and as carefully as I can, I scoop her up and carry her out.

I HATE FUCKING WAITING. I'm pacing the floor of the small waiting room the nurse showed us to after they took Cam in for examination. I didn't get a good look at the marks on her back, but I have a pretty good idea what they are. Every muscle in my body tenses and feels like it's going to snap when I think about that bastard laying his hands on her and hurting her. I want to rip him limb from limb, and then put him back together so I can do it over and over again. I wanted him to suffer, and although he did, it wasn't even close to the pain I would have inflicted on the man that killed my brother and hurt the woman I love.

The door swings open, raising my head slightly I see it's Seb with two mugs of tea. No doubt he sweet talked one of the nurses, the guy knows no bounds. I shake my head at him as I take the mug he offers.

"What?" he asks, innocence and disbelief lacing his tone.

"You. You're unbelievable, that's what," I say with a small smile, as I take a sip of the hot, sweet tea.

"Sit down, man. You make the place look untidy." Not in the mood to argue, I take the seat across from him. "So, while I was gone, I called that Jamie chick. She sounds hot. Like, she can ride my dick anytime, hot." I narrow my eyes at him, piercing him with a glare that makes it clear he's to stay the hell away. "Aww, come on, don't be like that. She might like me." He winks, bringing the mug to his lips.

"She would not like you. Jamie is a smart woman. Not at all like the bimbos you usually go for," I say, rolling my eyes. He scoffs at that and goes back to drinking his tea.

While we wait, I try not to think about how different tonight could have been if we hadn't had that tracker on Cam and Russ. After Jamie's attack and Cam's accident, I became suspicious of Russ. Some stuff just didn't add up, and when we did a little digging into the guy from the hotel, we came up trumps.

We managed to trace him back to a bar in the city that frequently ran behind doors poker nights, and who should be sat at the table with him? Russ. After that I had Scott keep a very close eye on Russ. We don't yet know how Russ was connected to Sean, but I will get the answers I need.

An hour later the nurse comes and gives us an update on Cam. Aside from the dislocated shoulder and the wounds to her back she's good. They have moved her to a private room, at my request, and though she's still woozy from the drugs we can see her.

I pause with my hand on the door, suddenly unsure about seeing her and what to say. I haven't forgotten our lovemaking, and that's what it was, the day she found out I knew about Faye. And even though I felt those words on the tip of my tongue, they never crossed my lips. I think that maybe if I had, then this would be much easier. Cam would know exactly how I feel about her, and that fucking recording that Sean played wouldn't have put any doubts in her head. I don't know how this is going to go, so I take a deep breath and push through the door.

Cam is asleep, left arm in a sling while the other lays by her side. The knuckles on both her hands are red, evidence of her fight with Sean. How the fuck she managed that with a dislocated shoulder, I don't know, but it shows just how strong she really is. If only she believed it.

I pick the only chair in the room up and move it closer to the bed, and when I turn around her eyes are on me. I offer her a small smile as I sit.

"Hey," I say, then clear my throat and swallow down the lump there. "How are you feeling?" Cam closes her eyes, wincing as she shifts in the bed. I try to wait her out, but the tension in the air is stifling. "Jamie is on her way. I told her you were fine and to let you rest, but she wasn't hav—"

"Why are you here, Ryder?" she questions, her voice quiet but strong, and I don't miss the slight bite to them.

"Your job is finished now. Sean's dead, so you don't need to check up on me anymore."

Fuck. This is going to be harder than I thought. "That's not fair, Cam. You were never just a job and you know it," I growl.

"Do I? Because from where I'm standing that's all I ever was to you, oh, and a good fuck." I leap to my feet, the chair scraping on the floor as it's pushed back. "I think you should leave." Cam turns her head away from me in complete dismissal, and my heart sinks.

I open my mouth ready to fire back at her, but I stop myself, knowing it will only make things worse. My chest aches, like someone just shoved a knife right through it at what I'm about to say, but I need to give her time.

"Okay, fine. I'll go, but don't for one second think that this is over, Cam, because it fucking isn't." The words burn their way out, and I have to physically force my feet to move away from her.

I stop at the door, turning to look at her. She's still facing the window, but I don't miss the tear that slips down her face. I clench my jaw, and my knuckles turn white with my grip on the handle of the door because all I want to do is go to her and hold her. Instead, I drop my head and walk away, praying that I'm doing the right thing. That giving her time will help her see straight and see the truth. That I love her.

As I step out, shutting the door behind me, I see Jamie rushing down the corridor. I walk down to meet her, and as I reach her, I see the confusion on her face.

"Hey. Is she okay? What's going on?"

"She's fine, Jamie. Well, not fine, but she's okay. You should go talk to her, she's awake. I'm sure she'll be happy to see you." I try not to sound bitter, but Jamie doesn't miss it in my voice. She scrutinises my face, and I don't think she realises how intimidating she can be.

"What did you do?" Jamie points an accusing finger at me.

"Look," I sigh, running my hand through my hair before continuing, "Cam will tell you, but you need to know that it's not true. And, yeah, I may have known some stuff I didn't tell her, but I did what I thought was right. None of it changes anything between us, not for me anyway." I go to walk past her, but Jamie's hand on my arm stops me.

"You love her, don't you?" she asks, looking at me with a knowing smile on her face.

I nod, then say, "Not telling her sooner was my mistake, and I intend on fixing that. When she'll fucking listen to me. Take care of her for me, yeah?" Her hand slips off my arm as I walk away down the corridor, and the knife in my heart twists with every step I take.

THIRTY-SIX

Camryn

The soft click of the door closing opens the floodgates, and my bottom lip trembles as the sob I fought to keep in breaks free. My whole-body hurts, my shoulder throbs, my back feels as though there are a thousand tiny fire ants dancing across it, but the most agonising pain is deep inside. It's the kind of pain that sits in the shadows, a dull ache that can be ignited to the heat of fire in an instant. I swipe at the tears on my face, angry at myself for allowing them to fall.

The whoosh of the door opening has me tensing, ready to tell Ryder to do one. When I turn around, it's not Ryder, it's Jamie. Jamie strides across the room and takes me into her arms. Talking softly and stroking my hair as I fall apart in her arms. When my head throbs and my eyes are swollen and gritty, I pull back. Jamie passes me the box of tissues, and I wipe the tears from my face. Not one to waste time or beat around the bush, Jamie dives right on in.

"So, you want to tell me why that broody hunk of yours just walked away looking like someone kicked him in the nuts?"

"Luckily for him, I can't get out of this damn bed, otherwise he wouldn't just look like he had, trust me." I push the button on the side of the bed to raise it up slightly, screwing my face up as the movement pulls on my shoulder.

Once I'm settled, Jamie sits in the chair next to me and waits for me to talk. I don't really want to relive everything so soon, but I know talking about it with Jamie will help. I tell her everything and feel surprisingly lighter after.

"So, he knew more about Sean than he told you, they have a history, and he knew about your past?" she verifies in short. I nod, expecting her to be as angry with him as I am but she's not. "Have you given him a chance to explain? Because I guarantee that whatever you're thinking about him knowing those things about you, will not be the same for him."

"What are you saying, Jamie? I thought you'd understand." I struggle to keep the irritation from my voice. Jamie's my best friend, and the one person that I thought would be on my side.

"I do understand, and you know I love you, Cam. But don't let your own hang-ups about what happened to you push the people that care about you the most away." I try to interrupt, but Jamie holds a hand up, stopping me. "You need to consider his reasons for not sharing with you. Let me ask you this, what was your biggest fear about Blue finding out?"

My immediate response is that Ryder would think differently about me, that he'd think I'm worthless and disgusting. But thinking more about it, that doesn't really add up. If Ryder has known all this time, and he actually thought that, then why would he sleep with me in the first place? When I tell Jamie my thoughts, she nods her agreement.

"That's my point, Cam. And how do you feel about yourself and what happened to you?" Her question comes out strong, but I don't miss the cautionary way she says it.

I know what she's asking, what she's saying. She thinks that I projected how I feel about myself onto Ryder. I realise she's not wrong. "I feel worthless and disgusting. Sean always told me I was a whore, and after everything that he... and his friends did to me I started to believe it." I look away, unable to hold her gaze.

"Cam." She waits for me to look at her before continuing. "You need to give him a chance to explain his reasons, and you need to start believing that you are worth so much more than what that fucker Sean told you. Sean manipulated you and used the ones you love against you to keep you under his control and by his side."

I know everything she's saying is true, but I'm not ready to believe it quite yet. I tell her that I'll hear him out, but I'm not making any promises. Then I change the subject not wanting to talk anymore about the man that makes me feel safer than I've ever felt before. The man that has a whole rabble of butterflies beating in my chest whenever he's near, and the man whose rough hands and rough touch make me fly.

Jamie wants to stay at her parent's house a little longer, not for herself, but because things are so strained between her parents right now. She's concerned about them and I totally understand.

I have no intention of going back to Ryder's. I need some time to sort out my feelings before I face him again. Jamie promises that she'll have my things returned to the house and arrange for a key to be dropped here for me ready for when I'm discharged.

After she leaves, I fall asleep for a while, and when I

wake Seb is sitting in the chair tapping away at his phone. Feeling immensely irritated that he's here, having just woken up and because my shoulder is throbbing like a bitch, means my welcome is not exactly, well, welcoming.

"What do you want, Seb?"

"Woah. Someone's snarky when they wake up." He slips his phone into his pocket. "A little birdie told me that you're pissed at them, so I'm here until you two kiss and make up." He gives me a wink then waggles his brows. I have to try damn hard not to smile at him, but then I remember who he's talking about and any thought of a smile disappears.

"Well, in case you didn't know, the bad guy is dead, and I don't need a babysitter anymore. So, you can go. Please let Rick know that I appreciate all his help, and I'll sort out payment with him soon." I shuffle the blankets on my bed for something to do with my one good hand, then turn to look out the window. The nurse comes in before Seb gets a chance to reply, small mercies.

I realise that I must have slept longer than I thought, it's now almost dawn, and I watch as the sun begins to rise over the city skyline. The nurse said that the doctor will be round shortly, and if he's happy then I'll be discharged later today.

Seb sits quietly in the chair, and when I sneak a look at him, I see he's fallen asleep. Head to one side, at an angle that's sure to give him a crook neck when he wakes. Serves him right.

I don't understand why Ryder would send him here. I'm not in danger anymore, am I? No, that can't be it. Despite how I feel about Ryder, I know damn sure he wouldn't have left, no matter how mad I am at him, if that were true.

I think back over my conversation with Jamie and she's right. I have been projecting how I feel about myself onto Ryder and that's not fair. But that doesn't excuse the fact he knew and didn't say anything, and it also doesn't explain why he never told me he knew so much about Sean or what their connection was.

It's obvious from Sean's comments that Tyler was working with Ryder and the guys, it's obviously how they knew about me, but what I don't understand is what Ryder's personal vendetta against Sean is about. Then the dots slowly connect. Kyle, Ryder's brother, that's the connection. It has to be. I'm not sure how I feel about being a pawn in their personal war on Sean. I hated the guy, and I'm glad he's dead. But now I'm thinking that Rick only agreed to help because I was the best way to get to Sean. I guess there's only one way to find out.

I doze for a while. The painkillers the nurse gave me are bloody good. Seb snores in the chair beside me, but as soon as the door to the room opens, he's awake and alert.

The doctor approves me for discharge, and I can't wait to get out of this place.

After the doctor leaves to arrange my discharge papers, I change into the clothes that Seb brought for me while he goes to make a phone call. I don't need to be a detective to work out who he's phoning.

Seb escorts me from the hospital an hour later, and when I tell him to take me to Jamie's there's not even the hint of an argument from him. I have to admit that I'm a little surprised and maybe a little disappointed too.

When we pull up at Jamie's there's no sign of the police tape from the last time we were here, and as I step out of the car, I realise I don't know what happened to Russ.

"It's okay, Cam, Russ is locked up. He's being charged with the attack on Jamie and several other things that we don't need to talk about right now. Come on let's get you settled. I don't know about you but I'm starving." I frown at the back of Seb's head as he carries my bag up the drive. I jog a few steps but stop when it jolts my shoulder. Seb pulls a key from his pocket, opening the door and stepping in.

"Hey. What do you mean other things?" I don't get to say another word as a little boy comes running down the hall, crashing into Seb, who drops my bag and picks the boy up. It's then I see its Max, Rick's son, and the smell of cooking hits me at the same time.

"Dad, dad, uncle Seb is here—with another girl," he says, rolling his eyes as he spots me behind Seb. I choke back a laugh as Rick enters the hall. "Hey, I know you, you were at our house that day. Uncle Ryder said you were hot." There's a cough from Rick, as he ushers Max back through to the kitchen, and Seb lets out a loud laugh.

"Now that is priceless." Seb picks up my bag from the floor, and I smack him on the back of the head as he rights himself. "Ow! What the fuck was that for?" Humour laces his words as he heads for the stairs, and I follow behind.

I don't offer a reply because I'm too busy trying to work out why Rick and his son are at my house. What the actual hell is going on.

Seb leaves me in my room, telling me Rick has made breakfast and to come down when I'm ready.

I stand frozen in the room for several minutes before heading for the shower. The hospital told me that the cuts to my back weren't deep enough to need stitches but not to soak them for too long, so a quick shower should be fine. Washing my hair with one hand is a nightmare, but one I've done before.

Once I'm clean and dressed, I hesitate at the door. I'm guessing Rick is here to go over what happened, and whilst I'm keen to find out, I'm also a little scared about what will happen.

After all, I killed a man and don't expect to go unpunished.

THIRTY-SEVEN

Camryn

Voices reach me from the kitchen as I near the bottom of the stairs. Max's being the most prominent as he tells Seb about his art project at school. A sharp stab of pain hits my chest as I listen to him, knowing that Faye would have been around the same age as him now.

I've avoided being around kids since Faye's death as it used to bring on awful panic attacks, but I don't feel anything now except sadness at her loss. It brings a smile to my face when I hear Seb and Max laughing, and I'm so lost in my own memories that I don't hear Rick approaching.

"Hey, you okay?" He stops in front of me, frowning in concern.

"Yeah," I say wistfully, watching as Rick raises his eyebrows not totally convinced. "Honestly, I'm fine, Rick. Now, Seb mentioned something about breakfast." Walking past him to the kitchen.

Rick has made enough food to feed a starving third world country, and I was worried about it going to waste seeing as my appetite isn't what it normally is. But I needn't have bothered as Seb, Rick and Max demolish it in the space of twenty minutes.

Once the plates are cleared away, Seb takes Max out to the garden, and I watch as they kick a ball around. I sit at the breakfast bar nursing the dregs of my tea as Rick comes and joins me. I know what's coming and think I'm ready, but I couldn't have been more wrong.

Rick avoids mentioning Ryder as much as possible, even though he was trying to be subtle about it. Rick tells me that whilst their main business is security and private bodyguard work, they have another side to their business. They take on jobs from other organisations that often involve undercover work and recovering lost or stolen items. I get the distinct impression he's not just talking about pieces of rare art or jewellery but people too.

Apparently, Sean had been wanted for some time, but nobody was able to connect anything to him. They were approached with the suggestion of sending in an undercover operative, Tyler, hoping they could gain enough evidence to put him away. That's why Tyler wanted information from Sean's laptop. Sean was connected to a sex trafficking ring; young girls snatched off the street or sold by parents to pay off drug or gambling debts.

I feel sick as I listen to Rick telling me how the man I once loved, and the father of my child was involved in such a disgusting business. When I think about all the terrible things he did me, and that he probably did or allowed to happen to other young girls, I almost vomit. I wish I could kill him again and make him suffer more.

"After Faye's death things got worse for you, and Tyler was worried that Sean would kill you. He came to me asking if there was a way to get you out, but we needed evidence, and you were the only one that could get close enough to get it. I'm sorry for that, Cam. I know how much of a risk you took when you retrieved that information from Sean's laptop.

"Your mum and Faye's death had always seemed suspicious to us, but we didn't have anything to go on until recently."

"What do you mean until recently?"

"I believe that you received some information that made you question their death." I nod. "We did too. Whoever sent you those articles and the autopsy report also sent them to us. We still don't know who that was, but we are looking into it. We believe that Sean never intended for Faye to be in the car that day and think the accident was meant for you and your mum."

I confirm Rick's belief when I tell him what Sean said about wanting me dead and marrying off our daughter. I'm torn between being grateful Faye was in that car and wishing she had survived. Knowing what I know now, I wouldn't have wished for her to suffer at the hands of that perverted arsehole, Daniel. Rick must see the torn look in my face.

"I need you to know that if Sean had succeeded in killing you, we would never have let him go through with his plan. I would have personally made sure that Faye was safe and taken care of." Rick rests his hand on mine, I squeeze his fingers to let him know I appreciate it as the lump in my throat prevents me from speaking.

I clear my throat and swallow thickly before asking Rick about Russ.

"Russ joined the team three years ago, and it looks like we weren't the only ones to think about having a person on the inside. What Sean didn't consider is that we keep a very tight ship and only the three of us know all the details of any of the jobs we do. Unfortunately, Russ had proved to be quite an asset, and when Ryder wanted security for you, Russ and Scott were the best we had available. Again, I apologise for that error in judgement."

Rick goes on to tell me that Russ had been using the house over the road to spy on Jamie and me. It had been him that had left the back door open and stolen the key from the kitchen hook. I question Rick about what Seb said about Russ being charged with other things, and he tells me that the estate agent for the house had been found dead in his apartment. That means Rick is being charged with his murder along with the attempted murder of Jamie.

"And what about me, I killed Sean, so I'm guessing that the police will want to talk to me?"

Rick shakes his head. "No, Cam. The police aren't directly involved and means that Sean's death won't be investigated. We have all given our statements to the organisation that hired us confirming Sean was killed in self-defence. You don't need to worry about anything else." I give him a sceptical look, but he doesn't say anymore on the matter. Given everything he's told me today my brain doesn't have the space to deal with it right now.

"There's one more thing, and no, Ryder didn't put me up to it. In fact, he'll probably throttle me for saying it." He holds his hand up when I go to interrupt him. I feel like a reprimanded child so shut my mouth and drop my head. "Ryder wasn't allowed to tell you about the details of our operation, nothing, not even that he knew about what you went through. That's not to say that he didn't want to, believe me, he did. And when I found about you and him and that he wanted to tell you, it was me that stopped him. I reminded him that this was a job, and that had to come first."

"Yeah, well it doesn't matter anymore, does it?" I say indifferently.

"That's where you're wrong, it does matter. He was scared, Cam. He'll never admit it, and if you tell him, I'll deny, deny, deny." Rick gets up from the stool, coming round to my side. "Give him a chance to explain, okay. That's all I'm asking."

I nod, "Just...tell him to give me some time, okay? I know we need to talk, but I want— no, I need to sort things out in my own head first." Standing, I give Rick a one-armed hug. "Thank you. I can never repay you for everything you've done for me. Oh, shit. I need to pay you," I blurt out, pulling back.

"Fuck, no, you don't. Don't you dare insult me by even offering." Rick smiles at me, leaning down and kissing me on the cheek.

"Are you going?" I ask, a little nervous about being alone.

"Yeah, I have some things I need to sort out here before going back home tonight. Don't worry, you won't be alone."

"What—" I look over just as Seb and Max fly through the back door. "Oh, no! No way." Rick just winks, calling out to Max that it's time for them to go. Seb comes over, throwing his arm round my shoulders but careful not to touch my left one.

"He told you, huh. You and me, princess. You and me." Seb chuckles, and I elbow him in the ribs. "Oomph! Hey, what's with all the hate today." Releasing me, he walks over to Max, crouching down to his level. "Okay, little man, you take care of your ole man. He's not as sprightly as he used to be." Seb ducks this time as Rick goes to cuff him round the ear. "Ooh, that was pretty quick, but not quick enough," he mocks, with a smirk on his face. "Now, I'll see you again real soon, and we can hang out some more. Miss you, bud." Seb holds out his fist for Max to bump.

Standing back up, him and Rick do the whole man hug, pat on the back shit, then head to the door. I hear Max ask his dad if I'm Seb's girlfriend. Rick picks him up and whispers in his ear. I can't hear all of what he says, but I do catch the name Ryder. Rick turns and winks at me as he steps outside.

"You're not funny, you know that, right." He just laughs, dropping Max to the floor, and he runs to the car that has pulled up outside.

"Sure I am. Look after yourself, and don't be a stranger, Cam."

"Hold on, what do I do about my name and ID?"

"That is entirely up to you. If you want to go back to Kasey, I can sort it for you." Rick tilts his head as he waits for me to reply. I already know the answer without really having to think about it.

"No. No, I'm not her anymore." I feel a flutter in my chest at that. I haven't been her for a long time. This is me now, and I get to start afresh. Rick nods, a smile lighting up his face. He waves as he gets in the car, and I call out a goodbye to them as the car pulls away.

Back inside, Seb is making tea in the kitchen and carries it into the lounge just as I take a seat on the sofa. Putting the cups down, Seb drops into the seat beside me and snatches the control from me as he does.

"Hey!" I grumble. "Give that back." He holds it up out the way as I try to take it back. My back stings as I stretch, giving up with a wince and gently resting back in the seat.

Seb refuses to give it back all day, even taking it to the

bathroom with him. Dick. He also refuses to let me do anything, even make tea, until I threaten to castrate him while he sleeps.

With no phone I can't message Jamie and beg for her to come and rescue me. I could call the landline, but I don't want to in case things are going off with her parents.

Seb makes sure I take regular painkillers, and he makes dinner while I snooze on the sofa. I haven't really had chance to think over everything Rick told me, but as soon as I slip into bed, my brain lights up like a freaking firework.

I hardly get any sleep, between my brain being unable to switch off, and the nightmares that come when I finally do sleep, I'm lucky if I got more than a couple of hours. But it has allowed me to think about what I need to do.

Seb slept on the sofa, despite me telling him to take Jamie's room. The thought of me telling her that a hottie slept in her bed without her brings a huge smile to my face. I might tell her anyway, just for kicks.

Seb is still snoring away when I slip into the kitchen to make tea before grabbing the phone and heading out to the garden to make a start on getting my shit together.

TWO WEEKS Later

Jamie came home a week ago, and I returned to work. Seb left when Jamie decided to come home. I heard him on the phone to Ryder, shouting about me not needing him here anymore. Neither of us spoke about their conversation, but I got the impression that Seb was pissed at Ryder for some reason.

Things have been going really well. I called a therapist after realising that I needed some help to accept what had happened to me and if I ever wanted to move on.

I still haven't spoken to Ryder, but Seb and Rick call regularly. I know I need to call him, but I'm shit scared. What if he's moved on? Found a girl with less baggage and —. I slam the brakes on those thoughts just like Haley, my therapist, taught me to.

Haley has been a god send. Helping me understand that none of what happened was my fault. I don't feel worthless anymore, I know that I deserve to be loved, and am lovable, and I can, and deserve to have another child one day. I had the biggest panic attack in a long time when she first suggested that to me, but now I realise that there's no reason why not. I understand that it won't mean forgetting or replacing Faye, and I can't live my life in fear of what might happen.

Jamie has planned a weekend away for us, and I can't wait. I make a promise to call Ryder when we get back, I owe him that much, and it's not fair to keep him hanging. I miss him. I can't sleep properly, and I get all teary eyed when someone mentions his name, which isn't often seeing as I told everyone to not talk about him.

Dragging my bag from my room, I pause outside Jamie's when I hear her talking to someone. "I'll message you when we arrive. Yes, okay, bye." Not wanting to get caught eavesdropping, I quickly knock before pushing the door open further.

"You ready?" Jamie is on her bed, and a look of concern flashes across her face before it's gone again. I don't ask, knowing she'll tell me when she's ready.

Her parent's relationship is over. Just before she moved back home, they sat her down and told her they were getting a divorce. She was devastated and always believed that her parents would be together forever. Since then her dad has moved out to an apartment closer to work in the city, and she barely talks to either of them.

"Absolutely. Let's go. Have you got everything?" she asks, as she picks up her own bag.

"I think so. Let's do this."

THIRTY-EIGHT

Camryn

It takes us almost four hours to get to Durham because the traffic was horrendous, but it was so worth the journey. The hotel is beautiful. But I can't admire it for too long as I'm bursting for the loo. Jamie says she can check us in while I find the toilet.

When I get back to the lobby, Jamie is waiting at the bottom of the stairs, and we head to our room together, almost getting lost on the way.

The room has a four-poster bed, and a balcony that looks out over the beautiful gardens. As Jamie explores the room, I open the doors to the balcony, stepping out into the sun and basking in its warm rays.

After freshening up, we head down for a quick lunch before we go out on some excursion that Jamie pre-booked.

As it's such a glorious day we decide to sit out on the terrace. Jamie seems nervous and distracted, and she doesn't eat much of her lunch either. Which is always a concern as she loves her food.

"Are you okay? You seem, I don't know...distracted," I say, laying my napkin on my plate.

"Huh. Oh, yeah, I'm fine. I didn't sleep well, so feeling a little tired."

"If you're not feeling up to it, we can always give the excursion a miss." I haven't got a clue what the excursion even is, so I'm happy to just explore while Jamie catches up on her sleep.

"No, no. I'm fine, the fresh air will wake me up. Besides, we don't want miss this." She checks her watch, then asks for the bill when the waiter comes to take our plates.

I don't say anymore, but there's definitely something going on with her. I plan to get it out of her by the end of the day. We pay the bill then Jamie suggests that I should change my shoes, so I head up to the room. Quickly switching out my flip flops for pumps and grabbing a jumper before meeting Jamie back downstairs. Only Jamie isn't there, and after searching the lobby for her with no luck, I make my way outside. I spot her leaning against the car with her phone to her ear, hastily ending the call before I reach her.

"What's—" She cuts me off before I get another word out.

"That's better. Okay, let's go." Opening the car and climbing in.

I get in the passenger side, suddenly nervous and certain there's something she's not telling me. We drive away, neither of us saying a word, and it's awkward as fuck. Just as I go to ask her what the hell is going on, we pull into a car park, and Jamie gets out announcing that we're here.

"That's it. What the fuck is going on, Jamie? I'm not going anywhere until you tell me." I stand in front of her, blocking her exit.

"What do you mean? There's nothing going on." I'm not buying it, and I raise a brow at her. "There's nothing going on. Just more shit with my parents, and I don't want it to spoil our weekend so come on." She practically drags me towards a small dirt pathway.

We walk a little way before Jamie stops suddenly. "Shit. I left something in the car. You go on ahead, and I'll be right back." Before I get a chance to tell her I'll come with her, she's gone. I keep walking as the sound of gushing water reaches me, and as the path comes to an end, I step out into a small clearing. I don't notice the man standing there at first, too taken aback by the stunning view of the waterfall in front of me.

My breath hitches when I finally see him standing there. I already know who it is before he even turns around. The butterflies are going crazy in my chest.

"Hey, Bambi. It's not exactly Niagara, but it's the best I could do." His deep, velvety voice washes over me like a balm, and I almost fall to my knees at the sight of him.

"Ryder." His name is a whisper on my lips, it's all I can manage. My heart is beating so loud I can hear it over the water fall below us. And as I step closer to him, my knees give out beneath me. Strong arms wrap around me, stopping me before I hit the ground. Finally, I find my voice. "I'm going to fucking kill Jamie. She knew, didn't she?"

Ryder nods as he leads me over to the blanket I've only now just seen. Ryder lets me go, and I sit before I fall again. He takes a seat opposite me, and I take him in. Looking at him is like a tall glass of water on a hot summer's day. One I've been dying for, and I didn't even know it. His hair is a little longer on top, scruff on his jaw that I love so much, and my core clenches at the memory of it between my thighs. Holy shit.

"What are you doing here?" It comes out a bit more angrily than I expected.

"I decided that you've had long enough."

I scoff at the arrogance of his answer. "Right, and what, you just get to decide when I've had enough time, do you?" This time the venom in my tone is certainly intended.

"No, I don't, Cam. But that doesn't mean that I'm going to sit back and do nothing. I know you're angry at me, but we need to talk, and you need to hear what I have to say." I can't deny that he's right, or that I had been thinking about him a lot more lately.

"You lied to me, kept things from me. Important things, and that's all I need to know." I tuck my legs beneath me.

"You're right, I did, but I had my reasons, Cam. You of all people should understand that."

I jump to my feet, in utter outrage at the audacity of the man. "No way, nah-huh. You do not get to sit there and justify what you did by comparing it to me. That's bullshit." I go to walk away, but his hand on my arm stops me. Tingles from his touch rush over my body, and I squeeze my eyes shut.

"I'm sorry. I didn't mean for it to come out like that. I just meant that we both..." he trails off, and I turn to see why. When I look up into his beautiful blue eyes, I'm completely mesmerised. "Fuck, I've missed you." He leans down, his lips brushing against mine. Oh, my god, he tastes divine. For a few seconds I get lost in the kiss, and then my senses come back to me. I push him away.

"No, that's not fair. Don't do that. You lied, Ryder."

"No, I omitted the truth."

"Yeah, but like I told you once before, a lie by omission is still a lie, Ryder.

"Yes, and I told you that sometimes people lie to protect the ones they love, Cam." He lets that statement hang in the air. And as the sound of the water rushing down the cliff fills the air, and a breeze rustles the long grass, I realise what he's trying to say. I shake my head in disbelief, then I close my eyes and try to remember everything that Hayley told me. I let Hayley's voice fill my head, and I'm so lost trying to calm myself down that I almost miss Ryder's next words.

"I love you, Cam." I feel him as he steps closer, but I keep my eyes closed, scared to open them. "I love you. I love you. I fucking love you, Camryn Moore," he shouts the last one, and I open my eyes to find him with his head thrown back, arms out wide as he shouts it again and again. I start to laugh, then look around as I start to worry someone will hear us. I slap my hand over his mouth, startling him. He knocks my hand away and tries to shout again, but I reach up gripping his shirt in my hand and slam my mouth over his.

Ryder lifts me up, and I wrap my legs around him as he carries me back to the blanket. Our mouths fused together and tongues warring with each other. I suck his bottom lip, biting down as a growl leaves him.

Laying me on the blanket, I immediately reach for the button on his jeans, desperate to feel him inside me, when his hand stops me, and it's like deja vu. When my eyes lock with his, I can see the question there. He's waiting, wanting me to tell him I want this. He grinds his pelvis against my core, and I lift my head up in ecstasy of the friction it causes.

"Tell me," he growls, grinding into me again. "I need to know, Cam. I can't do this if you're going to walk away. It almost killed me to leave you in that hospital, to not call you, hear your voice, to not be able to touch you or kiss you. So many times I reached for my phone, but I knew I needed to give you space."

"I'm sorry." I see the dejection in his eyes. "But I needed to sort my own head out, forgive myself and learn to love me again before I could let someone else do the same." I kiss his lips, and I know he thinks I'm saying goodbye but I'm not. "I love you too, Ryder." His eyes fly to mine instantly with hope that he heard me correctly returning. When I nod letting him know he heard right, he almost snaps me in two he squeezes me so hard.

His kiss is ferocious, just like him, and I give myself over to it. I forget where we are and within seconds, he has me naked and spread out before him. As he sits back on his heels, I run my hands over his abs as his lust filled eyes rake over my body, and it sends a shiver over me.

"You're so fucking hot. I've missed this and," he says, running a finger through my soaking wet folds, "I've missed tasting this." He slips his finger into his mouth sucking my juices off. He undoes his jeans, pulling his cock free and precum glistens on the tip. I reach out a hand, running my finger over it, then bringing it to my mouth and moan as the salty taste hits my tongue.

Ryder fists his hard cock, running his hands up and down the shaft, and without taking his eyes off me he leans forward swiping his tongue the length of my pussy.

"Fucking divine." Is all he says before feasting on my pussy till I'm writhing and screaming out his name. As I come down from my orgasm, I watch Ryder licking his lips, not wanting to miss one drop. "And I've missed this too," he says, as he thrusts his hips forward, ramming into me.

Bringing his lips to mine as he falls over the top of me, caging me in. He eases back out and in again slowly, and it's torturous, agonising pleasure. Ryder continues the pace until we are both on the very edge and then he speeds up, pumping in and out before we both fall over the edge.

This time those three little words don't hang in the air, they ring out, echoing around us.

EPILOGUE

Three months later

"Can someone get the door, please," I shout out, as I pull the quiches from the oven. Feet pounding down the hall tells me someone heard me. I place the hot tray on the trivet as arms wrap around my waist, and Ryder places little kisses all along my neck.

"Hmmm. You smell delicious. How about you and I disappear upstairs, and I'll just eat you, no one will even know we're gone," he whispers. I tilt my head giving him better access as he continues kissing, biting and sucking. No doubt leaving more marks on me. The man is a territorial beast and knowing that there will be other guys here today meant last night Ryder made sure everyone knows I belong to him. Despite the shit ton of concealer I used, you can still see the love bites.

"As much as that sounds like a really great idea, no. Your mum and dad will be here soon, and I still have more food to get ready." Pulling his hands from my waist I move to the fridge. He groans behind me, and I turn, giving him a quick kiss. "Go, drink, mingle and be merry," I tell him, turning my attention back to the mountain of food in this gigantic fridge.

We're at his house in Surrey, and it's a fucking mansion. The first time he brought me here I almost died. I thought Seb's house was big, but it's got nothing on Ryder's. Some might suggest that these guys are overcompensating for the lack of size in other areas. Obviously, I can't talk for Rick, or Seb really, although I did walk in on him in the shower, but anyway, it's not true in Ryder's case.

The barbecue was my idea, and I'm suddenly regretting it. I thought it would be great to bring everyone together. But now the butterflies have started, and I'm hit by a wave of nausea.

Max runs passed me as Seb chases him through the kitchen into the garden, and Max's laughter rings out, bringing a smile to my face.

Over the last three months, Ryder and I have spent a lot of time with Rick, Max and even Seb. I finally feel like my life is back on track and as it should be. In fact, I've never been happier, and I often wonder how stupid I would have been to let Ryder slip through my fingers.

Seb flies past me, Max now chasing him, and I have to lift the tray of drinks I'm carrying above my head before they end up in a sticky mess all over the floor. As I place the tray of drinks on the counter, I hear the front door open and close before heels click down the hall.

"Hey. Slow down you two," I shout, as they run past me again. "God, bloody big kid," I mutter to myself. Well, I thought it was to myself.

"You're not wrong there," comes my best friend's voice behind me. I spin around, stepping forwards and giving her a hug. "You look amazing," Jamie says, as she steps back taking me in.

The last three months have been immensely difficult for her. The shit with her parents has caused no end of trouble, and now she's not talking to her mum at all. Turns out it wasn't her dad that was having an affair but her mum.

Before I get a chance to reply, Seb runs into the room, skidding to a halt when he sees Jamie there. And there's another cause of her trouble.

The weekend away that resulted in Ryder and I getting back together was also the weekend that something happened between Seb and Jamie. But neither of them will say a word about it. Up until now, Ryder and I have tried to keep the pair away from each other.

Max smacks into the back of Seb, knocking him a few steps forward.

"Why'd you stop, uncle Seb?" Max asks, coming round to stand next to him. "I thought we were still playing. Can we still play? Come on let's go," he says, pulling on Seb's arm. I watch as a look passes between Seb and Jamie, and the tension in the room just ratcheted up a few thousand degrees.

"Max, can you please go and ask your dad to give me a hand, and tell Ryder that the food is almost ready." The timing couldn't be more perfect as the oven timer begins to buzz. Max spins away, grumbling under his breath about spoiling his game but heads towards where his dad and Ryder are talking beside the barbecue. Walking over to the oven, I switch it off and reach for the oven mitts, but Jamie beats me to it. Looking over my shoulder, I see that Seb has gone back outside.

"Are you ever going to tell me what went on with you two?" I ask, pulling a plate from the cupboard and beginning to pile the bread rolls on it.

"Nope. It's not important." Jamie puts the oven mitt

down before grabbing a beer from the fridge. "Now, how are you feeling?" Avoid and deflect. Shaking my head at her, I tell her I'm fine, and then point to the salad on the side as I walk outside.

As I step onto the patio, I see that everyone is seated at the long bench table. Just as I place the plate down, I hear the front door again, and then Ryder's parents' step outside. After a quick round of greetings and introductions, everyone digs in.

I push my food around my plate, barely eating anything. Ryder keeps throwing glances my way, but I avoid his gaze as much as possible. As people begin to finish their food my heart rate spikes, and I realise that if I don't do this now it will be too late.

Rising to my feet, Ryder stops talking and turns my way as concern lines his face. Offering him a warm smile, I clear my throat before asking everyone to wait here for two minutes.

Dashing inside, I find my bag and pull out the envelope I placed in there earlier. My hands are clammy with nerves as I make my way back to the garden. As I step out conversation ceases, and everyone turns to look at me. My steps are slow and measured as I walk towards Ryder, and when I reach him, I hold out my hand to him. When he goes to take it, he grabs the envelope instead. He looks up at me in question, and I nod my head for him to take it. I look up, catching Jamie's eye, and she winks at me settling my nerves a little.

I sit back down beside Ryder as he begins to tear open the envelope. I keep my eyes trained on him as he pulls out the card inside. I watch as he reads the words written across the front. As the words sink in his eyes widen, and his head snaps up at me.

"Do you mean...does this mean what I think it means?" he stutters out, and I nod my head unable to speak as the biggest, brightest smile lights up his face. "Holy fucking shit!" bursts from Ryder, and I hear a muttered 'watch your language' no doubt from his mum.

"What is it, son?" Ryder's dad asks from the other end of the table.

Ryder doesn't answer him, instead he jumps from the bench, snatching me up and spinning us around. A tear slips free, in happiness and a small amount of relief.

We never talked about kids before because of the secrets we were both hiding, but after we got back together and everything was out in the open, we discussed the idea of having a family. I had shared my fears about having another child and Ryder had fears of his own based on his experience when his brother died, but we decided that we would both love to have a child in the future. I just didn't realise it would be this soon.

Ryder finally puts me down when everyone starts demanding answers. He opens the card staring at the ultrasound picture inside. Turning to the table with his arm wrapped around my waist he finally puts them out of their misery.

"Cam's pregnant. I'm going to be a fucking dad." And as everyone begins congratulating us and chatter breaks out, Ryder carries me inside. I don't even question where we are going.

"I fucking love you, Camryn Moore, soon to be Hawkins," he whispers in my ear.

"Is that your way of proposing?"

"No, but watch this space, Bambi." I laugh as we fall onto the bed.

ACKNOWLEDGMENTS

First of all, thank you for reading my debut novel, and I hope you enjoyed reading Cam and Ryder's story.

I must thank my amazing family for all their support, and an extra big thanks to my husband for keeping me sane when I was stressed and crazy. I love you all.

Thank you to my fantastic friends, Janis Bevan, Felicity Wilkin, Kelly Maclean and Lisa Wesley for cheering me on and reading my first draft. Thanks for all your advice, support and being there for me.

Thank you to all my amazing Beta and Arc readers, you're the best. And a special thank you to Sophie Ruthven and Clayr Catherall for all your support and for always being there when I needed you.

A huge thanks to my friends and fellow authors, Raven Amour, Wendy Saunders and Becca Steele. I don't think this book would have made it out there if it were not for all your guidance, advice, support and your faith in me. Thank you for always answering my questions, no matter how silly they were, and for constantly reassuring me.

Thank you to Lou at LJ Designs for my amazing cover and graphics. An extra thanks for putting up with me too.

Thank you to all the readers, bloggers and bookstagrammers for all your support and help with sharing my first book baby with the world.

ABOUT THE AUTHOR

Imogen Wells is a dark romantic suspense author from the East of England, where she lives with her husband, three children and the family dog and cat.

After being a stay at home mum to her three children, Imogen decided to go back to school. Much to her teenage son's amusement. And earlier this year she graduated with a First-Class Honours degree in History and English Literature.

When she is not reading, she can now be found writing after turning her passion for books into her career.

Keep up to date with Imogen's latest news and up-coming releases, by following her author page on Facebook, stalking her on Instagram and Goodreads, or you can email her directly at imogenwells.author@gmail.com

Printed in Great Britain
by Amazon